Jacob's Place

Enjoy and God Bless.

H. C. Hewitt

— *a novel by* —

H. C. Hewitt

 FriesenPress

Suite 300 - 990 Fort St
Victoria, BC, V8V 3K2
Canada

www.friesenpress.com

You can contact H. C. Hewitt at
hchewittauthor@gmail.com or visit her website: **www.hchewittauthor.com**
You can also find her on FaceBook **H. C. Hewitt**,
Instagram and Twitter **@hchewittauthor**

ISBN
978-1-5255-1186-8 (Hardcover)
978-1-5255-1187-5 (Paperback)
978-1-5255-1188-2 (eBook)

1. Fiction, Cultural Heritage

Distributed to the trade by The Ingram Book Company

Acknowledgments

"With men this is impossible,
but with God all things are possible."
Matthew 19:26

I WOULD LIKE to thank Jesus for all he has done for me and my family.

To my husband and children, your love and support is my anchor. Mom and dad, thank you for all you have done and will do. Lorraine I can't thank you enough for all the hours of reading, editing and advice you have given me, you are a true blessing. Cathy, your many edits, advice and listening ear has been warmly welcomed and needed. Thank you Leona for your quick edits every time I need you! Helen, the best sales lady anyone could ask for, you compliment my work and recommend it to every one, thank you for believing in me. To my friends: your support means the world and you are always faithfully there for me.

Tony and Debbie Photography: Thank you for the wonderful author photo.

Thank you to FriesenPress for helping publish my second book. It's been an experience that I won't soon forget. Thank you Galia Zavgorodni, my account manager. We make a great team and it's a pleasure working with you. Also, thank you to my editor at FriesenPress for all your wonderful work.

Thank you, the reader for giving Jacob the opportunity to leave a little part of his life with you by following his journey. God Bless!

Dedication

To Mary Hartlin, my grandmother who was born in 1917, and is celebrating her hundredth year. And to Scarlett, my grand-daughter, who was born a hundred years later in 2017, the same year as our great country, Canada's 150th birthday.

Abbington Pickets

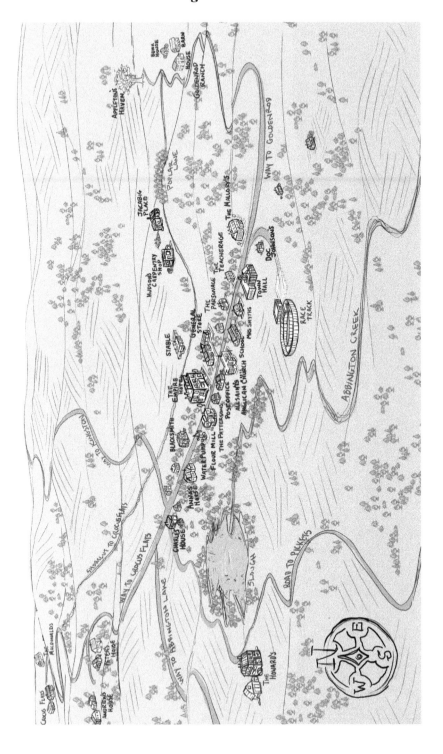

chapter one

"IT'S GOING TO be beautiful, Jacob!" exclaimed Abigail as she put her arms around his tanned neck and kissed his cheek. Her wavy brown locks draped down her back, covering her white lace-trimmed, blue cotton dress.

"I thought you'd like this one," Jacob said, giving her a dimpled smile. For months he had been designing their future home. They were getting married in six months and time was evaporating fast. Before their wedding, Jacob wanted to have their house built next to his well-established carpentry business. He had finished building the shop on the northeast side of Abbington Pickets the previous fall.

Jacob put his strong arms around Abigail's small waist, lifted her up, and twirled her around and around. He stopped, set her down, then looked down into her beautiful brown eyes.

"I love you, Girlie. You know that, right?" he whispered.

Abigail smiled and nestled her face into Jacob's neck. She always loved his nickname for her.

"I know," she softly said. "But I don't mind hearing it every day," she added.

Making Abigail happy was all Jacob desired. Since Abigail's return from England, they had spent as much time together as they possibly could.

It was a beautiful white Christmas morning when Jacob asked Abigail to marry him. He had already asked her father before popping the question. Once all the chores were done, breakfast was finished, and Christmas gifts were opened, in front of Abigail's parents and their guests, Jacob knelt down on one knee, facing Abigail. He took her hand in his, looked up at her smiling face, and gazed deep into her big eyes with all seriousness.

"Abigail, I have loved you since the first day I laid eyes on you," he began. "You are my dearest friend, my first love, someone who I receive my strength from." He looked down, took a deep breath, and glanced back up. "I missed you when you were gone from me. I never want to be without you." He nervously licked his lips. "Will you become my wife, Abigail?" His face lit up. "Will you marry me?"

Abigail squealed as she jumped to her feet, hopping up and down. "Yes! Of course, I will marry you, Jacob."

Jacob stood, grabbed her gently, and wrapped his arms around her, drawing her near him tightly. He leaned down and kissed her lips delicately. Everyone in the room clapped and roared. When Jacob let go, Abigail blushed from everyone watching them kiss.

"How exciting," exclaimed Alice as she and her husband Bert walked up to congratulate the happy couple. Alice was a petite-built young woman with sparkling green eyes. She had curly dark brown hair, which she wore in a loose bun. Bert, a small-framed, muscular man with dark-coloured hair and a handlebar moustache, used to work for Mr. Rodgers but had left to start a new job. An opportunity had come about for Bert to work at CN Rail, northeast of Abbington Pickets. Since Alice was going to have a baby that coming summer, they thought it was best to find their own home.

As well, Alice's brother Ernest was coming from England to homestead, and they would be making room for him to stay with them.

Although Alice missed working for Mrs. Rodgers, as they had become quite good friends, she and Bert were still part of their family. Abigail's ma and pa were happy about the engagement. They had always loved Jacob as their own son, and now he would be so.

Unfortunately, Jacob's siblings weren't there to witness the beautiful event. Peter, the oldest of the Hudson children, had gotten married the previous summer and he and his wife were spending Christmas at his in-laws'. Jane, the oldest of the girls, and Andrew had gone to spend the holidays with their younger sister, Sarah, in Kingston. She and her husband lived there with their new baby girl, Megan Lucy. Sarah loved being a mother and seemed to have found her niche in life. Jacob even received a letter every once in a while from her. Her selfish ways had subsided, and Sarah had blossomed into a responsible wife and mother, which Jacob was happy to realize. He was delighted that all the Hudson children were like a family again, not like it had been when he was sixteen years old and left Crocus Flats. He was sorry that they all would miss him proposing to Abigail.

It was a sunny day in mid-March when Jacob rode over to Goldenrod to show Abigail the drawings of his latest creation. There wasn't as much snow this year, so his horse was able to run swiftly. When Jacob arrived, Abigail was in the barn, brushing Rusty, her horse. Rusty was a beautiful sorrel horse with white socks and a white stripe down his forehead. He'd taken a shine to Abigail the day she'd met him at the horse race the previous summer. He really hadn't been for sale, but his owner could tell how much Abigail loved the horse, so Mr. Rodgers had made a deal with him.

Jacob and Abigail embraced for a few moments when the door flew open. At the noise of the door banging against the side of the wall, Jacob and Abigail released one another and turned quickly to see what it was.

"Abigail, Jacob, come quickly," shouted Bert. "It's your father. He has collapsed."

"What?" Abigail gasped, holding both hands over her mouth. "You go to Abbington Pickets and bring back Doc Johnson," Jacob directed Bert as they all ran out of the barn. "It's going to be alright." He stopped, looking at Abigail.

"I'll be back as soon as I can." Jacob's horse was standing outside the barn. Bert grabbed the reins, pulling himself up, he climbed on and rode out of the yard, heading for the village.

Jacob reached for Abigail's hand, then they ran quickly towards the stone house.

Jacob and Abigail raced into the kitchen where her father was lying. Mrs. Rodgers was sitting on the floor holding her husband's head in her lap, rubbing his forehead gently with her hand, speaking softly to him, quietly sobbing. Alice knelt down beside them both, consoling Mrs. Rodgers. Mr. Rodgers was very still, and his face was a greyish tone. It didn't look natural. His lips appeared to be outlined in blue. His eyes were shut. It was hard to tell if he was breathing.

"What happened?" Abigail looked desperately at them for answers. She quickly crouched down to her father's side, picking up his limp hand, placing it in hers. She started to cry as she held his hand, lifting it to her mouth and kissing the back of it. Her mama looked up with tears rolling down her face; she didn't say much. Jacob quickly knelt down, putting his head on Mr. Rodgers' chest to listen for his heartbeat. He could hear one, but it was extremely faint. *Bert better not take too long,* he told himself.

"He had just finished his tea," Alice began, "he stood up, and said he was going to go to the barn. There was a strange look on his face, a look of anguish, I suppose." She paused a moment. "Then he grabbed his left arm with his right hand, looked straight at your mama, and then he dropped to the floor." Alice appeared to be in shock, shaking as she recollected what had happened.

"Did he say anything else?" Jacob asked Alice.

"No," she shook her head. "It was like every other morning teatime."

"Let's pray," Jacob said as he reached over and held Abigail's hand, and placed his other hand on Mr. Rodgers' chest. Mrs. Rodgers laid both her hands on her husband's head. Alice put her hand on Mr. Rodgers' shoulder. Everyone closed their eyes, bowing their heads.

"Dear Jesus, we lift up Mr. Rodgers to you right now. Please heal his brokenness. We place him in your hands. We ask this in Jesus' name. Amen."

After what seemed like hours, Bert came back with Doc Johnson. "What happened?" Doc quickly crouched down on his knees to the floor beside Mr. Rodgers. Jacob backed away to give him room to work, as Alice explained once again what happened.

"You simply have to make him better," Abigail begged the Doc. "Like you did before." Her voice was desperate.

"We need to get him into bed," Doc Johnson said. "We brought a stretcher to help move him," he pointed to Bert, who was holding the homemade carrier in his hands. Jacob stood up and helped Bert place it by Mr. Rodgers.

"Careful," Doc warned them. "*Don't* drop him or make a sudden movement." The three of them slowly picked Mr. Rodgers up and placed him gently down on the stretcher. Jacob and Bert each took an end and lifted the stretcher, carrying him to the bedroom.

They took baby steps to get there, as to not startle him on the way.

Mrs. Rodgers, Abigail, and Alice ran ahead of them to open the door to the bedroom. The room was big with long drapes that covered the windows, floral wallpaper on the walls, and white crown moulding against the ceiling. Abigail pulled the drapes open to bring some light into the room. Alice drew the sheets back, and Mrs. Rodgers waited at the head of the bed. The men placed the stretcher on the bed so they could lift Mr. Rodgers and place him on the bed.

"Alright, everyone but Mrs. Rodgers out," Doc Johnson ordered as he pointed to the door. "I need to see what we can do for Mr. Rodgers."

Jacob put his arm around Abigail and pulled her close to him tugging her in the direction of the doorway. She was reluctant to go but, walked slowly with him. Sobbing quietly, she placed her head on his chest as they moved out of the room.

"I'll make a pot of tea," said Alice, not really knowing what to do. Keeping busy in the kitchen seemed the thing to do at this moment. Bert sat down at the table in silence. Everyone feared the worst would come to Mr. Rodgers. They had all come to be quite good friends since Bert came to Abbington Pickets. Alice made a good impression as well, and no one wanted to lose a good friend.

Jacob thought of Mr. Rodgers as his own father. Not that he could replace the one he had. Jacob had forgiven his father for the pain he'd caused Jacob all his life, but deep down he'd never had a close relationship with him. Jacob had found a fatherly figure in Mr. Rodgers. He remembered the first time they met. Mr. Rodgers had had a heart attack while riding with Abigail. Jacob had saved his life by getting him to Doc Johnson quickly. Now, five years later, Jacob felt more helpless than ever. He would be devastated if he didn't have Mr. Rodgers there to guide him, especially since he and Abigail were getting married. He wondered who would walk Abigail down the aisle if Mr. Rodgers died. He couldn't imagine how she felt, as his only daughter, and them being very close; closer than Jacob was with his mother. Jacob knew he had to be strong for Abigail's sake. He couldn't let her know he was as scared as she was. Jacob had to put it in God's hands.

"Oh Jacob," Abigail cried, "I don't know what I would ever do if anything happened to Pa." She held her face in her hands.

"It's up to the Lord now," Jacob told her. "You must have faith, Abigail." He held her close to him. "Come," he pulled her towards the chesterfield, "let's sit down."

"I can't sit still," Abigail cried. "I can't just do nothing. I want to be with my father." She ran from the room and headed outside. Jacob darted after her and grabbed her shawl from the hook next to the door on his way out after her.

"Abigail. Stop. Abigail," he called after her when he saw her running into the barn. He chased after her. It was getting colder outside. Neither of them should be out without a coat. As he caught up to her inside the barn, he walked up behind her, wrapping the shawl around her shoulders. He stepped in front of Abigail and gently pulled her towards him, holding both her arms with his hands. He looked down at her tear-stained face and swollen red eyes.

"Girlie," he'd given her that nickname the first year he worked for her father. "Listen to me." His deep voice was soft, already comforting Abigail. He lifted her chin with a bent forefinger. "I don't know what God's plan is for your father, but I do know you need to have faith in Him." Jacob held her close and stroked her long locks with his strong but gentle hand. "I'll always be here for you, Girlie. I'll never leave you."

"Jacob," Abigail sniffed, "I love you." She looked up at him, and even with the sadness in her eyes, her love for him shone through.

"I love you, too," Jacob said as he bent down and pressed his lips softly to Abigail's. For a few short seconds, they forgot about her father collapsing and not knowing if he was going to live or die. It was like Jacob and Abigail were in their own small world, where everything was perfect. That's the kind of love they shared, that's the kind of life they would have together.

Realizing the real world around him, Jacob lifted his head, cupping Abigail's face in his rough hands and said, "Now let's go back to the house. We want to be there when Doc finishes with your father." Jacob kissed her forehead then let her go. He was as worried as Abigail was, but he had faith his Heavenly Father would take care of his future father-in-law.

When Jacob and Abigail entered the living room, Bert and Alice were sitting in the two chairs beside the lamp table in the corner. There was a teapot, and two cups and saucers placed out for the two of them, along with the matching sugar bowl and creamer.

"Would you two like some tea?" Alice asked as she stood up to greet them.

"No, thank you," they both said simultaneously. "Have you heard anything?" Abigail asked.

"No," Alice looked down and shook her head with sympathy. She took Abigail's hand and said, "I am sure it'll be alright." She was trying to keep Abigail's spirit's up.

It was quiet in the living room. No one spoke for more than an hour. Jacob, Abigail, Bert, and Alice, sat in their chairs in complete silence. They each stared at the floor, impatiently waiting to hear any noise, movement, or news from the other side of the wall. The sound of someone walking towards the door was the first anyone heard. Abigail jumped from her chair, along with everyone else and darted towards the door, standing there hoping it would open. Seconds felt like minutes until the Doc and Mrs. Rodgers came through the doorway.

Their faces were solemn. It was clear Mrs. Rodgers had been crying for a long time. Her face was pale and showed every crease, making her seem older than she was. Her once-perfect bun was loose, her hair falling down her neck. Her dress was wrinkled, and her apron was askew. She was exhausted with fear and worry.

"Is Pa alright?" Abigail begged to know the truth. She searched her mother's face for answers, then looked at Doc Johnson.

"Your father," Doc Johnson began, "has had a massive stroke."

"A massive stroke?" Abigail repeated with confusion. "What does that even mean?"

"It is when there is a haemorrhage of a blood vessel that leads to the brain." His diagnosis was gruff. "He hasn't been well since his heart attack five years ago."

"I don't understand." Abigail's voice got louder; Jacob walked closer to her and lightly put his arm around her, trying to keep her calm.

"A stroke can cause paralysis or speech problems," Doc continued plainly.

"Are you telling us that he may never talk or walk again?" she demanded frantically. She stepped closer to Doc as her pleading eyes stared at him.

Calmly, the Doc said, "For now, we don't know what the damage is. We'll have to wait and see." He wiped his brow with his hanky, as he carried his black leather bag in the other hand.

Abigail turned to her mama and hugged her close. She began to cry.

Jacob felt his heart being tugged out of his chest. *Oh, how Abigail must be feeling,* Jacob thought as he felt sympathy for her.

"But he'll wake up?" Abigail grabbed hold of the doctor's arm as he tried to walk past her. "He'll walk, he'll talk again." Her eyes looked firmly at him.

"We'll know more when he wakes up," he said as he put on his coat. "Keep him comfortable." He looked at Abigail, then to Jacob. "And pray," Jacob nodded.

"Thank you, Doc," Jacob shook his hand. "I'll see you out."

"If there's any change, Jacob," Doc said, "send for me immediately." He tipped his hat, unlatched the door and left. Bert stood with Doc's horse ready for him when he got outside. He handed the doctor the reins.

Doc put his foot in the stirrup, pulled himself up, climbed on and trotted out of the yard. Jacob stood in the doorway, watching him slowly disappear in the distance. Jacob continued to pray for Mr. Rodgers, even though he secretly felt helpless. He went back to the living room where Abigail and Mrs. Rodgers were.

"Papa will be alright," Abigail consoled her mother, trying to be strong for her. "He'll be alright."

"I'll do anything you need, Mrs. Rodgers," Jacob stepped towards them. He patted her back.

"Oh, Jacob." Mrs. Rodgers cried in her hanky. "What would I do without you? What would Abigail do without you? You are a blessing to us both." She hugged him closely and kissed his cheek.

Bert helped Jacob do the evening chores. Alice made a light supper of sandwiches for everyone to eat, but no one felt like consuming anything. Bert and Alice headed home; they had their own chores to do.

Mrs. Rodgers sat in the most beautiful, but most uncomfortable chair in the house. The unusual piece was a Louis XIV-style beauty made of dark walnut wood upholstered in an exquisite paisley of green and gold with a hint of brown. Each arm had precise details of a carved ram's head. The curved stretchers across the legs were lightly carved. The straight back had a slight curve on the top, the rectangular seat was vast but had a matching pillow that would support the lower part of the back. It had been left in the house from when the Benedicts owned it. Rumour had it that the chair came from the elegant Langham Hotel in London. The King himself had sat in the "Ram's Chair," or so the story went. Now the beautiful piece of furniture sat at Mr. Rodgers' bedside.

Jacob stayed with Abigail until she fell asleep on the chesterfield outside her father's room. He spent the night in the guest room, not wanting to leave them alone. If anything happened, he wanted to be there, able to help. Besides, there would be chores to do in the morning.

chapter two

A MONTH HAD passed since Mr. Rodgers' stroke, and there had been no change in his condition. Abigail and Mrs. Rodgers sat by his side every hour of the day. Reverend Young came by to pray for Mr. Rodgers every few days. Jacob did the necessary chores, morning and night just as he did a few years earlier when he worked here. Alice and Bert had been experiencing calving problems, most of the month, and were unable to help as much as they wanted. Jacob had to temporarily close his carpenter shop, Hudson's Carpentry, in Abbington Pickets, as he couldn't juggle going back and forth to town for a few hours of work. He would barely get the fire started in the stove to warm up the room, begin a project, then it would be time to get ready to go back to the ranch.

Jacob felt it would be best to stay at Goldenrod, but the pressure of not being at his own work was starting to weigh on his mind. He had no income, and although his debt was minimal, he had wanted to continue saving his money for the home he was building for Abigail and himself. He wanted to finish it before their wedding in September, and it was going to take time to build the house. Jacob knew he had to talk to Mrs. Rodgers about hiring a hired man. He knew how delicate the situation was for both her and Abigail. He dreaded bringing it up, but it had to be done soon.

Jacob was walking from the barn towards the house when Doc Johnson rode up the lane, his breath coming from his mouth like puffs of smoke. It was cold, but there was little snow to trek through, which made it easier for the horses to trot.

Jacob nodded as he got closer to the doctor.

"Good day, Doc," Jacob greeted him. Doc Johnson stopped his horse.

"Jacob," he said, as he dismounted. "How is Mr. Rodgers today?"

Jacob shook his head as he looked towards the ground.

"No change." He didn't want to admit it out loud, not even to Doc. His mentor, the man he looked up to, respected, the one person who gave him a chance at a new life, might not ever wake up. Jacob didn't want to come to terms with it. He simply wanted the days to revert to when everyone was happy, healthy, and planning their lives together.

"Well, let's go see," Doc Johnson patted Jacob on the back sympathetically as they both walked towards the front door of the house. Both Doc and Jacob took their hats off when they entered the Rodgers' home.

Inside, Mrs. Rodgers was in the kitchen making breakfast. She looked up from stirring the porridge with a wooden spoon on the stove when she saw the two of them walk in the room. Mrs. Rodgers had aged ten years in the last month. She didn't seem to take the time with her hair as she usually did; there wasn't any time to iron either, so she and Abigail's clothes weren't as pressed as they would normally be. Her eyes were sad and tired, filled with a sense of loneliness. Two creases above her eyebrows curved across her forehead, the lines that drew away from the corners of her eyes added on more years.

"Come on in Doc," she murmured as she took the pot off the stove so it wouldn't burn. She walked over to them, kissed Jacob on the cheek, and shook Doc's hand. Jacob's face always brought a smile to hers.

"Abigail is with Mr. Rodgers," she murmured as they walked towards the bedroom. "She never leaves his side." She slowly opened the door.

Abigail was sitting in the chair beside her father's bed. She was leaning back on the chair, sleeping soundly with a book held open in her lap. Her beautiful brown hair was braided and lay down one shoulder past her chest. Her flawless complexion gave an illusion of an angel.

Jacob's heart flip-flopped, just seeing her peacefully sleeping. He always felt this way whenever he was in her presence.

Mr. Rodgers was lying on his back, just as he had been the last time Doc was in to see him. Abigail and Jacob moved him several times a day, to keep him from getting bed sores. Mr. Rodgers' dark hair with flecks of grey was getting longer since it had been over a month since his last haircut. As it grew longer, it started to curl as it came down the front of his forehead. Mrs. Rodgers sponge-bathed him once a day, and dry washed his hair, once a week, with cornstarch. Nothing they did seemed to make him move or wake up or do anything.

Abigail opened her eyes. She smiled when she saw Jacob. "Good morning, sleepy head." Jacob smiled at her.

"I thought I saw Pa's eyes open earlier this morning," Abigail told Doc eagerly. "It was for a few seconds." She stood up to make room for him to examine her father.

"Alright, let's see here. I'll have a look." Doc did all the usual things, lifting Mr. Rodgers' eyelids and looking at his pupils, listening to his heart, listening to his chest, touching the bottom of his feet to see if he reacted.

"There appears to be no change," Doc plainly stated as he put his stethoscope in his black bag. He reached into his pocket and took out his hanky and wiped his forehead.

"But I know what I saw," Abigail pleaded, as she grabbed Doc's arm. "He is getting better. I know he is," Abigail blurted.

Jacob grabbed hold of her arm gently and pulled her back towards him.

Doc headed towards the bedroom door to leave. He stopped and turned around. "Again, let me know if there is any change. See you next week."

"It's alright, Girlie," Jacob soothed as he watched Doc leave the room. He could hear the doctor saying goodbye to Mrs. Rodgers.

"Why won't anyone believe me?" Abigail turned towards Jacob as he put his arms around her and held her close.

Abigail sobbed tirelessly, feeling helpless, as if she were a small child.

It seemed to be a long day for everyone, emotionally and physically. Abigail stayed with her father, as she did every day. Mrs. Rodgers continued to keep busy with the household chores, and Jacob fed the horses, milked the cow, and chopped enough wood for the next few days.

Weighing on Jacob's mind was the fact that Mr. Rodgers didn't appear to be getting any better, and Jacob needed to get back to work. He wasn't sure how he was going to bring it up with Mrs. Rodgers, nor did he want to. Hiring a hired man was the perfect solution, at least for the time being. Once Jacob started the building of the house, he could possibly get his buddy Charles to help, then he could make time to come to Goldenrod to help out a bit more.

Jacob chopped enough wood for the next few days.

It was near dark when Jacob was walking towards the house.

As he reached for the latch to open the door, the aroma of supper drifted out from the kitchen. He took his hat and coat off and hung them up on the hook by the door.

"Hello," Jacob hollered out to let Mrs. Rodgers know he was in for the night.

"Oh good, Jacob. Supper is almost ready," she called back to him from where she was sitting at the kitchen table.

Jacob thought that this was the opportunity for him to speak with her. He walked over to the washstand that was on the right side of the doorway into the kitchen, lifted the pitcher of water, and poured some into the bowl. Jacob rolled up both the sleeves of his grey shirt. He reached both his hands in and touched the cold water, picking up the lye soap from the dish beside the bowl. He dipped it into the water and lathered up his hands, washing his face, neck, arms, and hands, then rinsing.

Grabbing the towel off the rod above the wash stand, he dried himself, rolled his sleeves back down and walked over to the table and sat down.

"Potatoes need a little more time," Mrs. Rodgers stated.

Jacob nodded. "Mrs. Rodgers," he said nervously. "I've been wanting to talk to you about something."

"Alright dear," Mrs. Rodgers answered.

"I was wondering," Jacob started as he shifted around in his chair uncomfortably, "if it were possible … if you could hire some other help." He glanced at Mrs. Rodgers to see her expression; her eyes were sad and concerned. "Ah, I mean, I love helping you, Mrs. Rodgers. That isn't the problem." He finished quickly. "It's just that I need to get back to my shop. I have orders to finish. Then there is the house to consider." He watched her closely to see her reaction.

Mrs. Rodgers looked down into her lap, then she suddenly burst into tears.

Jacob was startled. He hadn't thought she would take it like that. *What have I done? What now?*

Mrs. Rodgers brought her hands up to her face holding her apron and cried.

"I know … I know … I know Jacob," she wept.

"I am sorry, Mrs. Rodgers. I didn't mean to upset you," Jacob said sympathetically. "Please don't cry," he begged. "Forget I said anything." He didn't want her to cry. It reminded him of his own mama sobbing for Lucy for so long, it broke his heart.

"No, Jacob you're absolutely right," she went on to say between talking and sobbing. "You have been remarkable to

Abigail and I, not to mention Mr. Rodgers," she continued. "You couldn't be any more wonderful if you were our own son. We have been so selfish keeping you from your work as it is." Mrs. Rodgers kept wiping her tears with her apron.

"I don't mind really," Jacob assured her. "In fact, I love to do it." He got up, walked over to Mrs. Rodgers' chair, and crouched down to her sitting level, where he picked up her hand to comfort her. Looking up at her tear-stained face, he smiled.

"You and Mr. Rodgers are my family. You have been my family ever since that day, four years ago, when you opened your home to me."

"Jacob, you are sweet." Mrs. Rodgers tried to smile. "I am ashamed to tell you why I'm being so selfish with you."

Jacob then started to feel concerned. *What was she getting at? He wondered. Why does she think she's being selfish?*

"I don't understand," Jacob said. "You're not being selfish."

"Yes I am," Mrs. Rodgers insisted as she started to cry harder once again. "I can't even bring myself to tell you. You look up to Mr. Rodgers so much, and you'll never think of him in the same way."

"Please, tell me what you mean," Jacob coaxed. "There's no money," she blurted out plainly. "What?" Jacob asked confused. "What do you mean?"

"We have no money," she repeated. "That's why we had to let Bert go. That's why we can't hire anyone else," she cried, hanging her head. "We even owe Mr. Adair money, Jacob. He can't … he won't give us any more credit either, not that I blame him." Jacob was taken aback by this information, he knew that the Rodgers weren't as rich as the king, but he had thought they were pretty well off. He tried to think of something to say, something that he could be true to his word and make Mrs. Rodgers feel better.

"Look at me," Jacob spoke gently to Mrs. Rodgers. "Please, look at me."

She turned her head, wiped her swollen red eyes with her hand, blinking as she looked straight at Jacob.

"It's going to be alright, Mrs. Rodgers," Jacob firmly said to her. "There isn't anything I wouldn't do for you and Mr. Rodgers. I'll take care of this," he continued. "I don't want you to worry about this anymore."

"But Jacob, you can't—" She tried to say.

"Promise me you won't worry anymore," he repeated.

"I don't know what to say." Her sobbing broke Jacob's heart.

"The first thing I'll do when I get back to Abbington Pickets is talk to Mr. Adair. From now on, charge everything to my account. I'll take care of it, Mrs. Rodgers."

"Oh Jacob," Mrs. Rodgers was embarrassed and ashamed of the predicament they were in, but grateful for Jacob's generosity.

He stood, leaned over, and gave her a hug.

She grabbed both of Jacob's hands with hers, holding them tight. "Thank you, Jacob," her voice sounded relieved. "But please, don't tell Abigail," she begged. "It would break her heart. Promise me?"

"You have my word," swore Jacob. "Now you promise me, no more worrying, it's taken care of." He said it with such confidence that he even believed it himself. Jacob knew, with the grace of God, it would be alright. He simply needed to pray and have time to think.

"I thought I heard your voice." Abigail came up behind him.

Jacob turned around to greet her with a hug.

"Is everything alright? Why are you upset, Mama?" She looked at her with concern.

"Oh, it's nothing, my dear, just your mama being foolish again," Mrs. Rodgers told her daughter.

Abigail looked at her skeptically, but seemed to be satisfied with her answer.

All three of them sat down to eat supper. There wasn't much conversation that night at the table. Mrs. Rodgers couldn't stop thinking of how she had poured her heart out to Jacob. Jacob couldn't stop thinking of Mr. and Mrs. Rodgers' financial quandary and what he could do to help. Abigail thought about her father's health. They were hardly aware of the other's absence of conversation.

That night, Jacob lay in bed praying to the Lord, looking for guidance, thinking about the money he had saved since he'd started his carpentry business three years ago. He could give it all to the Rodgers, then he and Abigail would have to put off their wedding for at least another year, possibly two. Could he financially support both himself and Abigail and his future in-laws at the same time? What if he put off building the house, but they still got married? He didn't want to worry Mrs. Rodgers with the details. He'd promised her it would be taken care of, but had also promised that Abigail would never find out. How would he explain to her that they couldn't get married for two years? Or not build the house as he professed he was going to do. It was evident that both those scenarios were out of the question.

It was nearly daybreak when Jacob finally drifted off to sleep. His thoughts were lost amidst his dreams. He hadn't come up with a solution to his dilemma, but he knew, with faith and determination, God would open a new door. He believed in that.

chapter three

IT WAS A beautiful warm sunny morning in April. There
wasn't a cloud in the sky. The blue stretched from east to west,
and the sun's warm rays beamed wide. The previous day had
been stressful, so Jacob decided to go into the village, where
he looked forward to seeing a familiar face. He planned to go
see Mr. Adair, as Mrs. Rodgers needed some groceries, but he
would squeeze in a quick confab. The visit would also entail
speaking with Mr. Adair about Mr. and Mrs. Rodgers' account
and a hired man for them.

The breeze caressed Jacob's face as his horse loped into
Abbington Pickets. He had taken Poplar Lane, the path that
he and Abigail created after she came back from England. It
was their secret road to Abbington Pickets. It was quicker, with
hundreds of poplar trees shouldering the passage that only a
single horse could travel; hence the name. Although it was
early in the year, the air smelled so crisp and sweet, just like a
spring day. As he rode past the church, he waved to Reverend
Young who was standing in the churchyard. Over to his left
was Mrs. Smyth, walking down the street towards the Flour
Mill. Her long, grey dress swished as she took every step, and
her handbag hung over her forearm, where it bobbed from side
to side, Jacob tipped his hat and nodded as he passed by her.

The village was busy with people hustling around. *Must be the beautiful day. It brings people out I guess,* Jacob thought.

Jacob rode up to the front of the general store, where Mr. Adair was sweeping off the front porch. He looked up and stopped what he was doing when he saw Jacob climbing off his horse.

"Well if it isn't my favourite carpenter," Mr. Adair said warmly, greeting him with a smile.

"Good day, Mr. Adair," replied Jacob with a big grin. He always enjoyed seeing Mr. Adair. He meant a great deal to Jacob. If it hadn't been for Mr. Adair, Jacob would have never started up his own carpentry business, and of course, he wouldn't be as successful as he was without Mr. Adair's brother, David.

"How is Mr. Rodgers doing?" Mr. Adair asked.

"The same," Jacob said sadly. "There hasn't been any change since the day it happened, last month."

"What a shame," Mr. Adair shook his head. "What does the doc say?"

"Nothing really," Jacob said. "He told us to send for him if anything happens."

"Well, son, if you ever need anything," Mr. Adair said, feeling bad for their situation, "I'm always here."

"Thank you, sir," Jacob appreciated everything Mr. Adair ever did for him. From the start of his carpentry business through his darkest moments after Anna died, Mr. Adair was always there.

"Actually, Mr. Adair, I do need your help," Jacob started, "on a couple of things."

"You name it."

Jacob dropped his head. "I know about Mr. Rodgers' financial situation."

"Oh," was all Mr. Adair could say.

"I want to talk to you about paying for it."

"Are you sure you know what you're doing lad?"

"I am sure, sir," Jacob nodded.

"Come inside." Mr. Adair leaned the broom against the wall. He opened the screen door, and Jacob took off his hat as he went through the doorway.

"I'll get their account card."

Jacob followed him into the office and stood waiting while he watched Mr. Adair reach in the solid oak filing cabinet. He turned around and handed Jacob Mr. Rodgers' account card.

"Thank you." Jacob took it from Mr. Adair, looked at the amount, and tried not to show his shock. He shook it off as he reached into his back pocket for his wallet. He counted enough cash, which was almost every dollar bill he had, to pay the debt. "Also," Jacob added, "anything that's for the Rodgers, please put on my account."

"You are one of a kind, lad, one of a kind." Mr. Adair shook his head as he took the money. He was in awe of Jacob's heart for the Rodgers family and grew a whole new respect for him at that moment. Feeling as though Jacob was his own son, Mr. Adair felt his chest seem to pop out of his shirt with pride and love for the boy he never had of his own.

"Please, don't say anything to anyone about this," Jacob requested.

"It'll be our secret." Mr. Adair smiled. "Now, what else did you need?"

"I was wondering if you knew of anyone that was looking for a job?"

"As in carpentry?" He asked.

"No," Jacob put his head down and smiled, slightly amused despite the seriousness of the situation. "No. Farm hand, or hired hand," he finished.

"Oh, I see," Mr. Adair said realizing what Jacob was asking. "You know, now that you mention it," he said with a wide-eyed look on his face as if he had a bright idea. "There was a young lad in here the other day. He was talking to Mrs. Adair. I think he was new in town and looking for work."

Jacob was happy to hear that.

"Let me check with the Missus. Come on," Mr. Adair said as he stepped back to the office doorway. He called out to his wife, who was in the front of the store dusting.

"Hello there, Jacob." Mrs. Adair smiled when she saw Mr. Adair had company with him. "It's wonderful to see you, lad." She walked over and gave him a hug. Mrs. Adair was a tall, slim woman with dirty blonde hair. She had a distinct look about her, but her sharp cheekbones and naturally red lips made her undeniably attractive. She had definitely aged well, Jacob had always thought. He respected both Mr. and Mrs. Adair and they knew it and admired the young lad themselves.

"Jacob here is looking for a farm hand for the Rodgers," her husband explained to her. "Didn't you speak with someone a few days ago?"

"Yes, I sure did," she looked at Jacob. "What a nice-looking lad, much like you, Jacob, and about your age, too." She smiled. "He said he was new in town and staying at the Empire Hotel. He was hoping to find work so he could make Abbington Pickets his home."

"That's great," Jacob said with as much enthusiasm as he could muster. "I'll go see if he's still there," he added as he held his hat in his hands. In reality, he wasn't looking forward to going over to the Empire Hotel. He hadn't set foot in that part of the Empire since his nightmare of getting over Anna. He didn't want to go there again to remind himself of how he'd acted, how he'd treated his closest friends, who were like family to him. He didn't want to be reminded that he once had been lost, very lost.

"Did he happen to mention his name?" Jacob asked as he stood at the door ready to leave.

"I can't remember." Mrs. Adair hesitated as she tried to recall his name. "Now isn't that silly." She couldn't get over herself not remembering.

"That's alright," Jacob reassured her. "If he's still in town, I'll find him." He handed Mrs. Adair the list Mrs. Rodgers gave him for supplies.

She took it from him, reading it over quickly. "I'll get these for you, wait here," she told him.

Jacob put on his hat, and stepped outside, Mr. Adair followed. While Mrs. Adair gathered the merchandise, the two men visited out on the porch and caught up on all the news from the village. Mr. Adair picked up his broom and began to sweep as they chatted along.

Jacob sure missed chatting with him every morning before work started, as he did before Mr. Rodgers' stroke. Mr. Adair, along with Jacob's friend Charles, and both Jacob's brothers, Andrew and Peter, had helped build his carpentry shop northeast of the general store.

Mrs. Adair came back with the sack full of goods in her arms.

"Thank you, Mrs. Adair." Jacob paid her, threw the sack over his shoulder and turned around to leave as she went back inside.

"I'll walk with you, son." Mr. Adair put on his hat as well.

They stepped off the porch and were walking on the wooden sidewalk when Mrs. Adair came hollering out the screen door. She opened it, and it slapped shut behind her. "Claude Beaumont! I remembered that's what his name is." She stopped and seemed pleased with herself for remembering.

"Thank you, Mrs. Adair." Jacob nodded and tipped his hat in appreciation. "I'll go over there right now."

"Hope to see you around more often, Jacob." Mr. Adair patted him on the back as they got closer to his horse. Jacob tied the sack to the saddle horn on his horse. He gave his horse a couple pats on the shoulder as he turned to Mr. Adair.

"Is it all right if I leave my horse here while I go next door to see about that lad?" Jacob asked.

"Of course," he answered with a smile. "Hope you find your man."

Jacob nodded in agreement, then started to walk across the street towards the Empire Hotel. As he got closer, he could hear laughing and music coming from the building. He held his breath while reaching for the door latch on the front door. Closing his eyes, he pulled the door open. The first person he saw was the bartender, wiping the counter top as he looked up and saw Jacob.

"Well, look what the cat dragged in," the bartender sneered.

"Thought you'd never grace us with your presence again," his voice taunted Jacob. The bartender knew full well that Jacob didn't go there anymore, and he also knew the reason. The gruff-looking man, who always appeared to have not shaved for at least two weeks, loved to tease with a sense of being miserable. Jacob ignored his sick sense of humour and simply said what he was there for.

"I'm looking for a young fella named Claude Beaumont," Jacob said plainly.

"Oh, that French lad from Quebec," he answered. "He doesn't come in here other than to go to his room. I think he's in room five."

"Thank you," Jacob said politely as he headed towards the door at the back of the saloon, which led him to the stairs to the rented rooms on the second floor. The hallway was dark wood with wainscoting that abutted leather-covered walls, separated by carved wood trim. All the doors were nicely carved dark wood as well with gold numbers in the middle and elegant glass door knobs. Jacob reached door number five and knocked with three raps in rhythm and waited while the footsteps on the other side of the door grew closer. The door opened, revealing a tall, dark haired young man. He had dark eyes and distinctive eyebrows.

Cleanly shaven, he was a little overdressed for the job Jacob had in mind for him. Maybe he wasn't in the market for a labour position.

"Bonjour, can I help you?" The young lad stood holding the door open looking at Jacob with a curious look on his face.

"Hello there," Jacob started, "my name is Jacob Hudson. I heard from the General Store over there," he pointed towards the east, "that you were looking for work?"

"You heard right," he answered shortly.

"What sort of work are you looking for?" Jacob wondered if this was such a good idea. He didn't seem to be eager to work.

"Well, you don't look hardly old enough to be offering any sort of job." The man's French accent grew with his skepticism.

"I am looking for a hard worker." Jacob ignored his comment. "My father-in-law to be needs a hired man to help at Goldenrod Ranch, east of Abbington Pickets."

"Pays cash?" the stranger asked.

"Yep, at the end of each week." Jacob felt he needed to be a little firm. "As long as the work is satisfactory, that is."

"Oh, it will be." He answered with extreme confidence.

"So you'll take the job?" Jacob asked.

"When do I start?"

"Tomorrow morning."

"Sounds good. Let me know how to get to this ranch, and I'll be there at daybreak." He reached his hand out to Jacob. "Claude Beaumont's the name."

"Pleased to meet you, Claude." Jacob shook his hand firmly then gave him directions to the Goldenrod Ranch. The young lad seemed confident that he would find the place easy enough. "By the way," Jacob said, "you'll be dealing with me about the work at Goldenrod, and for your pay as well."

"As long as I get paid, that's all I care about." Claude seemed to only have one thing on his mind.

"My carpentry shop is a little east of here. That's where I'll be working. I'll come out when I can. There's a bunk house where you'll be staying at the ranch. But we can go over the details tomorrow."

"Thank you. See you in the morning."

Claude closed the door to his room, and Jacob turned around and walked back down the hallway to find his way out of the hotel. Happy to be out of the saloon, he walked over to his horse, climbed up onto the saddle, and urged the horse to proceed home.

During the ride, Jacob did a lot of thinking. It was difficult for him to hire someone else to take care of his family. The relief of not having to do everything himself was a comfort, but letting go to gain what was really his hardly made any sense at all to him. Jacob wanted to be married to Abigail, make his carpentry business a success, and have a wonderful family together. With, of course, Mr. Rodgers being well again and everything back to the way it was. That was his prayer as he rode home, talking to God.

chapter four

A WEEK HAD gone by since Jacob had hired Claude to take care of Goldenrod while Jacob was working in the village. For the most part, Claude caught onto everything that Jacob requested him to do around the ranch, including the understanding that the house was off limits except for at meal time. Claude said that was fine with him as he liked his alone time. He was going to school to be a lawyer and wanted his evenings for studying. Being the only one left to take care of his mother financially, made it difficult for him to go to university. So he borrowed the books from a professor he'd become friends with and came to the prairies to make a living while learning at home. When he had saved enough, he was planning to go back to Quebec, back to his mother and finish university.

Jacob hadn't really seen Claude much since the day they had met at Goldenrod to show him the ropes. He had spent most of his time working at the carpentry shop catching up. He worried about leaving Abigail and her mother alone with a stranger, but he sensed that he could trust the young Frenchman. He seemed to be stuck on wanting to make his money and carry on with life, so to speak. Jacob did worry that Abigail would need his support since they hadn't been as close as they had been before. It broke his heart to have to work away from her and her parents, but it was the only way.

Saturday, Jacob went back to the ranch for the first time to see how Claude was handling everything. Mrs. Rodgers said that he was quiet, but polite and kept mostly to himself, but always had meals with them. He did take longer to cut the wood than Jacob did. She also wondered if he had ever milked a cow in his life, because the first day he was there he had gone to the barn early in the morning, not returning until almost noon with hardly a half a pail of milk. Mrs. Rodgers said she didn't want to criticize, and he did a better job the next day. Her comments made Jacob smile to himself a little. Mrs. Rodgers told Jacob not to worry though, she knew Claude would catch on soon.

The following day, Sunday, Jacob took Mrs. Rodgers to church. Abigail didn't want to leave her father and said it would do her mother more good than herself to get out of the house.

"Hello, Mrs. Rodgers," Reverend Young greeted them at the church door with a handshake. He had just rung the church bell to remind the community that service would be starting soon.

"Good morning," Jacob said, standing behind Mrs. Rodgers. "Good morning, Reverend," Mrs. Rodgers said, her voice quiet and her smile reserved. It was the first day she had gone out since Mr. Rodgers had his stroke. She needed to get out of the house, but she felt everyone in the congregation staring at her with sympathy. She didn't like the way that made her feel.

Jacob took his hat off before he walked in the church door and set it on the hat rack in the entryway of the church with all the other men's hats. They walked past the pews together and sat in the third pew from the front on the right side. That was Mrs. Rodgers' favourite spot to sit, and she wasn't going to stop now.

"We will now sing, 'Amazing Grace,'" the Reverend instructed and motioned upwards with his hands to let everyone one know to stand to sing. The choir consisted of ten local ladies and one gentleman, who was Mr. Patterson the owner of the flour mill in Abbington. He was a tall, stout man with a full beard and a deep voice that could be heard throughout the church and even outside. It was a good thing that there was even a chorus to guide the congregation because it seemed no one else could carry a tune, much less all at the same time. Mrs. Smyth was an excellent organist, which also helped the vocalists out. The song ended, and everyone took their seats.

"I would like to welcome all of you in Jesus' name," Reverend Young began to speak. "It is wonderful to see all of you out here today, especially Mrs. Rodgers and Jacob," He smiled down at them, which embarrassed them both to no end. "We are all praying for Mr. Rogers and know what a trial this has been for all of you."

Mrs. Rodgers smiled and nodded at the Reverend.

"Psalm 91 is a prayer of protection…" he started his sermon when the door came open with a bang as it hit the wall behind it and in came a stranger. Well, he was a stranger to most in the village. Everyone turned around in their seats to look at what, or better yet who was so rudely interrupting their church service.

"What is the meaning of this?" Reverend Young sternly asked the young lad. "Why have you barged in here?"

"It's Mr. Rodgers." The young man stood there, holding his hat in his hands, feeling somewhat out of place despite the urgency of his visit. He scanned the room quickly to see if he could see Jacob or Mrs. Rodgers. Once he found Mrs. Rodgers, he ran towards her and blurted out, "He is awake!" The whole room spoke at once, in awe of what they had just heard.

"Are you sure?" Mrs. Rodgers questioned Claude. "Are you really sure?" she repeated, trying not to get her hopes up.

"I'm sure as I'm breathing, ma'am," Claude said. By this time Doc Johnson was up from his pew and running towards the door.

"Well, we'd better get going." He grabbed his hat on his way out, as Jacob, Mrs. Rodgers and Claude quickly followed. By this time, the whole congregation was astir, and everyone was talking to each other, while the Reverend tried to quiet everyone down.

"The wagon is over here," Jacob directed the doctor.

"I have my own, lad. Thank you," Doc said as he quickly walked over and climbed into his carriage. Claude was already on his horse and headed back to Goldenrod before Jacob even helped Mrs. Rodgers onto the covered wagon. She sat in front with her hands on her lap. Jacob climbed on, knowing how anxious she was to get home.

"Hee-yaw!" Jacob said to the horses. They didn't waste any time and began to trot, then were at full pace, hard work for a team pulling a wagon on the rough, still-wintered path. All Jacob could do was pray under his breath, hoping this was the miracle they were asking for. No one said a word on the way to the ranch. Both of them were praying their own prayers.

The trip seemed to take twice as long as usual, but finally, Jacob could see the house in the distance. The surrounding trees weren't covered in leaves yet, so it was easy to see the yard from farther away. As the team of horses pulled them up to the front step, Jacob could see Claude's horse tied up at the post in front of the stone house. Doc had pulled in front of Jacob and Mrs. Rodgers.

Jacob jumped off the wagon and turned around to help Mrs. Rodgers. Doc didn't wait for either of them and ran into the house, leaving the door open. Jacob and Mrs. Rodgers weren't far behind him. Everyone was scared, worried, and excited about what they were about to see behind the bedroom door. They followed Doc into the room where they found Abigail standing beside Mr. Rogers, holding his hand, smiling from ear to ear. As soon as she saw them all, she had such a satisfied look on her face.

"See! What did I tell you!" Abigail beamed, "I knew he would wake up! I told you his eyes opened for a moment, didn't I?" She was so full of life at that moment as she looked down at her father's face.

He looked back at her with tired eyes, not saying anything, simply looking around at everyone with a slight bit of confusion. However, he was holding Abigail's hand back, with a weak grasp, but a grasp all the same.

"Didn't I tell you, Mama?" Abigail looked at her Mama, who was as excited as she was.

"I know you did dear." She grabbed hold of Abigail's other hand and squeezed it tight as if to say "you were right." She took her husband's hand and held it as Abigail let go and made room for Doc.

"All right, everyone out while I examine him," Doc Johnson firmly said. "Give the man some space here." He dug into his black bag to retrieve his stethoscope and other tools he was going to use. Mrs. Rodgers stayed to assist him with anything he might need.

Jacob took Abigail by the hand and gently tugged her, to indicate that they should leave the room. He was beaming inside and was so grateful to see Mr. Rodgers awake. It had been such a long time since he had seen a smile on Abigail's face that it warmed his heart. They walked into the living room and stood in the middle of the floor. They both were too excited to sit still.

"Praise the Lord," Jacob said to Abigail. "God is good, isn't he?"

Abigail smiled back at him with relief, but she didn't speak about praying to the Lord as Jacob did.

Jacob hugged her tight, not wanting to let her go. He hadn't seen her much in the past week, not to mention the past month. He had missed her laugh, her non-stop chatting about the day, and her sense of humour. He didn't realize how much stress he really was under until he felt that relief, knowing that Mr. Rodgers was getting better.

"Let's make a pot of tea," Jacob suggested in an effort to keep them busy. He stopped and thought for a minute, and then laughed out loud. "Listen to me, sounding like Bert." Jacob remembered how Bert loved his tea and firmly believed that tea could fix anything. He also remembered how Bert had been such a good friend to him over the few years he had known him. It was a good thing he'd come to Anna's house during that terrible blizzard night, or they may never have met. *There is not another fella like him,* Jacob thought to himself. *He loves the Lord, he loves Alice, and he loves to help anyone he can. God knows how he helped me,* Jacob told himself.

Abigail laughed at Jacob's comment. "Here, you go, get the water." She handed him the water pitcher. "I'll put the tea leaves in the teapot." For a moment, everything seemed to be back to normal. Despite both of them keeping busy, in the back of both of their minds was what was going on behind the bedroom door.

Jacob and Abigail were sitting at the table, finishing their tea and boiling the kettle for another pot when Doc came out of

Mr. Rodgers' room. Abigail got up from her chair and rushed over to meet Doc in the middle of the room.

"Well? Is he going to be fine?" she asked him with a bit of desperation in her voice, as if it were up to Doc to make him better or worse.

"Don't get so excited, young lady," Doc said plainly. "Time will tell how much damage has been done."

"What does that mean?" Jacob asked. "He's awake. Isn't that a good thing?"

"Yes, it's a good thing," Doc replied, "but as I told you before, a stroke can do so much damage."

"But he squeezed my hand," Abigail said. "That's also a good thing."

"He has some movement. It's in half of his body, though," Doc explained. "The other half isn't moving much. I explained exercises to do with him to see if the mobility will start in that half."

Abigail left the room to see her father and talk to her mother.

"I have seen this before, Jacob," Doc said, still looking sympathetic. "A person has a stroke, but is left like a vegetable; it's a sad thing and hard to watch. Keep praying, lad," he said, patting Jacob on the back. Doc always seemed so harsh and gruff on the exterior, but everyone knew he had a soft heart. He really cared for his patients, and he kept his heart protected from all the loss he had seen over the years. In a close-knit community, such as Abbington Pickets, it was difficult to lose some of his closest friends. Doc hadn't always been that way. When he was a young doctor, new to Abbington Pickets, he had been full of life and excitement at being the community doctor.

He thought he could save the world. It didn't take long for him to realize that he couldn't save everyone.

When one of his dearest friends, Mr. Summerfield's son, was killed in a wagon accident, it almost ripped his heart out. Mr. Summerfield's hired man and son had been in the field spreading manure. Near the end of the day, on their way back to the farmyard, the hired man got off the wagon to open the gate. The boy asked if he could help, but the hired man shook his head giving him strict instructions not to drive the horses through. Mr. Summerfield's son disobeyed, taking the reins and starting to drive them through the gate. The horses began to gallop; the boy lost his balance and fell backwards off the wagon. When Doc got to him, he thought the boy could be saved. He was a fairly inexperienced doctor at the time and didn't realize that the lad was slowly bleeding inside. Just when they thought he was better, the boy died. It was a senseless death, and that experience was the start to Doc hardening his heart. At that point, he decided to protect himself from any emotions.

"I'll come back in the morning," Doc said as he put on his hat and coat, "unless there is another drastic change of course." He looked at Jacob as he opened the door. "You're a good lad, Jacob. You've done the work of ten men, and still, you have a smile on your face." With that compliment, he left the house.

Jacob didn't feel as honourable as Doc made him out to be.

He wished there was more he could do. With that thought, he wondered where Claude was. He hadn't been around since they got back. Jacob put on his coat, boots, and hat and opened the door. It was still light out, but the sun was going down; he could see the horizon towards Abbington Pickets. The light was on in the bunkhouse, so he knew that Claude was there. *He must be done all of the chores,* Jacob thought to himself. He reached the door. It felt a little weird knocking since it used to be the place he'd called home. Claude answered the door.

"Hello there, Claude," Jacob started. "I wanted to come and thank you for coming so speedily today."

"It was nothing," Claude said plainly. "I didn't want to get in the way, so I came out and finished the chores."

"It was more than nothing," Jacob insisted.

"How is Mr. Rodgers doing?" Claude asked.

"Well, he still has a ways to go, but he definitely has improved," Jacob explained. "We're still praying."

"Good," Claude said as he stood at the door. "By the way, did you say you would pay weekly?"

Well, it did seem that money was mostly what this lad thought of, Jacob thought to himself. *This really isn't the best time to ask, but I guess he doesn't know Mr. Rodgers from Adam, so it doesn't mean much to him.* "Yes, I did," Jacob answered as he reached into his pocket for his wallet. He was prepared to pay Claude then anyway because it was a week since he had started to work. "There you go." Jacob handed him several paper bills.

"Thank you," Claude said as he took the money, counted and folded it, and put it in his pocket.

"Umm, I am not sure what we'll be having for supper," Jacob started to say. "The ladies have been busy with Mr. Rodgers-"

"That's alright," Claude stopped him. "I have food here I can eat."

Jacob couldn't get over the stranger's unfriendly manner. *I guess he was raised differently or possibly it was because he was French,* Jacob thought. He'd heard they were rather frank and a little unfriendly.

"Well, have a good evening, Claude," Jacob said. *I guess you meet all sorts of people in the world and no two are alike. You learn something new every day, but Claude better get a little friendlier if he wants to get along in Abbington Pickets for long.*

Jacob went back to the house. He had decided to spend the night in case Mr. Rodgers needed the doctor. He would get up early and go to work in the morning. He took his outside clothes off and washed his hands in the porch. He walked through the kitchen, then the living room, anxious to see how Mr. Rodgers was doing. He knocked on the closed door, opening it slowly.

"Is it alright if I come in?" he asked.

Both Abigail and her Mama looked at him and simultaneously said, "Yes."

He felt like he had to walk slowly as he got closer to the bed. He could see Mr. Rodgers looking around, much as he was before. This time, he lifted his hand up as if to wave to him. Mr. Rodgers tried to smile, but all of it was such an effort for him to do.

"Good to see you so well, Mr. Rodgers," Jacob said, smiling. "I knew you would be up in no time."

"Of course he would," Abigail agreed.

"I'll go get some supper started. You two stay here with your father," Mrs. Rodgers said like a little old hen.

"We will, Mama," Abigail reassured her as her Mama left the room.

"Doc Johnson showed Mama exercises to do with Papa to make him stronger," Abigail explained, "but only a little each day."

"He'll be up and walking in no time," Jacob said. "Won't you, Mr. Rodgers?" Jacob spoke loudly as if Mr. Rodgers were deaf.

"Let's pray for him right now," Jacob suggested. He held Abigail's hand; she was holding Mr. Rodgers' one hand, and Jacob held the other.

"Dear Jesus, please continue to heal Mr. Rodgers, comfort him, protect him, and give him strength. In Jesus' name, Amen."

"Amen," Abigail said as well.

Mr. Rodgers' eyes seemed to get bigger, and they looked like they were smiling. He was trying to say something to Jacob, but he got exasperated and finally stopped trying. Jacob thought he was being grateful for the prayer, and he was trying to thank him for it, but only Mr. Rodgers and God would really know what he was trying to say.

chapter five

THE FOLLOWING WEEK went by quickly. Jacob was anxious to get his work done. It was a beautiful sunny Friday, and he wanted to ride to Goldenrod. Claude and he were planning on doing some much-needed chores over the next couple of days. Of course, seeing Abigail would be the highlight of the weekend. Every day that Doc Johnson was out to see Mr. Rodgers, Jacob would talk to him, and he had been encouraged by the progress Doc said Mr. Rodgers was making. It might only be baby steps, but it was an improvement.

When Reverend Young visited Mr. Rodgers, he let Jacob know as well. Jacob felt blessed that he had so many people watching out for him.

Normally the barn would get cleaned sometime in the middle of winter, but because of the circumstances, that job had been put off for a while. Saturday, Jacob and Claude were going to pull out the stone-boat and clean the barn. Bert was coming to help as well. Alice was itching to get out of the house for a day and couldn't wait to see Mrs. Rodgers and Abigail for some "woman" talk. They hadn't seen each other since Mr. Rodgers first fell ill, so they had a lot of catching up to do.

That night, when Jacob arrived for supper, he was surprised by Mr. Rodgers' progression. It was far more advanced than

Doc had let on. Mr. Rodgers was more awake, propped up in his bed, and moving his right arm, even squeezing Jacob's hand. He could say a word here or there. It was truly a miracle from God.

Abigail was beaming proudly as she stood beside Jacob, watching the interaction between her father and husband-to-be.

"You are looking mighty good there, Mr. Rodgers," Jacob said, smiling.

Mr. Rodgers nodded with an uneasy bob of his head. "Y-E-S," he slowly said, almost spelling it out, with an excitement he hardly could contain.

Jacob bent over and reached for his hand, giving it a gentle squeeze. He was thrilled to see his soon-to-be father-in-law doing well. *What more can I do for him? He's been stuck in isolation for almost two months. What if? Hmm … I think I know how I can help Mr. Rodgers,* Jacob said to himself.

"How was your week at the shop, Jacob?" Mrs. Rodgers asked as the four of them were eating supper. "I am sure you have many things to catch up on," she said as she took a bite of chicken stew.

"Very well, thank you, Mrs. Rodgers," Jacob smiled as he buttered his biscuit. "And," he looked over at Abigail with enthusiasm, "I ordered the lumber to start the house today." Abigail's eyes lit up in a way Jacob hadn't seen in a while.

"That's wonderful, Jacob." Abigail stopped pouring the tea, put down the pot, and swiftly walked over to Jacob leaned down and hugged him.

"Uhh unh," Mrs. Rodgers interrupted their brief embrace as she gave Abigail a look of disapproval for her unladylike lunging at Jacob.

Abigail sheepishly and slowly got up and continued to pour everyone their tea.

"And Mr. Adair said it'll be here a week from Wednesday." Jacob wiped his mouth with his napkin and took a sip of tea. "He has a wagon coming from Kingston earlier than usual. It was great timing."

"I can't believe you can build a house that quickly," Claude put in his two cents. Usually, he was pretty quiet at meal time but today Jacob was present, and a little male conversation was something Claude looked for.

Jacob was surprised by Claude's comment, considering he hadn't confided in him about his personal life. Claude sensed the confusion Jacob was feeling.

"Abigail mentioned you wanted to have it built before you two were married," Claude said.

Jacob looked at him again with curiosity.

"Well, since the wedding is planned for the fall," Claude continued.

"So, I take it you have built many houses?" Jacob said.

"Well," Claude shifted uncomfortably in his chair. "Actually, no."

"I see." Jacob dropped the rest of the conversation. "I'm going to go have a visit with Mr. Rodgers." Jacob stood up from the table, placing his napkin on his plate. He walked over and kissed the top of Abigail's head.

"Thank you for supper, Mrs. Rodgers." Claude got up from the table as well. "See you in the morning." He walked into the porch and put on his coat, boots, and hat, and left.

Jacob carried a cup of tea and sat down in the ram's chair beside Mr. Rodgers in his room. He set the tea cup on the small table beside him. Mr. Rodgers watched him closely from the very moment he walked into the door. Jacob knew Mr. Rodgers would come back to them, he had faith he would.

"You're doing better each day, Mr. Rodgers," Jacob started. Mr. Rodgers nodded in agreement.

"We pray every day. I believe the Lord has been answering our prayers," again Mr. Rodgers seemed to agree.

"Winter is almost over, and it'll be time to get the crops in."

Mr. Rodgers' face changed from agreement to disagreement to concern.

Jacob knew what he was thinking. Money. Jacob didn't want to hurt his pride by telling him he was taking care of his financial affairs; it was hard enough for him to watch the world going on around him without being able to do a single thing. Jacob wanted to ease his burdens but at the same time keep his reputation, as well as his pride intact. But Jacob was also feeling the pressure of building the house, making sure the crops got planted, and not to mention the wedding in the fall, along with making a living all at the same time. It felt somewhat overwhelming. It made his heart start to pound as he thought of the many things he needed to do in the next six months. Jacob took a deep breath and smiled at Mr. Rodgers.

"Soon the weather will be nice, and maybe we can take you outside," Jacob continued as he picked up the cup and blew on the tea, making sure it wasn't too hot. Jacob got up and leaned over to reach Mr. Rodgers, offering him a sip of tea.

Mr. Rodgers awkwardly opened his mouth to consume the warm liquid. Some of it flowed into his mouth, while the rest spilled down his chin, onto his shirt.

"Whoopsie daisy," Jacob made light of it as he wiped the tea off Mr. Rodgers with his hanky. *Each day is progress for Mr. Rodgers*, Jacob thought, and he was going to do his very best to help him all the ways he could.

"I'll see you in the morning, Mr. Rodgers," Jacob promised as he took the empty tea cup and left the room. Jacob could tell Mr. Rodgers was tired. He wanted to let him rest for the night.

He could hear Abigail and her ma still doing the dishes. Anxious to get started on a surprise for Mr. Rodgers, Jacob decided to go to the barn and work on it for a while.

The barn was cold and frosty; there was the smell of dusty, mouldy hay in the air, almost taking Jacob's breath away. Jacob climbed the ladder up to the loft. He thought he remembered seeing the chair he'd made for Abigail four years ago when he was up there last. Mr. Rodgers stored quite a few extra items up in the corner such as old furniture that needed repair, in hopes that one day it would happen. Of course, there was also hay that hadn't been used up yet this year.

Ah ha, Jacob said to himself, as he spotted the chair propped up against the wall with a few other things sitting alongside it. He stepped carefully between old furniture to reach over to grab the chair and pull it upwards and out of its spot. Jacob almost fell backwards when he tugged a little too hard on the wedged chair. Finally, he retrieved the awkwardly shaped chair and carefully climbed down the ladder, balancing the chair in one hand and holding onto the ladder with the other.

"What are you doing out here?" a familiar voice came from below, scaring the dickens out of Jacob. He almost fell off the ladder and dropped the chair.

"Whoa, don't ever do that." Jacob's heart pounded as he reached the floor of the barn and set the chair down. "You nearly scared me to death." Jacob grinned, not meaning to upset Abigail.

"I'm sorry. I didn't mean to." Abigail grinned back. "What are you doing with that?" She pointed to the chair.

"It's a surprise." Jacob smiled, grabbed hold of Abigail's hands, and pulled her nearer to him. "What are you doing out here? It's freezing," Jacob asked, trying to change the subject. He didn't want to tell anyone what he was doing in case his idea didn't work. He wrapped his arms around Abigail, and she rested against him to keep warm.

"I have been missing you, Jacob," Abigail quietly said to him. "I know we haven't been able to talk much. I just wanted you to know," She smiled as she lifted her head, looking up into his eyes.

Jacob stroked her hair with his rough hand as to say it was alright.

"With Pa being sick–"

Jacob put his finger over her lips, "Shhh, I know, Girlie," he consoled her, not wanting her feeling any worse than she already did. Jacob wished he could do more for her and her parents.

"I simply want it back to the way it was." Tears stung her eyes, but she didn't shed a one.

"Me too," Jacob agreed, "but unfortunately, it'll never be." He was thinking of the long road ahead of them. "It'll only make us stronger. Soon we'll have a house of our own, and we'll be married," Jacob reassured her. "Your pa will be better, quicker than you think."

"I hope you're right, Mr. Hudson." Abigail liked to pretend to be formal when she was playing around with Jacob.

"You better go back in the house." Jacob tapped her on the tip of her nose with his finger. "You'll catch a cold, Girlie."

"Alright, Mother," Abigail teased as she reluctantly backed away from him, turned around, and left.

Jacob pulled the chair over to the back corner of the barn where Mr. Rodgers kept his tools. He got to work right away. It was already late in the evening, and they had a big day planned for tomorrow.

"Good morning, ladies." Jacob walked into the kitchen, which was filled with a delicious aroma. Claude was already sitting at the table. "Morning, Claude," Jacob nodded.

"Morning," Claude looked at Jacob then back down to his plate.

Jacob couldn't figure out Claude. He seemed so distant from others and so unemotional in every way. It was like he has no feelings. *Maybe if he does, it's all for himself*, Jacob thought. "I'll be right back." Jacob walked out to the porch and pushed the newly finished wheelchair in through the kitchen. As he walked in, Abigail and her Mama stared in wonder. Jacob rolled the chair through the living room and into Mr. Rodgers' room.

Mr. Rodgers was lying in his bed with his head propped up with a pillow, his eyes wide open, watching every move Jacob made. Abigail and her Mama followed Jacob without saying a word. Even Claude lingered behind the women.

"Come on, Claude," Jacob delegated without hesitation. "Give me a hand here." He directed him towards Mr. Rodgers.

"You're kidding me," Claude said. "You're not going to get him to sit in that thing." He seemed to mock Jacob for even having the idea.

"Are you sure you should be doing this?" Mrs. Rodgers asked.

"It's a fantastic idea," Abigail intervened with a big smile on her face. "You are a genius, Jacob. I never thought of it, but what a great idea." She turned to Mrs. Rodgers. "Don't you see, if we can get Pa up and sit him in the other parts of the house, or better yet outside, he'll improve even faster. Well, Claude, let's get going," Abigail ordered as she stood beside her father's legs, ready to lift.

"Well," Claude hesitated, not liking being told what to do. He walked over to the other side of Mr. Rodgers, across from Jacob, to lift Mr. Rodgers' upper body. Mrs. Rodgers stood opposite Abigail, and on the count of three, all four of them lifted Mr. Rodgers into the homemade wheelchair. Mr. Rodgers had a somewhat terrified look on his face at first, but once he realized he was on safe ground, he relaxed. Then right at that moment, his lips formed a slight smile. He looked over at Jacob's grinning face, gratitude in his eyes and love in his heart for his almost son-in-law. Everyone cheered for the small victory.

Jacob felt his chest swell a little, knowing this could change Mr. Rodgers' life for the good. Jacob was a humble young man, never wanting credit or a big deal made over anything, but he couldn't help feel proud of himself at that moment.

Bert and Alice reached Goldenrod not long after Mr. Rodgers was in his moveable chair and sitting in the kitchen, watching the ladies make dinner. Jacob and Claude were outside, pulling the stone-boat out from behind the barn with the work horses. The stone-boat had been left at Goldenrod by the Benedict brothers, built by two local men. It was eight feet wide and ten feet long, with skids underneath the planks that ran side to side. It was originally built for picking stones in the field and hauling hay, but when the barn needed to be cleaned, the stone-boat helped get the job done.

Bert was eager to help clean the barn, and Alice was anxious to help Mrs. Rodgers and Abigail with anything. She was happy to be there to spend time with them.

"Good morning, lads," Bert said to Jacob and Claude. "What a beautiful day it is."

"Well, hello Bert." Jacob looked up and smiled to see his good friend walking closer to them.

"Bert, this is Claude," Jacob directed a hand towards Claude, "Claude, this is Bert."

"How do you do?" Bert put his hand out to Claude. "Bonjour." Claude shook his hand.

"A Frenchman," Bert noted. "Are you from France?"

"No, Quebec," Claude clarified. Once he spoke, no one would mistake his French Canadian accent.

"Ready for a big day?" Jacob smiled.

"You bet," Bert answered. "I see Mr. Rodgers is improving. What a blessing that is."

"That it is." Jacob nodded.

"That was a wonderful idea you had with the chair."

"Well, we won't know that for sure until he's used it for a while." Jacob tried to be modest.

"Did Alice's brother get here from England?" Jacob asked.

"He sure did." Bert smiled. "It's wonderful to have Ernest here. He'll be with us until his fiancée arrives from England."

"That's great." Jacob said.

"Do you think we could just get to work?" Claude interrupted the long overdue visit.

"Hold your horses, lad." Bert laughed. "There's plenty of time for work. Jacob and I have a little catching up to do."

"I am here for the work. That's it." Claude didn't lighten his mood in the least. "Although the view in the kitchen isn't that bad," he added under his breath.

Jacob wasn't sure if he'd heard right. "What was that?"

"Nothing," Claude turned away.

Jacob ignored the comment, but couldn't figure out why Claude was so unfriendly most of the time. Unfriendly and unsociable. Jacob wasn't sure what kind of lawyer he was going to be—definitely not a nice one. Jacob was beginning to think that maybe he'd made a mistake hiring Claude.

"Pull the stone-boat in front of the barn door," Jacob ordered Claude while he smiled at Bert as if to say, *Well, if you want, you can work.*

Jacob and Bert walked in the side door to the barn. Jacob grabbed a five-tine fork that was leaning against the wall and handed it to Bert, picked up another one, handing it to Claude, and then he picked up the last fork. It had a broken tine, so Jacob would pick up the slack that would be caused by the defective tool.

"Let's get to work, then," Jacob announced matter-of-factly.

The three men spent the day lifting horse manure onto the stone-boat, then driving the horses to the pasture to unload. It took until supper, with a break at dinner and a three o'clock lunch to finish the barn. It was a job well done, and Jacob was relieved it was completed. Once the stone-boat was put away, the horses fed, and the chores done, everyone sat around the supper table. This time Mr. Rodgers was there to join them. It was the first time in a while Jacob felt the family was all together.

With the lateness of the hour, Bert and Alice decided to spend the night and would leave bright and early in the morning. Since Alice's brother Ernest was at home to take care of the chores, they were able to do so.

chapter six

THE DAY ARRIVED when the lumber for Jacob and Abigail's new home came. A team of horses drove into the village, right up to Jacob's carpentry shop. There were perks to knowing Mr. Adair personally; he managed to talk the driver into dropping off the load at Jacob's doorstep, or at least the invisible one, for now.

Jacob hadn't been to Goldenrod for two weeks. Once the lumber had been unloaded, he got to work right away. He also had furniture orders to finish, but he managed to do both. He was getting up every morning at four-thirty, working in his shop until after breakfast. He then worked on the house until supper. Once he had something to eat, he went back out to the shop to continue working on the furniture. Jacob was still sending his specialty tables to Kingston to be sold at Mr. Adair's brother's store. That was his biggest source of income at the moment. Good thing he had been saving for three years. Paying Claude weekly made it seem like the money was leaking out of the bottom of the bucket like water, but Jacob knew God would supply all their needs and left it in His hands. He would work as hard as he could, knowing it would pay off in the end. He and Abigail would be married, and they would live in their beautiful new home and start a new family. That was what kept Jacob going, that was what kept him strong, that was what he believed.

Jacob, along with Charles, Bert, Mr. Adair, and a couple of neighbours, had already dug the footings for the foundation of the house the previous fall after his shop was completed. Jacob knew he would be building a house there, even before he proposed to Abigail. It was his little secret plan. It wasn't going to be a huge mansion; however, it wasn't going to be any ordinary house either. Jacob knew he couldn't afford to be lavish and fancy, but he had an idea. If it couldn't be the biggest and fanciest place in Abbington Pickets, it could at least be the most unique. With much planning and a lot of discussion, along with some detailed advice from Mr. Adair, Jacob designed a residence that would not be found anywhere else in the province.

Over the previous few days, Charles and Jacob strung the floor joists and then laid the subflooring. Charles had indeed been a big help to Jacob. He was still a bachelor himself and lived in town. His father owned a local business and Charles worked for him when he wanted, which was why he was able to help Jacob. The days seemed to pass by so quickly. Although Jacob missed Abigail terribly, he knew it wouldn't be long before they would be able to spend all their time together. He was determined that the house was going to be finished in September.

That morning, Jacob and Charles began constructing the house's exterior walls. Since the house was going to have two storeys, the walls were going to have to be at least seventeen feet tall. Charles was going to help him, as he couldn't do a lot of the lifting by himself.

"You had to make it different, didn't you?" Charles laughed as the two of them struggled to construct the bow-shaped wall.

Jacob hadn't told Abigail everything about their house. He'd showed her diagrams of the house he designed but failed to mention one minor detail. He wanted to surprise her with a one of a kind abode. He wanted all of Abbington Pickets to ride or walk by in awe of the place they lived, and to want to get a peek inside.

"Of course." Jacob smiled back with a hammer in his hand, crouching down on one knee. "You know I am a peculiar fella." They both burst out laughing.

It was a beautiful sunny day, which was in their favour. Jacob was also in a particularly great mood as he was going to Goldenrod for the night, after work. He felt he needed to check on Mr. and Mrs. Rodgers, see how Claude was making out with all the chores, and of course, see his beautiful Abigail.

By supper time, Jacob and Charles were finished one of four walls for the outside of the house. Jacob stood up from being hunched over most of the day, stretching out his back by reaching up into the air with his hands.

"I bet you're excited to see Abigail tonight," Charles stated.

"Without a doubt." Jacob grinned from ear to ear.

"I'm sure she'll be happy to see your dirty mug as well," he teased as he threw his hanky at Jacob.

Jacob reached out in front of him and caught the dirty cloth in his hand. "You better get home, or your Mama will be looking for her baby," Jacob teased.

"Oh, go on," Charles said seriously. "You know she won't look for me … until … at least six o'clock." They laughed again at his joke.

"Thank you for your help," Jacob said with all seriousness.

"Any time, my lad," Charles said as he picked up his tools and placed them in his wooden tool box.

"If you want to get this place up before the big day," Charles began, "we have a lot of hours to fill."

"We'll get it done," Jacob said plainly.

"If you say so." Charles got the point quickly. "We will," he agreed as he walked away to head for home for the night.

Jacob went into his carpentry shop to change, have something to eat, and pack his bag for the ride over to Goldenrod. He hurried as he was anxious to see Abigail. Although he wanted to see how Mr. Rodgers was doing, all he could think about was Abigail. It reminded him of when Abigail went to England. Oh, how he missed her.

Since it was by then the middle of May, the days were getting longer. It didn't get completely dark until around nine o'clock. Jacob climbed onto his horse and rode swiftly through Poplar Lane to Goldenrod. It was still light out when he stopped in the yard. No one was around. It was apparent the chores were done, but he knew supper would be over. There were two windows lit up in the house, the kitchen and the room Mr. Rodgers occupied. Jacob put his horse in the stable for the night and walked up the path to the door of the house. He unlatched the door and went inside. Mrs. Rodgers was in the kitchen.

"Well, Jacob, my boy," she exclaimed, happy to see him. "It's good to see you." She rushed over to him and hugged him tight. Jacob couldn't help but feel, as his arms were around her, that she had lost weight.

"How are you doing, Mrs. Rodgers?" Jacob asked with concern but didn't want her to know why he was asking.

"I'm good, Jacob." She stood there, lying to him as he'd guessed she would. "What about you? You're the one working so hard. How are you?" She touched his cheek in a motherly fashion as her worry lines increased above her brow.

"Don't be worrying about me, Mrs. Rodgers," Jacob told her. "A little work never killed anyone." He grinned.

She shook her head at his logic and ignored his comment. "Mr. Rodgers is doing so well; you must go and see him." she smiled faintly. "Abigail has been so happy to see her pa getting well. He's speaking more and more every day."

"Great news, Mrs. Rodger." Jacob squeezed her clammy and trembling hands.

"Are you sure you're alright?" Jacob persisted.

"Of course, why do you ask?" She looked pale as she regarded Jacob.

"Just making sure," Jacob said. "Now let's go visit Mr. Rodgers." He let Mrs. Rodgers lead the way as they both headed towards the bedroom door.

"We have tucked him in his bed for the night," Mrs. Rodgers said. "Claude has been a great help around the house lately," she added.

Jacob was confused by this statement. He had specifically told Claude the house was off limits except for meals. But then again, maybe it wasn't as bad as it sounded. Not wanting to alarm Mrs. Rodgers, Jacob let it go.

"That's good."

"Mr. Rodgers, you look so good," Jacob said with a smile that lit up the room.

Mr. Rodgers was happy to see Jacob. He was like a small child delighted to see his parents after they had been gone for days. Mr. Rodgers was sitting up in his bed, with the crocheted bedspread covering him from his chest past his toes. He was more alert, with the colour back in his cheeks; his hair was parted on the side and combed neatly.

Jacob thought he was beginning to look like himself again.

It did his heart good to see this man, his mentor, be healed. God was good!

"Well, I better let you get some sleep," Jacob said. "I'll be back to help put you in your chair in the morning." Mr. Rodgers nodded.

"Alright … my … boy," Mr. Rodgers said, much like he used to say to Jacob, only a little slower.

"Good night," Jacob said as he left Mrs. Rodgers to be with her husband.

"Good night," they both responded at the same time.

Jacob wondered why he hadn't seen Abigail yet. Maybe she was in her room sleeping already? Jacob headed down the hallway, towards Robin's Roost, the billiard room where he and Mr. Rodgers had played pool together the very first time he visited Goldenrod. He thought maybe a walk through the room would give him strength. He walked into the already lit room.

Abigail was leaning against the pool table as Claude stood closely adjacent to her. They were both smiling at one another as they spoke quietly until Abigail looked past Claude's shoulder and saw Jacob standing in the doorway.

"Jacob!" Abigail exclaimed, almost shouting with excitement. She brushed past Claude and ran into Jacob's arms.

Jacob felt the warmth of her body pressing to his as he put his arms around her, drawing her near. The smell of her hair made his heart go flip flop as it had when he'd first met her. Abigail was wearing a two-piece dress—a white cotton blouse with three- quarter-length sleeves and ankle-length burgundy skirt. She had a black lace shawl draped over her shoulders. In Jacob's mind, she was a vision of a perfect angel. Although the person who was standing across from her wasn't to Jacob's liking, it didn't change the fact that he loved the beautiful woman he held in his arms.

"When did you get here?" She stood back, not wanting to embrace too long in front of Claude.

"Just a few minutes ago." Jacob explained how he had already visited with her father.

Claude shifted from one leg to the other in an awkward way. He and Jacob were both thinking the same thing.

"What are you doing here?" Jacob looked at Claude firmly.

"We were just talking." Claude never forgot his rudeness.

"I'll be going now," he said to Abigail and headed out the door.

"Jacob, he was simply helping me carry something." Abigail grabbed Jacob's arm to stop him. Jacob wasn't listening to her as he continued to follow Claude. Abigail let go and stayed in the room as Jacob caught up to Claude.

"Remember our agreement?" Jacob didn't want to mince words.

"I remember," Claude said. "She asked for help. What was I supposed to do?"

"Help with what?" Jacob asked. "What could she possibly need help with in Robin's Roost?"

"Ask her," Claude didn't care to answer Jacob's question. He turned around and walked away quickly.

If I wasn't so desperate for someone to look after the ranch, I'd fire him right here and now, thought Jacob. Claude knew this as well, hence his cocky attitude. This burned Jacob from the inside out, of all the nerve of him. Not wanting to cause a scene in front of Mrs. Rodgers, who was now in the kitchen, he let Claude go. He didn't want to admit it to himself or to anyone, but he was slightly jealous that Claude was able to see Abigail each day when he could not. Jacob shook it off and walked back to the billiard room to see Abigail.

"I am so happy you're here," Abigail told Jacob. She pretended that the conversation between Jacob and Claude had never happened.

"Come," she grabbed his hand and tugged it towards the hallway. "I'll make some tea and serve you some cookies I baked today."

Jacob slowly moved one foot in front of the other behind her as if she was dragging him. Holding his hand, she led the way to the kitchen. Jacob sat at the table, while Abigail filled the kettle with water and placed it on the wood stove. He couldn't stop thinking about Claude, his rude ways, his greediness, and now his interest in Abigail.

Abigail placed the sugar and cream in the centre of the table and then set down a plate of cookies. To Jacob's surprise, they were uniform in shape, not burnt, and looked very inviting. As she poured the boiling water into the teapot, Jacob picked up a cookie, brought it up to his nose, and smelled it. It smelled delicious. He took a bite. The cookie was soft and sweet, melting in his mouth. It was good! Darn good. For a brief moment, Anna came to mind. She could bake the best cookies, roll the lightest biscuits, and make the sweetest, mouth-watering lemonade. For a split second, time stood still as Jacob remembered the woman he had almost married, the woman he'd loved second, the love he'd lost so tragically.

"Well?" Abigail's voice brought him back to present while she impatiently waited for Jacob to say something.

"Wow, these are tasty," Jacob complimented Abigail, waiting for her to say her mama had really made them.

"I guess I never told you how Aunt Gladys taught me how to bake, did I?" Abigail admitted.

"No, you didn't." Jacob looked at the second cookie he held in his hand, then took another bite. "She's a great teacher."

He smiled lightly, still thinking about Anna. As Abigail put the teapot on the table to wait for the tea to steep, Jacob took another cookie.

"What kind of cookies are they anyway? I don't believe I have had such a cookie," he said as he took another bite, still observing its texture.

"They're an English cookie," Abigail explained. "Aunt Gladys said they were her good friend Alma's recipe. They're called English Raspberry Cookies."

"Well whatever they're called, they're scrumptious." Jacob winked at Abigail as he finished the moist coconut-flavoured cookie with raspberry filling.

"I'm happy you like them," Abigail beamed. "She also taught me a little about cooking too," she added.

"Well, how come you haven't told me this before?" Jacob asked in amusement.

"I don't know. I guess I never thought about it." She smiled as she sat down and poured the tea into three teacups.

"Mama." Abigail looked over at her mama, who was washing a few dishes before bed. "Come sit and have some tea."

"Yes, Mrs. Rodgers. Please, come sit." Jacob stood up and pulled out a chair to let Mrs. Rodgers sit down.

"Thank you, Jacob." Mrs. Rodgers smiled as she looked up at Jacob as if he were her hero. "Abigail is quite the cook now," she stated as she smiled over at her daughter. Mrs. Rodgers looked so frail, and Jacob wondered how she could look like that in just two weeks, since the last time he'd seen her.

"Well, that's good," Jacob said. "After all, she is going to be my wife." The three of them chuckled.

At that moment, the door swung open as fast as a jackrabbit jumped into a hole. Everyone's head turned toward the porch to see what the noise was, with the same thing going through their heads: what was going on at this time of night?

Bert stood in the doorway. "Jacob!" he hollered, "I'm so glad to see you, lad. It's Alice."

By this time, Jacob was standing in the porch with Bert, along with Abigail and her mother.

"What's wrong, Bert?" Jacob asked. He could see that Bert was out of breath. "Calm down, breathe," Jacob encouraged.

Bert gasped to catch his breath. "It's Alice, she is having the baby." Bert started to panic.

With that, Jacob slipped on his boots and ran outside. Bert followed, yelling, "I thought I could get her to Doc, but I think we've run out of time."

Jacob reached the back of the covered wagon and looked inside. Alice lay on its floor, covered with quilts. Jacob could see the pain in her eyes; she didn't want to make it known how much she was suffering. Alice was such a polite lady who didn't say too much.

"Quick Bert, let's carry her into the house." Jacob climbed up into the wagon with Alice, lifted her petite body in his arms, and passed her down to Bert. Alice winced with the movement, but tried so hard to keep it to herself.

"It won't hurt to yell, dear Alice," Bert told her sympathetically as he held her.

Jacob jumped off the wagon and ran towards the house door, where Abigail and her Mama were standing.

"Bring her into the bedroom, Bert," Abigail directed him towards the room beside her father's. Bert laid her down on the bed.

"I'll go and get Doc," Jacob announced. Everything seemed to be happening in fast motion. He ran out the door.

Abigail knew nothing about birthing babies, her mama on the other hand had given birth once, but wasn't familiar otherwise. Neither of them dared admit they had little knowledge in that department and each of them was scared to death, something else they kept to themselves. They had the water on the stove to boil, knowing that was the first thing to do when a woman was in labour, then they gathered up as many sheets and rags as they could.

"Well, I do know about birthing calves," Bert said lightly with a slight smile.

Hopefully, that's the same thing, thought Abigail. Normally men weren't allowed in the room with the mother to be, but this was a different situation. Abigail tried to make Alice as comfortable as possible, and Bert stood at her side, holding her hand and praying quietly with her. Mama gathered more blankets and sheets. Poor Alice couldn't help but cry out in pain every few minutes as the contractions got closer and closer together. Abigail placed a wet cloth on Alice's forehead to try to soothe her. She was hoping Jacob would get there soon with Doc.

The wind blew Jacob's hair back as he leaned forward while his horse ran fast and steady. He held onto the reins tightly.

Darkness made it harder to see, but Jacob knew the way to Abbington Pickets by heart. Jacob prayed for Alice's safety as well as her unborn baby. He knew the baby wasn't supposed to come for at least two more months. He recalled when his mama had had a miscarriage; he had been barely old enough to remember it.

When Jacob reached Doc Johnson's house, he jumped off his horse and ran to the door, calling Doc's name before he got close enough to knock. Right away Mrs. Johnson answered the door.

"What's all the racket about?" she asked as she opened the door.

"We need Doc real fast," Jacob blurted out.

"But he's not here."

"Where is he? We really need him, now."

"He's on a house call. I'm sorry, Jacob." Mrs. Johnson seemed to sympathize.

"Mrs. Hibbert is having her baby. She's at Goldenrod now." Jacob's eyes begged Doc's wife for a solution.

"I can help," Mrs. Johnson said as she quickly reached into her desk drawer for a piece of paper and pen. She wrote a short note and left it on the table. She then grabbed her sweater and coat.

"I left Doc a note to come to the Rodgers' as soon as he gets home," she told Jacob as they ran outside and climbed on Jacob's horse. Like the wind, they headed east towards Goldenrod Ranch. *Hopefully, we aren't too late*, Jacob worried.

It seemed like forever before Jacob returned to the ranch with help. He helped Mrs. Johnson off his horse as fast as he could, and both of them ran towards the house, Jacob unlatched the door, held it open for Mrs. Johnson, following her inside.

"We're here!" Jacob yelled from the porch, knowing everyone would be relieved for him to be returning. Mrs. Johnson washed her hands before going into the bedroom where Alice was. Jacob stayed in the kitchen.

"Where's Doc?" Abigail asked as she came out of the bedroom. She hadn't wanted to ask in front of Mrs. Johnson. "Alice is in terrible pain; we need him." She looked terrified.

"Mrs. Doc knows what she's doing," Jacob reassured her. "Don't you think she's experienced this in all the years she's been married to Doc?" Jacob was nervous himself; he just didn't want to say so. Jacob hugged Abigail and kissed her forehead.

"It'll be alright, Girlie." He squeezed her hand.

Bert came from the bedroom, drained and pale. A thin sheen of perspiration coated his forehead, and the sleeves of his white shirt were rolled up.

"Mrs. Johnson wants more water please, Abigail." He looked disheartened. "She also wants you, not me."

"It'll be all right, lad, as you would say." Jacob patted Bert on the back.

"She said men shouldn't be allowed in the room when babies are born," Bert shook his head. "Alice needs me."

"She's in good hands. Let's make some tea," Jacob suggested. Bert shrugged his shoulders and shook his head.

"Come on," Jacob slapped him lightly on the back again. "Wasn't it you who told me everything looks better after a cup of tea?" Jacob tried to get Bert's mind off of the situation at hand, knowing full well that it wouldn't do the trick.

Jacob made tea, while Abigail, Mama, and Mrs. Johnson were in the room with Alice. Very little noise came from the room, which worried both of the men all the more. Good thing it was during the night, so they didn't have to worry about Mr. Rodgers. Jacob had been into his room to check on him a time or two, but each time he was sound asleep.

Another hour had passed with no news from the other side of the door. Jacob was really concerned and could understand why his friend would be worried sick, but he tried not to show his emotions.

There was a knock at the door. As Jacob got up to go answer it, the door came open.

It was Doc. He quickly took off his coat and boots. "I came as fast as I could," Doc said, looking for guidance on where to go.

"Thank you!" Bert quickly went over to him. "Alice is in there," he pointed towards the door. "We haven't heard much from them for quite some time," Bert said as they walked quickly towards the door.

Doc opened the door, went inside, and swiftly closed the door behind him.

"But I want to see Alice," Bert said loudly through the door so they could hear him. Silence was all the only answer.

"Don't worry, Bert," Jacob told him. "You have faith in our Lord. Doc will do his very best."

"I know you're right, Jacob." He scratched his head with his right hand and sat back down on the kitchen chair. "I love my dear Alice so much. I'm nothing without her."

Jacob wanted to do something for his friend. He wanted to do the same as Bert had done for him when he was at the worst time in his life. "Let me pray." Jacob stood beside Bert and put his hand on his shoulder. They both bowed their heads.

"Dear Heavenly Father, we know you are a merciful God," Jacob started to pray. "We know you love all of us. Please take care of Alice in this time, and bring this baby into the world graciously and unharmed. Give Bert and Alice strength and peace. In Jesus' name. Amen."

"Thank you lad," Bert looked up at Jacob. "You're a good friend." Jacob felt embarrassed at the compliment.

"I haven't done anything that you haven't done for me, Bert" Jacob had no sooner said that when there was the burst of a baby's cry, loud and strong, coming from the bedroom. Bert looked at Jacob, both smiled, and Jacob shook Bert's hand.

"Congratulations Papa!"

"Thank you, lad!" Bert said beaming as he shook Jacob's hand.

Abigail came out of the room, white as a ghost with a tired smile on her face. She looked exhausted.

"Bert, Alice is asking for you," Abigail told him. "Doc said you could come in."

Bert didn't take any time as he raced into the room.

In the living room, Jacob put his arm around Abigail. She rested her head against his strong arm. He sensed something was wrong.

"What is it, Girlie? What's the matter?"

Abigail looked up at him. A single tear rolled down her left cheek. "Jacob, that was one of the most terrifying things I have ever witnessed. The helplessness I felt … I didn't know what to do."

Jacob pulled Abigail close to him, stroking her hair with his hand, as she pressed her cheek against his chest. He couldn't imagine what it was like, and he didn't know if he could have handled the situation.

"And what's worse," Abigail continued looking up at Jacob's face, "is Doc said because the baby came so early and only weighs about three pounds, she may only live to be three years old."

"Oh no," Jacob said quietly, not really knowing what to say. *Poor Bert, poor Alice, how devastating for new parents.* "Doc could be wrong," Jacob consoled Abigail. He believed the Lord would look after their new little bundle of joy.

"I hope you're right, Jacob," Abigail faintly smiled at him.

She went back into the room to help clean up and see what else she could do.

Bert came out of the bedroom holding the smallest baby Jacob had ever seen.

"Meet our little one." Bert beamed, showing off the newest member of their family. "Grace Evelyn. After Alice's younger sister, who passed away when she was a young girl," Bert explained.

"She's beautiful," Jacob smiled. He wasn't saying that to be polite; he really meant it. Grace had such petite features with a button nose that he thought she was the most delicate person he had ever seen, like a porcelain doll. Jacob was happy for his friends. What a gift from God. Despite what Doc said, she was a miracle indeed. It reminded Jacob once again how precious life was and he was more determined than ever to get their house finished and marry his beautiful Abigail.

chapter seven

IT WAS A gorgeous day on the seventh of June. The sweet-smelling air was slightly cool, the fragrance reminding Jacob of how he used to feel in the early mornings of spring when he was a boy. It was funny how a smell could make people feel. In Jacob's favour, spring had been good to him.

Three weeks had gone by quickly. Abigail's father was healing every day, speaking more clearly with longer sentences. Even Bert and Alice were having a good spring. Baby Grace was growing strong and healthy every hour since she was born. Bert and Alice were so proud of their tiny sweet baby. Ernest, Alice's brother, had worked hard to get his crops in and broke ground for new fields for next year. Bert worked for the Canadian Pacific Railway and tended to his cattle.

With the help of a couple of neighbour boys, Jacob's brothers, and Claude, Mr. Rodgers' fields were plowed and seeded. Jacob worked hard every hour of each day to build his tables and work on the house. Charles helped when Jacob needed it, and when he wasn't helping his father. Jacob didn't want to admit it, but it was all he could do to keep up with the orders for Mr. Adair and juggle helping at Goldenrod while also working on the house. Jacob seemed to be spreading himself very thin. Fortunately, the crop had been put in early that year, so he'd be able to spend the extra time on the house.

The workload at Goldenrod was now down to a minimum and Claude would be able to handle it on his own. Although Jacob didn't like him being there any more than he wanted to cut off his right leg, he didn't have any choice. Full-time help was hard to find. The only thing that kept Jacob going was he knew that when the house was finished, he and Abigail would be married.

Jacob awoke extra early that morning. He and Charles were planning to start on the roof now that the walls were erect and the second storey floor was finished. The walls had six windows with two door openings on the main level and four windows and a balcony door on the second floor. Of course, there were no windows in yet or doors, for that matter, but the openings had to be framed in ahead of time. The roof would take a bit of extra work since the house was round. Jacob did the figuring that was needed to construct such a building. It wouldn't be the first one to be built in Canada, but it was the first one to be built on the prairies and definitely the only one in Abbington Pickets.

Abigail was one of a kind, a very special lady. Jacob thought she should live in a one of a kind castle.

Charles was there by eight in the morning, and as always he smelled a little rank from alcohol. This wasn't new for Charles; he liked to have a good time, but it never affected his ability to work the next day, which is why Jacob never said a word about it.

Jacob had time to varnish a half dozen tables before breakfast. He'd then have to sand and give them one more coat before they would be ready for delivery. Jacob felt good about it because the wagon from Kingston would be coming in three days.

Jacob and Charles worked hard as the sun beat down on their backs. Both of them had sweat beading down their foreheads, and their shirts were wet under their arms and on their backs and chests.

"Well, how about some dinner?" Jacob asked Charles as he began to climb down the ladder from the roof.

"You bet," agreed Charles as he followed Jacob. "You don't have to ask me twice."

Jacob walked towards the shop and into the kitchen part of his building. Charles washed up at the washstand by the doorway. Jacob took out a loaf of bread from the cupboard, along with two plates and set them on the table. From the icebox, he grabbed the plate of sliced pork and onions, placing it beside the bread.

Reaching for the butter and salt and pepper on the top shelf above the sink made him stop and think for a second. While he stood there and held the butter in his hand, he thought of Anna making butter, sitting on her front porch during the summer. Her smiling face with rosy cheeks, blonde hair neatly braided down her back, oh sweet Anna, so domestic and in the loveliest way he had ever seen anyone. For that split second, Jacob saw Anna as clear as anyone standing right before him.

"Hello?" Charles snapped his fingers in front of Jacob's face. "Anyone home?" He laughed as Jacob came to the present.

"What's so funny?"

"I thought you must have left for la la land." Charles smirked.

Jacob turned towards the table and set everything down, then walked back over towards the door and washed himself.

"I was just thinking," Jacob admitted, but not wanting to tell Charles what he was really thinking about. "I have a lot to do in a short time," he talked louder so Charles could hear him.

"Don't worry," Charles said as he started making his sandwich. "You will."

Once dinner was over and cleaned up, Jacob and Charles continued on the roof. They got a lot accomplished in one day, although they were far from being done. It was a great beginning to the roof.

"Oh my goodness, Jacob! It's wonderful!" A woman's voice came from below. There was Abigail, smiling as she held a basket over her arm while she sat on her horse. She was wearing a white blouse with men's britches. She always liked to wear britches when she rode her horse; she didn't feel proper wearing a dress. That always made Jacob feel even more attracted to her—she was different from any girl he had ever met because she had a style, along with a mind of her own. The men were so busy, neither Jacob nor Charles had heard her ride up.

Jacob was surprised to see her, and also slightly disappointed as he hadn't told her yet about the shape of their home and he had been hoping to get a little further on it before she came to see it up close. *I guess there was no getting away from it since the house was being built so close to Abbington Pickets that anyone who rode by could see it*, he thought. Abigail had been so occupied with helping with her father and mother that she hadn't been in town much other than to church sometimes.

"Well, look who's here," exclaimed Jacob. *I guess now's the time to give the tour of the house,* he thought to himself. Jacob made his way to the ladder.

"Wow! Jacob, you didn't tell me the house was going to be round!" Abigail declared.

"Do you like it?" Jacob asked.

"I love it!" Abigail climbed off her horse quickly to take a closer look, meeting Jacob at the bottom of the ladder.

"What brings you to Abbington Pickets?" Jacob asked.

"Mama needed some things, and I volunteered." Abigail was looking more beautiful every time he saw her. She seemed to be back to her usual self for the first time since her father had fallen ill, and Jacob was thrilled to see it.

"I feel so housebound, and I thought I was going to go crazy if I didn't do something. Today is such a beautiful day. Claude offered, but I wanted to surprise you with some cookies and tea."

"Well, I'm happy you did." Jacob took his hat off with one hand, scooped his other arm around Abigail's small waist, and kissed her cheek. "I must admit, I wanted to surprise you when I showed you the house a little further down the road."

Abigail quickly closed her eyes and covered them with one hand. "I didn't see a thing," she joked.

"It's alright." Jacob smiled.

Abigail never tired of seeing his dimples. Abigail laughed at her own silliness. "I never dreamed it would be this huge." Abigail couldn't get over the uniqueness of the upcoming abode.

"Are we going to eat lunch or not?" came a voice from above came. "We aren't getting any younger."

Abigail could see Charles's curly red hair, which sprouted out from under his hat over his ears, and his freckles were showing more every day from the sun.

"You'll have to be patient, my lad. We're doing a tour of our castle on the hill," he matter-of-factly told Charles.

Technically, the house wasn't on a hill, but there was a slight hump in the ground where Jacob had started building the house; it looked much higher than it appeared, so he thought of it as the house on the hill.

"Well, excuse me, your royal highness." Charles rolled his eyes with a smile and continued to hammer on the roof while he waited.

Jacob took the basket from Abigail and set it on the ground in a safe place. He put his left arm across his stomach and bent over with his right arm stretched out as if to bow to her. He took her by the hand and directed her towards the inside of the house.

"This way, your royal highness." He could hardly contain his laughter. Abigail smiled and went along with his little interlude.

"This is the kitchen," he said as they walked through the first doorway into the inside of the shell of a house. He gestured to the area to the left. He grabbed her hand and pulled her towards the right, which was the southeast quarter of the house.

"This is the dining room." Jacob pointed to the whole area. "Here is where you'll play the piano." He drew a pretend shape of a piano with his hands on the southeast wall. "You'll play for all the children."

"Oh really?" Abigail laughed. "What children?"

"Our children," Jacob said, so sure of himself. "All ten of them." He looked so determined.

"Ten children?" Abigail gasped. "Are you crazy? We can't have ten children."

"Why not?" Jacob asked. Then he cracked a smile, and Abigail realized he was really fooling.

"And just a minute." Abigail pretended to clear her throat. "Why do you think we'll have a piano?"

"Your mama told me you play," Jacob stated quite quickly. "Oh she did, did she?" Abigail tickled Jacob under the arm.

"What else did she tell you about me?"

Jacob ran from her, into the next quarter of the house. "And this is the living room," he said quickly, trying to get away from Abigail's tickling fingers. "And over here there will be a fireplace," he pointed to the northeast wall.

"I am not done with you, mister." Abigail ran after Jacob. He grasped both of her hands and pulled her tightly towards him so she couldn't move. "Hey, that's not fair; you're stronger than I am," Abigail played the damsel in distress.

Jacob smiled and kissed her forehead. "Give up?" Jacob raised his eyebrow. Abigail didn't answer. "Give up?" He repeated.

"Would one of you give up so we can have some lunch?" A voice from above faintly came through the upper floor.

"Would you stop thinking with your stomach?" Jacob hollered up towards the ceiling.

"Yes, I give up," Abigail blurted out and gave him a pouty look.

"I knew you would see it my way," Jacob teased. "Now can we finish the tour without interruption?" He let go of her grasp and held just one hand. "And these are the stairs towards the upstairs," he pointed towards the upper north wall to the invisible staircase.

"There is an upstairs?" Abigail seemed surprised.

"Of course," Jacob beamed, knowing this surprise would excite her. "That is where you'll have countless books on bookshelves."

"Really?" That got Abigail's real attention. She had learned the necessary things in life, such as cooking, baking, and even cleaning, but reading and learning were really the things she loved to do. She had been smart in school and always thought one day she would write a book. "That would be so lovely," Abigail said.

Jacob was happy she was pleased by this. He wasn't certain that that's what the upstairs was going to be for; it was just a hunch that she would like that idea. But now he knew for sure.

"And how about towards the south? A balcony, so you can step out and see all of Abbington Pickets and the beautiful prairies?"

"How wonderful that would be," Abigail, stood almost mesmerized by the picture she drew of it in her mind.

"For you, my beautiful," Jacob turned towards Abigail.

Looking at her face, he lifted his dark tanned hand and swiped the hair from her forehead, pushing it to the side of her face. "I would do anything." For that moment, the two stared at one another, like there was no one else on earth but the two of them.

"Jacob, you are too good to me," Abigail whispered.

Jacob, remembering Charles was waiting, thought he better get a move on. "Let me show you the last room," he said as he pulled her towards the last quarter of the house, which was the northwest. "Our room."

For a second, it appeared to be somewhat awkward for the two of them to be standing in their so-called bedroom before they were even married. Even Jacob felt rather uncomfortable and was thankful when his trusty friend appeared.

"Did you say you had cookies?" Charles smiled at Abigail. "Yes, Charles, I did." Abigail laughed. She was also relieved he had come in the room when he did. "Let's go sit in the sunshine and have some tea and cookies, and by now it's going to be iced tea." Abigail smiled as she led the way to the outside of the house. Jacob and Abigail sat on a tree that had been cut down and was lying on its side. Charles sat on the ground across from them. Abigail took out the things she'd brought. First a small table cloth that she placed on the ground. Then the mason jar of tea and a jar filled with cookies.

"Hey, those don't look like English Raspberry cookies,"

Jacob stated, now that those were his favourite thing to eat. "That's because they're not," Abigail teased. "Today they're peanut butter cookies. It's my grandma's 'famous' recipe, Mama said," Abigail proudly passed the jar to Jacob. He took the container from her, reached in, and pulled out a cookie. He sniffed it and looked at it strangely.

"It's good!" Abigail declared. "Stop goofing around and just eat it." She gave him a stern look, then smiled in anticipation.

"Oh, all right, if you insist." Jacob winked at her with a slight smile, then took a bite of the peanut-flavoured morsel.

"Mmm, you are right." Jacob put the rest of the cookie in his mouth and reached for another before he passed the jar to Charles. Charles took the jar and took one out. Jacob sipped from the mason jar, a sweet taste of tea, just the way he liked it.

Tea with a bit of lemon and honey.

"You are a sweet girl, Miss Abigail." Jacob slid down off the tree trunk onto the ground, leaning against the rough bark, stretching his legs out in front of him. "You sure can spoil a guy."

"You know it," Charles agreed as he drank his tea in a few large gulps. He lay on his side with his arm propping his upper body.

"Well, you're worth it," Abigail said as she stood up, dusting off her britches. "But I have to get going. I'm going to the store for a few things for Mama."

"Thank you for the lunch," Charles said with a grin.

Jacob stood up to say goodbye. "You take care; give my regards to your Ma and Pa." Jacob gave her a kiss on the cheek. He didn't want to make a big show of affection in front of his friend. Jacob walked her to her horse. Once she was mounted, he handed her the basket.

"Hope to see some windows in those walls next time I'm in town," Abigail winked, teasing Jacob as she trotted away.

"Well … maybe you will!" Jacob called after her with a laugh. "Come on, lad. Let's get back to work."

Jacob smiled at his sidekick. "We have a house to finish!" he shouted up towards the sky.

Both of them were back up on the roof working when they heard a horse walking. Since they weren't expecting anyone, Jacob had to stretch his neck over the rafter to see who it was coming to visit them. To his surprise, it was Abigail again. Jacob carefully walked over all the bottom boards to reach the ladder and make his way down.

"I thought you would be on your way home by now." Jacob smiled at Abigail as he climbed down.

"I was. I mean, I am." Abigail seemed not herself, something was troubling her. Jacob could sense it before he even got close to her.

She stayed on her horse as Jacob walked to her. He looked up at her worried face, touching her arm lightly.

"What is it? What's wrong?" Jacob asked.

"Well, I'm not sure," Abigail started. "Maybe it's nothing. When I was at the general store, Mrs. Adair said she would put it on 'your' account. What did she mean by that? Papa has his own account there. I don't understand."

Jacob realizes she could find out that minute about her father's money troubles. Mr. Adair knew it was a secret. He couldn't let her find out.

"Well, since your papa has been ill, I've been picking things up for him," Jacob began. "That's probably what she meant."

"No, she specifically said, 'Jacob's Account.'" Abigail's concern disturbed Jacob, especially since he'd made a promise and he intended on keeping it.

"Since your ma couldn't come to the village, she asked me to deal with the account whenever I picked up goods for the ranch," Jacob said, being careful not to lie.

"It appeared weird; I had a different feeling about it."

"Don't worry, my love," Jacob reassured her. "Give your mama and pa my best, and I'll see you next week," he said, hoping Abigail got that idea out of her head. He thought he could hurry her along. If he didn't appear worried, maybe she would think there was nothing out of the ordinary.

Abigail bent down to kiss Jacob on the cheek before she trotted off.

"What was that all about?" Charles stood at the roof top, overseeing everything.

"Nothing," Jacob said plainly without explanation. He climbed back up the ladder for a few more hours of work.

chapter eight

THE WEEK HAD been a productive one. Jacob and Charles, along with both Jacob's brothers, Peter and Andrew, finished the roof in great time. The weather cooperated, and since it was the middle of June, Peter and Andrew could afford to be away from their farms to help their little brother.

Jacob was going to go to Goldenrod for the weekend to see what Claude needed help with and make sure things were going well. The glass Jacob had ordered to construct the windows would hopefully be in Abbington Pickets on Monday. The building of the house seemed to be on track now. Jacob was starting to feel a little more relaxed than he had been a month earlier.

Since the outer part of the building was complete, once the windows and doors were put in, Jacob would be able to work on the inside construction. He could at least get the main floor complete before fall, then he could work on the upper level over the winter.

The days were longer, keeping Jacob working later in the day, but still arriving at Goldenrod before sundown. His horse loped down the grass lane into the ranch. Jacob was anxious to see everyone and give them an update on the house. Not only was he excited to see Abigail, but he was eager to see Mr. Rodgers' progress as well.

Jacob knew Mrs. Rodgers would have a plate of supper waiting in the oven for him when he got there. As sure as his stomach was growling, he walked in, and Abigail's mama met him at the door.

"Come, Jacob," Mrs. Rodgers gushed over the sight of him. "I saved you a plate. It's been kept warm." She directed him to the table.

Jacob washed up, anxious to see Abigail, but not wanting to appear rude. He wondered where Abigail was. "How are you doing Mrs. Rodgers?" he asked as he sat down at the table in front of a plate of potatoes, fried chicken, and yellow beans that had been canned the previous year. Of course, there were buns, butter, and hot tea to drink. Jacob bowed as he quietly said Grace.

"I'm good, Jacob." She sat down quietly at the table with her cup of tea. "I hear the house is really coming along."

"It sure is." Jacob beamed. He couldn't help but feel proud of the work he had accomplished. He took a bite of the light and fluffy buttered bun.

"Abigail made those today," Mrs. Rodgers said with a light smile. "She's doing a great job around the house. In fact, she and Clau-" she stopped there. "Well, I mean it's great to have her help."

"What do you mean?" Jacob asked.

"Oh, it's just that Abigail has been a great help to me," she tried to explain. "Mr. Rodgers and I are so proud of how she has been handling things."

The door swung open and in came Abigail.

"Hey." Abigail's face lit up upon the sight of Jacob. "When did you sneak in here?" Jacob stood up as she walked into the kitchen and they embraced briefly. Abigail was wearing her famous britches and a white blouse with lace on the neckline and sleeves. Her brown hair was braided and fell down her shoulder to one side.

"I got here about ten minutes ago," Jacob said. "Just long enough to try out these fantastic buns you made." He gave her a wink.

"Well, I guess I'm a natural," she modestly said.

"I was out in the barn, brushing Rusty." She seemed a bit sheepish as she spoke.

Despite her presence in the barn, Jacob could still smell her sweet fragrance. He wondered, *Why is she out here so late, and where's Claude?*

"I have something to show you." Abigail changed her disposition to run to her room and back. She placed what looked like a piece of paper on the table in front of everyone.

Jacob Daniel Hudson
and
Abigail Mary Rodgers
request your presence
as they become united as one.
Sunday, September Ninth,
Nineteen hundred and eleven
At two thirty in the afternoon
At the All Saints Anglican Church
in
Abbington Pickets, Saskatchewan.

"The invitation is perfect, Abigail." Mrs. Rodgers smiled down at the ivory-coloured paper lying on the kitchen table.

"I'm so pleased with them." Abigail beamed uncontrollably. "I never knew that was your middle name." Jacob stood behind Abigail with his arms wrapped around the front of her waist, linking his fingers together, his chin resting on her right shoulder.

"I'm named after my grandmother, Papa's mama," Abigail proudly explained. Abigail never knew her grandmother; she'd passed away when Abigail was a little girl, but she always knew she had a special bond with her, especially since they shared the same name.

"When you have them ready, I can mail them for you," Jacob offered.

"Thank you, but no." Abigail smiled mischievously. "I'm going to take them myself, as I want to have a look at *my castle* while I'm there," Abigail teased. "By the way, do you have the list of guests you want to invite?"

"Ah," Jacob felt his breast pocket to make sure he hadn't forgotten it. "Yes, I have it." He pulled it out and handed it to her with relief. For a second, he thought he had left it at home. He had spent a great deal of time on the invitation list of his side of the family as well as friends. They wanted to have a beautiful wedding—nothing elaborate but something they both would fondly remember. It was going to be the best day of their lives.

"I'm going to retire," Mrs. Rodgers said, and she took her apron off and hung it on the hook on the inside door of the pantry. "I see you have a few things to talk about, and I'm tired tonight."

"Good night, Mama," Abigail turned around, hugged her mama, and kissed her cheek. "Sleep well." Abigail had noticed that her mama looked more tired than usual and that she had lost some weight.

"Good night, Mrs. Rodgers." Jacob hugged her.

"You know you're soon going to have to start calling me Mama," she stated.

Jacob blushed. "I know," he said, as she headed towards her bedroom.

"I am so happy you're here." Abigail turned to Jacob and hugged him tight.

"Me too." He hugged her back, kissing the top of her head, taking a deep breath of the aroma of Abigail's hair; she smelled so good.

"Can we talk?" Abigail asked as she looked up at Jacob. "About some things."

"Of course," Jacob answered with worry in his heart. "Let's go into Robin's Roost," Abigail pulled Jacob by the hand as they walked toward the hallway and into the billiard room.

"Is everything alright?" Jacob asked as they sat down on the lounge side by side. He took Abigail's hand in his and held it gently as he turned to her.

"I'm worried about something," Abigail began but hesitated to express the next sentence. "I don't know how to say it."

"Abigail," Jacob started, "you never have to worry about anything. I *don't* want you to ever worry about anything. You can tell me whatever it is that's troubling you, and we'll work it out, no matter what it is."

"I know, I know," she agreed. "It's so hard to say."

Jacob waited for her to explain. He didn't want to pressure her into telling him, but his stomach was turning around and around, as he wondered what it was that she was so concerned about.

"Jacob," Abigail hesitated, but slowly continued. "Remember when I came to our house for the first time?"

"Yes." Jacob knew she was speaking of the time she'd shown up unexpectedly and he'd given her the tour of the house.

"Remember how you said we were going to have ten children?"

Jacob laughed, "Yes, I do."

"Don't laugh," Abigail scolded him. "I'm being serious."

"I'm sorry. I thought you were fooling." Jacob tried to be more sober about the conversation. "Alright, let's start again. Ten children."

"That's my point," Abigail was very sober. "Children seem to be important to you."

"Of course they are," Jacob agreed. "Aren't they to you?"

Abigail ashamed of not really knowing how to say what she wanted to. "I guess they are, if you want them."

"What do you mean? If you want them?" Jacob stared at her. "Don't you?" Jacob was confused. Never in a million years did he think Abigail wouldn't want children. The notion had never crossed his mind. Didn't all women want babies?

"Well … no … not … really …" Abigail answered him with her head down, not wanting to face him.

Jacob didn't know what to say, he didn't know what to do.

You could have knocked him over with a feather he was so stunned.

"Are you saying you don't want children?" Jacob bluntly asked as he bent over with his elbows leaning on his knees, holding his head in one hand.

"Jacob, don't make it sound like that," Abigail pleaded with him to understand.

"Ever?" He turned his head back to look at her.

She looked down at the hardwood floor ashamed, shaking her head no. Jacob thought long and hard for several minutes. His vision, or so he thought his ideal fantasy, was to be married, have children and live the Canadian dream by becoming the best he could be, and for him, that was to be a skilled carpenter, marry his first love, and he *thought,* have a family to fulfil his life. A beautiful, curly haired brunette little girl, the spitting image of her mother, or a precious blonde, curly haired girl who resembled his baby sister, Lucy. Maybe a sweet blue-eyed boy with smiling dimples to match his father's. It was all laid out perfectly in his mind, or so he'd thought until that very moment. Jacob took a deep breath, closed his eyes, and faced Abigail, small tears slowly rolling down her cheek. Jacob lifted his hand touching her cheek as he wiped the tears away with his thumb.

"Abigail," Jacob began, "I love you." Never had he thought he would be saying these words to her. "It doesn't matter if we have no children or ten. I will always love you. I want to marry you for you, and only you, no matter what."

"Oh, Jacob." Abigail threw her arms around his neck and hugged him close. "I didn't know how to tell you, and I thought you wouldn't want to marry me once you knew. But it wasn't fair to you if I wasn't honest with you."

"It's you I love," Jacob consoled her. "I always will. Nothing can change that."

"I love you too, my love." Abigail closed her eyes, pressing her cheek against his chest, as Jacob held her in his arms.

He didn't want to show his disappointment, his heartbreak. *What could be wrong that she doesn't want to have children?* he wondered. *I guess she never said she did want them, but then again she didn't say she didn't.* Jacob was confused, and this made him somewhat resentful of Abigail, but he loved her more than himself and would do anything for her. If that meant respecting her wishes to not have children, then so be it. He would have to live with that.

The rest of the summer went by smoothly, as did the building of the Hudson abode. Some days were scorching hot and others plain hot. The warm weather suited Jacob just fine. There was the odd rain storm that held up progress, but the crops needed it, so there wasn't much use in complaining about it. The warmer weather made it easier to work on the house and helped get the haying done at the ranch as well. Jacob's brothers were able to help a couple days a week for the month of July, then August brought harvest. Jacob himself had to slow down with his working in Abbington Pickets to help with cutting, stoking, and finally the week of thrashing. The usual neighbours all gathered as they did every year. This year a few more men pitched in since Mr. Rodgers was still recuperating from his stroke.

Charles had been there every day Jacob worked on the house. Besides finishing the upstairs, the house was complete. Although they didn't have any furniture, Jacob knew he could remedy that when he had the time.

It was time to prepare for the wedding. Abigail had a few requests. It might not be a royal wedding, but Jacob wanted Abigail to have the wedding of her dreams. It was traditional for the parents to pay for the wedding, of course, everyone knew that but Jacob, knowing the circumstances, gave money to Mrs. Rodgers to give to Abigail so she wouldn't be suspicious of their financial predicament. As promised, Jacob came through with paying off their debt, paying for their amenities and of course their hired man.

It was two weeks before the wedding and Jacob had a surprise for Abigail. He had been planning it for weeks. He asked Mrs. Rodgers to make them a picnic, and he told Abigail they were going on an outing. Of course, Abigail was curious, and she asked question after question about what they were doing and where they were going. Abigail had a lot of great traits, but patience wasn't one of them.

"You'll see," was all Jacob told her; patience was something he possessed.

He had got the horses and wagon ready and then loaded it with the basket, Abigail's favourite quilt, a couple of pillows, a tablecloth, a bouquet of wildflowers that were still in season, and lastly, the most important thing. The whole reason Jacob planned this little outing was packed neatly and protectively in the wooden box that he set in the wagon last.

"Where are you taking me, Mr. Hudson?" Abigail persisted.

"Be patient, my love." Jacob smiled as he blindfolded her and helped her up into the wagon seat.

"Well, can't I even see where we're going?"

"Nope." Jacob walked around to the driver's side of the wagon and climbed up into it and picked up the reins.

"Giddy up," he commanded the horses, Myrt and Gert. Abigail held onto Jacob's arm with both hands, giggling as they left the yard.

"I don't know why I can't see where we're travelling," Abigail persisted on bugging Jacob. She knew he wasn't going to tell her where they were going, but she had fun teasing him.

Jacob, on the other hand, thought it was entertaining and kept on going without saying a word. He drove down a path he'd made when he started to work for the Rodgers, to get wood for the winter. In fact, it was a familiar path he and Abigail had taken a few years ago.

The day started off crisp with a lot of dew on the grass, but they were having an Indian Summer, so the afternoon was sunny and very warm. Poplar trees were turning yellow, and the maple trees were starting to turn red. The grass wasn't as green anymore, but it had a somewhat mystical dried appearance and made it seem beautiful. Birds were singing around them with the sound of the horse's hooves as they crushed grass and dried out twigs.

The Canadian geese were flying overhead in their traditional "V" shape, already starting to head south for the winter. *They must be sensing an early winter.* Jacob thought. It only took about fifteen minutes for the horses to pull the wagon to where Jacob wanted to stop.

"Whoa," Jacob said to the horses as he pulled on the reins. "Are we here?" Abigail asked.

"Just stay here," Jacob said with a smile. "I'll come and get you out of the wagon when I'm ready."

"Where are you going? Wait!"

"I'm right here and won't be far. Stay here and no peeking!" Jacob jokingly ordered. He jumped off the wagon, walked behind it, and started to unload. Abigail thought it took him an hour but was only ten minutes before he came back to the side of the wagon to retrieve her.

"Alright, Miss," Jacob held his hand up to Abigail as if she were the Queen of England. She gently reached to touch Jacob's hand, grasped it and slowly got off the wagon with his help. Once she reached the ground, Jacob kissed her cheek as she stood there, still blindfolded.

"Are you ready?" He teased.

"Yes!" She couldn't stand still and wanted to jump up and down with impatience.

Jacob stood behind her and untied her blindfold. As he took it off, he stepped back anxiously, waiting for her reaction to his surprise.

"Jacob!" Abigail saw the view then turned towards him, "You're the sweetest."

Jacob blushed at the compliment. The place Jacob had brought her to was under the tree where they'd had their first picnic.

The most memorable one, the time she fell out of the tree and broke her leg. Despite the terrifying experience, they had both wanted to make that place "their place." Over the past few years, Jacob had cleared the road that led to the tree. He'd picked up all the fallen trees and trimmed the dead branches from the tree Abigail had fallen from. The number of trips he made to clean up the wood made the pathway clearer and drivable. It was much different than the day he'd ran on foot to go get help, and Mr. Rodgers could hardly get his wagon through it to pick Abigail up.

Jacob had built a wooden sign that read "Appleton's Haven" and hung it on the tree. He laid out Abigail's favourite quilt on the ground directly below the sign, with the basket of food set in the middle and two pillows on either side. The wooden box was sitting on one corner of the quilt, out of the way, with a pink tablecloth hanging over it and the jar of wildflowers set on top as if it were a table.

Jacob offered his arm to Abigail to walk her gracefully to their solitude.

"When did you plan this?" She looked at Jacob with love. "It's so beautiful here."

"This was always our favourite place to be, and now it'll remain ours forever." Jacob and Abigail always referred to the tree they had picnics at and walked to, to be alone, to have long talks at, as "Appleton's." William "Bill" Appleton owned the land on the other side of the fence that lined up perfectly beyond their favourite large limbed umbrella. In fact, the tree was almost on his land. It was farm land on that side, and hardly anyone came there. It was very secluded, except for when seeding and harvesting occurred. Despite Abigail falling from the tree some years ago, it was still their most desired whereabouts.

"This was always our favourite place to be, and now it'll remain ours forever." - Jacob

Abigail gracefully sat down on the quilt, her dress skirt on either side, so she didn't sit on it, with her legs to the side.

She fixed the fabric so it perfectly circled around her. Jacob sat close; he unpacked the basket of yummy morsels that Mrs. Rodgers had prepared as a favour to Jacob. Of course, she had been happy to do it for him, and there was a method to his madness. He had a surprise gift for his wife-to-be, one that was special to him that he wanted to give to her in private.

"Well, as always, your Ma out did herself." Jacob finished the last bite of the cookie he was eating and licked off the tip of each finger and winked at Abigail.

Abigail was taking a sip of her tea, enjoying every swallow. "I knew you didn't pack this yourself!" She laughed and gave him a play slap on the arm. "Here I thought you slaved away at this party." She reached over to flip his hat off his head and her arm gave way as Jacob leaned backwards to miss her attempt. She fell right on top of his chest. They were face to face, inches between his lips and hers. She surprised herself and Jacob tried hard not to burst out laughing at the expression upon her face.

"Whoops, I didn't mean to do that." Abigail blushed, speaking politely as if Jacob were a total stranger. She was just about to get up when Jacob reached for her hand.

"Wait," he said softly. "I didn't bring you here just for a picnic," he began. Abigail looked surprised. Jacob got up and walked over to the wooden box he had hiding under the tablecloth and flowers. Removing each of the items and lifting the box with little effort, he walked back over to where he had been sitting. He sat it in front of Abigail, with a bit of excitement in his heart, but also worried that Abigail would think it was silly.

"This is for you," Jacob began. "An early wedding gift," Jacob smiled and revealed this dimples.

Delight spread across Abigail's face. "Really?" She didn't know how she was supposed to open the box. She looked at it real close, examining every side to see if there was an opening. Jacob was intently watching her in amusement.

"Um, Mr. Hudson," Abigail said in her serious, playful manner, "there seems to be no way of getting into this secret crate."

Jacob laughed, then stood and walked over to the wagon to retrieve a hammer. "I forgot," he shook his head. "It was too much fun watching you try to get into the thing." He continued to chuckle despite the unimpressed look on Abigail's face.

"Here, allow me." He pried the lid open with the claw of the hammer where each nail kept it shut tight. All Abigail could see were wood shavings in the box. She looked up at Jacob's smiling face with confusion.

"Keep looking," he reassured her.

Abigail moved some of the wood shavings to the side to see if she could discover what was inside. There was something black, which piqued her curiosity. She scooped out some of the shavings so she could reach in to pull out whatever was hiding. It was heavy, though, and it wasn't something you could grasp with one hand either.

"Well, I must say, Mr. Hudson. You're good at packing things."

"It's fragile, my dear Abigail," he said with slight sarcasm.

At last, she was able to fit both hands in the box and hold onto the mysterious item inside. As she pulled it out, Jacob grabbed hold of the wooden box so Abigail could freely lift the item.

"Oh Jacob, it's gorgeous!" Abigail exclaimed as she set down the brand new, shiny black mantel clock. She admired it thoroughly, looking at its every angle. The ornate brass legs, the brass lion's head handles on each side. The beautiful pillars that decorated the front of the clock on either side of the ornate face.

"There's a key." Jacob showed Abigail the envelope in the box, which held the key. "It needs to be wound once a week," he explained.

"How marvellous." Abigail was thrilled to have such a piece for their new home and couldn't wait to be married and be there together.

"It chimes on the hour and dings every half hour," Jacob continued. "It's called a 'Sessions clock.' I thought it was very unique because they have only started making them about eight years ago in the United States."

Abigail looked at the envelope with the key. She noticed there was a note inside. She looked over at Jacob, then back at the note, slowly unfolded it and began to read the handwritten words.

You now hold the key,
the key to my heart.
And as time passes by,
You will always be mine.
As the clock tick tocks,
So will my love for you.
And it will never stop,
This is our time,
Our place, our love.
As time passes by,
I am yours, you're mine.

-All my love,
Jacob

Abigail now knew the significance of the clock. It wasn't only a pretty piece of furniture to decorate their new house. It was important to Jacob, and now it was very important to her.

"Jacob," Abigail said quietly, as she was almost speechless. His symbolism of his love for her was overwhelming. She had never been more in love with anyone than she was at that moment. "I'll cherish it forever."

Jacob leaned towards her as if to kiss her. "I'm so glad you like it," he said.

"Like it? I love it," Abigail gushed. "Thank you."

"You're very welcome, my love." Jacob blushed. With his finger, he pushed the hair from her forehead to the side. Then he kissed her cheek. He knew how important it was to be respectful to women, especially when they were alone together. As much as he desired Abigail, they weren't man and wife yet.

Abigail smiled warmly at Jacob and then she turned around in the spot she sat in and leaned back against his chest.

Jacob held his arms in front of her as they both sat in the beautiful moment, under their refuge, daydreaming about their life together.

chapter nine

"JACOB!" HIS BROTHER Peter's familiar voice came from outside the shop. Jacob was still living in his workshop's living quarters because he wanted Abigail and himself to move into the house together, once they were married.

"Aren't you ready yet?" His brother asked as he and his other brother Andrew walked in the door. They were both dressed in their Sunday best.

"Almost!" Jacob joked as if he was irritated by them. He was trying to tie his tie in front of the chipped little square mirror above the washstand.

"You can't be late for your own wedding," Andrew spoke up.

"You're right," said a new voice.

Jacob spun around. "When did you get here?" he exclaimed, excited to see his older sister, Sarah. He picked her up and twirled her around and around, hugging her. Even though they wrote a lot, Jacob hadn't seen his sister since she got married. She hadn't changed much, still beautiful as ever. Her curly blonde locks were pinned up in a bun with a large hat covered in flowers and a stretch of netting across the front. Her dress was pale pink with a wide, light blue ribbon around her waist.

"I wasn't sure you were coming. Where's little Megan?" Jacob asked.

"She's out in the wagon with her father," Sarah said.

"We all came to make sure you weren't late for your own wedding." Jane walked through the doorway. Behind her was Missy, Peter's wife.

"And dressed right," Peter added.

Jacob walked over to give his other big sister a hug. She was dressed as she always was; plain brown dress, black boots, and a small hat with her hair pulled tightly in a bun. She reminded Jacob of his second-grade school teacher, who had loved to put anyone in the corner when they so much as looked at her wrong. Missy wore a two-piece burgundy dress. Her hat was much like Sarah's, and she carried an ivory-coloured homemade crocheted purse. She was attractive in her own way, brown hair that she wore in a loose bun; her eyebrows were distinct as they were so thick, almost joining in the middle. She had a petite nose and plump lips. Jacob nodded to Missy and gave her a small hug.

"What, you don't think I can get dressed for my own wedding?" Jacob asked with a joke.

"This is the most important day of your life, I will have you know, and you'd better be ready," Sarah informed Jacob.

"Alright, alright." Jacob laughed, thinking Jane was usually the bossy one in the family. "I give in, what do you want me to do?" First thing Sarah did was tie his tie right for him and then she looked him over to make sure his trousers were pressed and that his suit jacket matched. Indeed, Jacob did know how to dress up, that was for certain, but he didn't need much help to look handsome; that came naturally.

"Here, I have something for you," Peter handed Jacob something wrapped in an old hanky.

"What is it?" He looked at his brothers, confused. They appeared to be very serious.

"Well, look and find out," Andrew spoke up.

Jacob pulled back one corner of the hanky, then the other until it revealed a beautiful silver, open-faced pocket watch.

"It was Pa's," Peter explained. "Jane found it in his things at the house, and she thought you should have it."

"*We* all thought you should have it," spoke up Sarah, "especially today, your wedding day."

This brought back the last bittersweet memory of his father.

He'd been on his death bed when he'd asked for forgiveness for all he had done and gave his life to The Lord that very day. It brought a tear to Jacob's eye, but it was a good memory, one that erased all the pain and anguish his father had put him through.

All had been forgotten and forgiven. The watch meant a lot to him and the fact his siblings wanted him to have it meant the world to him. He clipped the chain onto the button of his vest and looked at the watch to make sure it was the right time, then placed it in his inside pocket.

"Here," Jane held out her closed hand to Jacob. Curious, Jacob opened his hand and held it out to her. Jane dropped something into his palm.

Jacob looked at it closely. He glanced at Jane, then looked back down at his hand again. A lump formed in his throat and tears came to his eyes, but Jacob blinked them away. Jacob knew exactly what it was: Mama's wedding ring. Jane could see the question on Jacob's face.

"She would want your bride to have it," was all she said, trying not to get any more emotional than she already was.

"Thank you," was all Jacob could say as he looked at each one of them. He placed the ring in his breast pocket. He shook each of his brothers' hands and hugged his sisters.

"You'd better shine those shoes!" Andrew announced to break the silence of their close moment. Growing up, nobody hugged and kissed much as a rule; it had to be a special occasion or possibly a death before anyone did. It felt embarrassing and unnatural. Despite the awkwardness, Jacob felt warm inside and thought he was truly blessed to have such wonderful brothers and sisters. He thanked the Lord daily for his family, especially for Abigail and the many talents that God gifted him with.

"Hey, I polished my shoes, thank you very much!" Jacob looked over at his brother, who was quickly wiping a tear away from his eye, trying not to be noticed. Everyone laughed.

Jacob finished getting ready, with plenty of time to get to the church in the horse and buggy that he had borrowed from Mr. Adair. It only took one horse to pull it, and he wanted to decorate it to surprise Abigail for their departure from the church. Of course, he had help from Mrs. Adair with the decorations. Jacob had also spent a great deal of time preparing their new home's furnishings, making sure they were ready for their wedding day. Instead of going away for their wedding night, they were going to spend their first night in their new abode.

Jacob wanted it to be one of the most memorable days of their lives, and everything had to be perfect.

"Well, brother, are you ready to tie the knot?" Peter slapped Jacob on the back in a joking way.

"You bet," Jacob smiled from ear to ear.

"Well, let's get you to the church on time," interrupted Andrew.

"You know the bride is always late." Jacob laughed.

"You're not the bride!" Sarah informed him. "Now let's get going." The once carefree, conceited girl was now rather serious and quite grown up. This made Jacob smile.

"I can't believe you're getting married," Jane added as they walked out the door.

The carriage was only big enough for two people, so Jane and Jacob drove together. Sarah, Dennis, Sarah's husband, Peter, and Andrew drove in the wagon. They could have walked, but since they would be leaving from the church to go home, it only made sense.

The churchyard was humming with people arriving with their horses, wagons, and buggies. It was a beautiful day for a wedding. The sky was blue, the trees had turned their palette of autumn colours: yellow and orange. It was quite stunning. There was a refreshing wind, a particular light breeze of familiarity, that of which fall brings.

Fifty-some locals were seated in the beautiful grey and white church that centred the village. Everyone knew every-one, and of course, everyone knew just about everything *about* everyone else. As with most small communities, there was one thing that made them special, their support for each other. If someone needed help, a neighbour would be right there to help them out.

Outside, everyone could hear Mrs. Smyth playing the organ for all the guests as they waited for the wedding to begin. Jacob was feeling more nervous as he and his family entered the church. His siblings found their seats, and Jacob walked to the front of the church to stand in his place to wait for the bride. Reverend Young and his best man were already there.

"Good day, lad. How are you feeling?" Bert whispered with only the enthusiasm Bert had. Bert was wearing his suit as well. It was the one he'd worn when he married Alice.

Jacob had considered quite a few people to be his best man, but he settled on Bert. No, he hadn't known him his entire life. No, he wasn't his brother. No, he wasn't even related. But Bert was his life saver. If it hadn't been for Bert, Jacob to that day didn't know where he would be. Bert had shown him that Jesus loved him no matter what he did or what he was going through.

Bert had shown him that God was his Saviour. For that, Jacob would be forever grateful; he'd always hold Bert in high regard. He knew his brothers would understand, plus how would he have chosen between the two of them. Charles had been his childhood friend, and to this day he would be there to help Jacob. But there were some things he and Jacob didn't quite agree upon.

Jacob knew their paths were going in two different directions. Jacob turned around to face the crowd. Looking at all the familiar smiling faces made Jacob feel grateful and loved. His stomach fluttered with anticipation and excitement at the same time. He couldn't wait to be married to his love.

Andrew, Peter, Missy, Jane, Sarah, Dennis, and little Megan sat in the two front pews on the right side. Mrs. Rodgers and Aunt Gladys sat in the front pew on the left side. Aunt Gladys had come from England to attend her niece's wedding, of course, but also to stay awhile to help Mrs. Rodgers since Abigail would be gone. Ernest, Alice's brother, was holding baby Grace and sitting behind Mrs. Rodgers. Alice was Abigail's matron of honour. Jacob spied Mr. and Mrs. Adair behind Ernest, along with Mr. Adair's brother David and his wife, Lily. Charles, his ma and pa, Mr. and Mrs. Mac Donald, had been neighbours of the Hudsons for years.

Jacob continued to scan the room quickly and saw Doc and his wife, Mr. and Mrs. Marley and, of course, large as life, there sat Claude, smug as always. It didn't matter to Jacob. Nothing was going to ruin this day for him. In the back pew, near the wall, was Anna's father. Jacob felt sadness for a moment as he remembered his Anna. He felt sorry for Anna's father: he'd never have a son-in-law, never have grandchildren, and never walk his daughter down the aisle.

Jacob reached into his pocket and pulled out his pocket watch. He held it in the palm of his hand, looking at the time. It was two thirty on the dot. Any moment his beautiful bride would be walking through that door, and both their lives would be changed forever.

Alice came down the aisle first, walking slowly to the organ music. Her neatly pressed grey dress, with long sleeves that hugged her arms, touched the top of her black boots. There was a row of lace sewn two inches from the hem. Alice's bun was perfectly formed with a brimmed hat covered in large flowers. She reached the front of the church and smiled at Jacob as she took her place.

Mrs. Smyth started playing the introduction to the "Wedding March"; the guests all stood and turned towards the back of the church in honour of the bride entering the building. As the music played, Jacob watched Abigail, dressed in a long-sleeved A-line gown that almost touched the floor. Ivory lace overlaid the empire-waist bodice. The high neckline of tulle was trimmed with narrow, flat lace. A four-inch satin ribbon tied neatly at the back and draped down the length of her dress. The skirt was satin, trimmed with two-inch flat lace around the hem. Abigail and her mama had re-made the design from her mama's own wedding dress.

Abigail was adorned with a sheer veil attached to a thin silver crown that sat on the top of her head and draped down her back. Her hair was in a loose bun, Victorian style. She was arm in arm with her papa.

Mr. Rodgers had been slowly recovering from his stroke.

Rehabilitation wasn't easy, and he had worked hard to be able to walk his daughter down the aisle on her wedding day.

He wore a dark grey wool suit and white shirt with striped grey tie and a vest. His trousers were pinstriped with fine black lines. The two of them walked together in time to the music, with Mr. Rodgers clutching a cane in his other hand. His steps weren't perfect, in fact, he stumbled many times, but as the dignified man that he was, he didn't want help from anyone. This was the one honour every man should be able to do on his own.

Jacob was so proud of the progress Mr. Rodgers had made.

Watching the two of them come up the aisle made his heart swell.

Abigail held autumn flowers in her other hand as she and her pa made their way to meet Jacob.

Jacob's heart pounded as he took in the beauty of his future wife. Abigail's flawless complexion with rosy cheeks brought a smile to Jacob's face.

Mr. Rodgers and Abigail stopped two steps before reaching Jacob. Mrs. Smyth finished the "Wedding March," and the Reverend motioned everyone to sit down. Reverend Young stood to the right of Jacob as he spoke.

"Who gives this woman to be married to this man?" he asked out loud.

"Her mother and I do," Mr. Rodgers said. He leaned down and kissed his daughter on the cheek and hugged her. As he turned on his heel, putting the majority of his weight on his cane, he slowly and awkwardly walked back to sit with Mrs. Rodgers. Mrs. Rodgers smiled and helped Mr. Rogers sit down; they sat side by side, holding hands. Mrs. Rodgers had a hanky in her other hand, ready for use.

"We are gathered here today, in the presence of God and all these friends and loved ones, to see the unity of Jacob Daniel Hudson and Abigail Mary Rodgers in holy matrimony."

Reverend Young continued as he spoke about how he had known Jacob all his life, how his family contributed to the community, what a hard-working young lad he was, and that he was an asset to Abbington Pickets. He went on to say that Abigail was the beautiful young woman who came to Abbington Pickets and stole his heart.

"Marriage is a sacred union created by God between a man and a woman, which is also a union between Christ and the Church."

Then there was the apprehensive moment when he asked, "Is there anyone here who thinks this man and this woman should not be married..."

Jacob held his breath. Not that he thought anyone would stand up and argue, but he held his breath just the same.

Finally. Jacob thought they would never get there.

"Please face each other," Reverend Young instructed the couple.

Abigail passed her flowers to Alice and turned to face Jacob as they held both hands.

"Jacob, do you take this woman to be your lawful wedded wife? To have and to hold, in sickness and in health, for richer or for poorer, from this day forward, until death do you part?"

"I do." Jacob looked at Abigail with a twinkle in his eye and a dimple in his cheek. He held Abigail's left hand in his left hand and slipped the wedding ring on her ring finger with his right hand.

"Do you take this man to be your lawful wedded husband? To have and to hold, in sickness and in health, for richer or for poorer, from this day forward, until death do you part?"

"I do," Abigail said as she slid the wedding band on his ring finger.

"By the power vested in me, I now pronounce you man and wife," he smiled at them. "You may kiss the bride!" Reverend Young looked directly at Jacob.

Jacob and Abigail looked at each other as if they were the only ones present. Not an ounce of embarrassment did Jacob feel, like he thought he might, about the brief intimate moment between him and his bride in front of all the community. Jacob reached out towards Abigail, placing his hand around her waist, drawing her closer to him. As he tipped his head, leaning down slowly, he gently placed his muscular hand on Abigail's neck as his thumb cradled her jaw. Jacob's lips touched hers. Abigail blushed. It was a quick kiss, but when they stood back and looked at each other, they smiled for the first time as man and wife.

"Ladies and gentlemen, I give you Mr. and Mrs. Jacob Hudson."

Jacob and Abigail held hands as they turned towards the crowd, while everyone cheered and clapped. They walked together down the aisle, Bert and Alice followed. As they passed through the doorway, the church bells started to ring. What a glorious day. Jacob and Abigail stood outside the church to meet their guests in a receiving line.

The rest of the afternoon was spent outdoors enjoying music by Bill Thomas and his orchestra, local musicians. Songs such as "Haste to the Wedding," "The Minute Waltz," and "Turkey in the Straw" were favourites, but there were particular pattern dance tunes that were to everyone's liking. Jacob did like his Joplin music, but Bill Thomas was well-known in the area for his fine fiddle playing, and the music was enjoyable. Delicious food, brought by all the church ladies, consisted of roasted beef, roasted pork, potato salad, devilled eggs, homemade buns, beet pickles, and several kinds of relishes. Desserts were Maid of

Honour tarts, carrot cake, raisin pie, and many other different kinds of pies including, of course, one of Jacob's favourites, Saskatoon pie. Abigail had, however, insisted on making their wedding cake. She had made a moist fruit cake that was usually made for both Christmas and weddings. She covered it in almond paste, then decorated it with white icing. It was plain but beautiful. Jacob has been quite impressed with how domestic Abigail has become. Despite the absence, Jacob felt when Abigail had gone away to England, she had sure learned quite a few new things.

Jacob and Abigail visited with each guest and thanked them for coming. He was especially pleased to see David and Lily Adair from Kingston. Jacob sent David Adair tables every month to sell in his store, but Jacob hadn't seen the Adairs for a year or more. Anna's father shook Jacob's hand in the receiving line, but Jacob watched as he put his hat on his head and left the churchyard, heading towards home. Jacob shared his pain.

At three-thirty, everyone gathered around the bride and groom as they sat in chairs with all the gifts. They spent the next hour opening gifts, laughing while sharing the afternoon with the people who were important to both of them. The young children helped by handing each gift to Jacob and Abigail for them to open, then they passed it along for the guests to admire.

"Oh, my," Abigail exclaimed as she carefully unwrapped a handmade quilt. "It's gorgeous." Jacob helped her hold it up to show all who were watching. It was made in warm colours with traditional squares. There were two appliquéd hearts in the centre, along with words of love and affection embroidered in particular places.

"Jane, Missy, and I worked on it together," piped up Sarah. "It was something of a long-distant quilting experience if you want to say."

"I love it." Abigail looked at Jacob. "*We* love it."

Abigail gave the quilt to Jacob to hold while she quickly ran over to each of her new sisters-in-law, hugging them tight in appreciation for their thoughtfulness and generosity. When Abigail sat back down next to Jacob she heard a voice call out to them.

"Our gift is waiting for you in your new home," spoke up Mr. Adair. "The Missus picked it out." he winked at Abigail then looked over at his wife who was smiling proudly.

"I can't wait to see what it is," Abigail said as she looked curiously at Jacob thinking he might be in on the secret. Jacob knew what it was and simply smiled to his bride.

Jacob and Abigail received many wonderful gifts from their friends and family, such as silverware, a set of blue willow dishes, tablecloths, dish towels, a beautiful bowl and pitcher, a flower vase, baking pans, pots and pans, a cast iron kettle; all gifts to create a home. Jacob and Abigail finished opening the last gift.

"I would like to congratulate Jacob and Abigail on their wedding day." The guests hushed when they heard Mr. Rodgers' voice. He had stood up close to his chair to say his speech.

"I want to thank Jacob for all he has done for our family," Mr. Rodgers eyes began to tear up. He cleared his throat to avoid the embarrassment of crying in front of a crowd of people. "I don't know what I…" he stopped and looked over at his wife, "what *we* would have done without you during my illness and my recovery.

I needed a miracle, and Jacob you were that miracle. I needed strength, and you were that strength. I needed support, and you were that support. You're a good man, Jacob Hudson, and I am honoured to call you my son. Welcome to the family." Mr. Rodgers smiled from ear to ear as he watched his daughter and new son-in- law accept his words of love and praise.

Everyone clapped in agreement with Mr. Rogers. Jacob walked over and hugged his new father-in-law and mother-in-law. Of course, Mrs. Rodgers was wiping the tears with her much-needed hanky.

"Now, you two lovebirds go enjoy your evening," stepped up Peter. "We'll clean up the church yard." He walked over to Jacob and slapped him on the back. The rest of his siblings and their families were behind him.

The crowd huddled around the newlyweds as they said their goodbyes and started walking towards their decorated buggy. As they climbed in, everyone threw rice towards them.

"Giddy up." Jacob shook the reins, and the horses slowly began moving. Jacob and Abigail smiled, waving to all who were there. As they rode towards their castle on the hill, tin cans tied to strings dragged behind the buggy. Charles smiled to himself as he stood in the crowd, watching them drive away.

Jacob drove the buggy up beside the front step on the east side of the round house. Jacob and Abigail wanted to name their home, so they agreed to disagree, on naming it "Jacabig Place." It was made up of both their names. Jacob liked it so well he made a wooden sign with Victorian letters painted on it. He placed it at the end of their pathway towards their home. It was one of the surprises he had for Abigail on their wedding day.

"Wait, Wait," Jacob said as he tried to stop the horses and climb off the buggy to run to the other side to help Abigail off. "I'll give you my hand." Jacob stood firmly on the ground beside the carriage, reaching his hand up to Abigail. Abigail began to chuckle at his little game; he was the King, and she was his Queen.

"Why, thank you, my lord." Abigail placed her hand in his and grasped her dress at the side, lifting it up so she wouldn't trip on it. She stepped down to the step with Jacob's help, and then down on flat land. Jacob put his arm around her waist with one hand and scooped her up with his other.

"What are you doing?" Abigail laughed.

"Carrying you over the threshold," he informed her seriously.

"Isn't that only in books?"

"Well, this is *our* fairy tale, and you, my love, are entering our new home in style."

Jacob walked up the step and reached the door. Fumbling with his hand, which was holding Abigail, he managed to unlatch the door. He pushed it gently with his knee, and as the door swung open, the smell of fresh-cut lumber tickled their noses. He looked at Abigail's big brown eyes, leaned his head forward, and kissed her lips softly.

"Welcome to your, *our*, new home," he whispered.

"I love you, Jacob Daniel Hudson," Abigail whispered as if someone could hear them, but of course no one else was there.

Jacob set Abigail down on her feet so they could explore the new place.

"This is wonderful," Abigail exclaimed as she looked through the kitchen. Jacob took the chimney off the oil lamp sitting on the washstand beside the doorway. He lit the wick with a match, then set the chimney back in its place and adjusted the flame with the knob on the side. The room lit up as the flame flickered and cast a silhouette of two of them on the wall.

"Oh my goodness!" Abigail saw the gift from the Adairs right in the middle of the room. A brand new, white enamel cookstove.

She would be the first woman in Abbington Pickets to have such a beautiful new stove. Not only would it cook, but it would also heat the whole house.

"Oh, Jacob." She hugged him. "We must thank them as soon as we can," she said, as she pulled the handle of the door to have a look inside the oven. She then looked it over, back to front, side to side. Abigail felt very blessed to have such a piece of new furniture.

"Welcome to your, our, new home," he whispered.

"It was Mrs. Adair's idea. She thought you would love it, and I would say by the look on your face, she was absolutely right."

Abigail couldn't get enough of absorbing every item there was to see in the house built especially for her. Along the north wall there was a wooden cupboard that held flour, sugar, and baking supplies as well as a counter top built below the upper part, and then a door and three drawers below the counter.

"I can't wait to mix up a batch of cookies on this new cupboard." Abigail gushed.

In front of the window against the west wall was a small breakfast table made of fresh pine. Under the ledge of the table in the centre was a small drawer that held cutlery. Abigail couldn't believe the details that Jacob had thought of while building their abode.

"Come, let me show you the rest of the house." Jacob took her by the hand and walked her into the dining room. There was a beautiful, handcrafted maple wooden table with two chairs, one at either end.

"I only had time to build two chairs," Jacob said coyly. "I'll build you the rest over time."

"You made this?" Abigail asked as she rubbed her hand along the smooth surface. She felt so grateful to be loving a man who could create such beauty with his hands. "It's beautiful," she said softly. "I don't know how you found all the time to do all of this, you must have never slept." Her heart was overflowing.

As Jacob promised, a piano sat along the east wall of the dining room.

"Oh Jacob," Abigail gasped when she saw it. "You weren't joking." She ran over to the piano and sat down on the stool. The upright cherry wood piano was plainly crafted, but perfect, in Abigail's mind. "This must have cost a fortune," Abigail fussed before she played a piece of Joplin's "The Entertainer."

"No, it didn't." Jacob smiled with a wink. He wasn't going to reveal the secret that he'd traded several of his tea tables for the piano.

"I am the most blessed woman."

"No, I am the one that's been blessed."

"My beautiful clock is going to look wonderful on the piano," Abigail envisioned.

"It sure will."

Abigail continued to look around when she noticed a familiar chair in the living room. There, next to the fireplace, was the chair that had been in her father's room while he was recovering.

"Your Mama and Pa thought we should have it for our new home," Jacob informed her. "You spent many hours in that chair sitting by your father's bedside; it was only fitting you should have it," Abigail was touched by the gesture and gift from her parents. Next to the chair was a beautiful tea table that was very obviously made by Jacob.

"I love it," Abigail told him. "I can't wait to curl up and read a book with a cup of tea."

Jacob was pleased that Abigail was satisfied with all that he had done.

"The fireplace is beautiful," Abigail added. She admired the fieldstone fireplace, with a long maple mantel above the hearth. The stone chimney, made with smaller stone than the fireplace itself, continued to the ceiling.

"Peter and Andrew contributed." Jacob smiled. "They brought all the stones. I don't think they had a stone left in their fields." He laughed.

"You did a wonderful job, Jacob." Abigail was impressed.

"Well, I did have some help," Jacob admitted. "I can't take all the credit."

"Oh, don't be modest." Abigail grinned.

"No, really," Jacob continued. "Mr. MacDonald helped me work on it."

"Well, it still looks wonderful to me," Abigail insisted. "What's this?" Abigail ran over to the north wall where an elegant, yet odd-looking long settee was sitting.

"That's a chaise lounge," Jacob informed her. "I bought it from a local fella. Isn't it a neat piece of furniture? I thought I might try to build one myself." Jacob left out the detail that the gentleman he bought it from had purchased it at an auction a few years back. The gentleman had gotten it real cheap because another older man had laid down on it during the sale and died.

That was going to be Jacob's little untold story.

The last room was the bedroom. Jacob had moved his bed there, along with a dresser and a tallboy that had belonged to his ma and pa. Jane had offered it to him when he was working on the house. At the end of the bed was an old trunk with Jacob's name printed on it from when he was a young lad. The writing had some wear to it, but you could see it was definitely Jacob's name. It was an almost square trunk, with a lot of things Jacob saved over the years, keepsakes and the like. Along the northeast wall, Jacob had built Abigail a small closet for her to hang her clothes.

"This is amazing." Abigail couldn't get over how much work Jacob had done to the house in the short time he'd had.

"I know there isn't a lot of furniture yet, and it could use some curtains," Jacob reassured her, "but I know you will have this house looking like a castle when you're done decorating it."

"No, Jacob you're the one who has made it a castle." Abigail was teary eyed as she spoke. "It's beyond words the work you have done for me, for us."

"I would do anything for you." Jacob walked up behind Abigail and wrapped his arms around in front of her waist, kissing the nape of her neck. "I love you more than anything in this world. I want to build a wonderful life with you."

"You are too good to me, more than I deserve," Abigail whispered.

Jacob held his wife with all his might. The love he felt for her at that moment tripled in seconds. God was truly a good God.

"Let us pray together," Jacob suggested. They both walked over to the bed and sat on the edge, holding each other's hands as they bowed their heads. Jacob prayed.

"Dear Heavenly Father, we thank you for this glorious day that you have given us. Please anoint us with your holiness.

Protect our marriage, our home, and our families. Make us the husband and wife you want us to be. Bless us and keep us, in Jesus' name. Amen," Jacob knew this would be a daily routine as well as a sacred moment between him and his wife and the Lord.

They both looked at each other with excitement in their eyes. The two of them were as one, to have and to hold until death did them part. What wonderful life did God have in store for them? Where would He take them? Today was the first day of the rest of their lives.

Jacob touched Abigail's forehead with the back of his fore-finger slowly moving to her temple. He ran his fingers through the length of her brown locks, then he gently pulled her close to him and kissed her lips. The two of them had waited a long time to be together, this close, this alone.

chapter ten

IT HAD BEEN a wonderful week of married bliss for Jacob and Abigail. Abigail was the happy wife and a good little home-maker, working hard to decorate the new house and make it homey. Jacob was the hard-working grateful husband to the woman he had always longed for. Jacob awoke extra early each day to finish sooner so he could spend time with his new bride. They took walks, went horseback riding through Poplar Lane, and bought groceries for the first time together at Adair's General Store.

It was a marvellous start to their marriage, but the honey-moon had to come to an end, and they had to get into the swing of regular everyday life. A week turned into a month, then the next month. Table orders were coming in every day. Jacob had spent the winter months catching up.

Abigail made friends with Mrs. Adair since the general store wasn't that far from her. Whenever she would go in for grocer-ies, she and Mrs. Adair would have tea. In fact, Abigail planned her visits for the afternoons, bringing freshly baked scones or biscuits with her. They talked about each other's families, exchanged recipes, and had a mutual love for gardening. That spring, Mrs. Adair gave Abigail her first perennial. She planted it in her flower bed on the southeast side of the house. As the beautiful, dark burgundy hollyhock started to bloom, Abigail had Jacob build a wooden stake to support the tall spike. Abigail also grew pansies, sweet peas, marigolds, and sunflowers for the birds. She ordered all the seeds that winter from the general store. Her flowerbeds were her pride and joy.

The winter had been a long one. It started snowing in the middle of October and hadn't stopped. They visited Goldenrod every two or three weeks to see if there was anything they could do to help. Claude remained the hired man but still seemed like a stranger to them all. Mr. Rodgers' mobility had been improving, but he still needed a lot of help. His speech had come back a hundred percent, which was a real blessing. Jacob had once thought maybe they should sell Goldenrod, but with all Mr. Rodgers' improvements, Jacob thought things would get back to the way they had been.

Another Christmas was spent at Goldenrod, with Alice, Bert, Grace, Ernest, and Aunt Gladys, with the addition of Claude, and two of Jacob's siblings, Andrew and Jane. Jacob was very pleased Andrew and Jane had joined them since Peter and Missy were going to her family's again and as Sarah was expecting her second child, she would be staying in Kingston.

Jacob and Claude still didn't see eye to eye, but they seemed to keep out of each other's way. Claude also appeared to stay away from Abigail, which suited Jacob just fine. Jacob couldn't figure out what it was about Claude that he didn't like but he knew there was something.

Jacob gave Abigail a beautiful treadle sewing machine for Christmas that year. She spent a lot of her time making curtains, tablecloths, and napkins, and she even taught herself to sew her first quilt. Mrs. Adair was great about helping her pick out fabric. She would let her work off the cotton batting and fabric by helping at the store when Mrs. Adair wanted to do her errands. Easter weekend, a late April snow storm was moving in, so Jacob and Abigail were going to celebrate their first holiday without family. They had invited Mr. and Mrs. Adair to come for dinner after church. Abigail cooked a stuffed roasted chicken. She wasn't real sure how to do the whole holiday meal herself, but she managed with a little guidance from Mrs. Adair, who even offered to prepare some of the meal. Abigail insisted she wanted to make her first dinner for company all by herself.

Abigail tried to remember from when she'd helped her mama make a meal, but as far as any cooking recipe, well it was all in her head. She did, however, consult with her new Five Roses cookbook, which she had received as a wedding gift.

"What a delicious meal, Abigail." Mr. Adair leaned back in his chair rubbing his belly.

"Thank you, sir," Abigail proudly accepted the compliment. She had worried so much about everything being perfect.

"It was a beautiful dinner, Abigail," Mrs. Adair agreed.

"That's my Girlie." Jacob beamed.

"Those sweet potatoes were excellent; I can't say I ever had them like that before," Mrs. Adair added.

"Well, I learned that from my Mama. I didn't really have a recipe," Abigail blushed, "but I remembered how she did it, apparently." She laughed. "I hope you left room for dessert."

"Oh, there's always room for that." Mr. Adair smiled as Abigail got up from the table, picking up the dinner plates in front of them.

"Let me help you." Mrs. Adair helped her clear the table, then placed before each of them a plate filled with fluffy white meringue; a perfectly cut brown-sugar-coloured dessert.

"Mmm, that looks mighty good," Jacob spoke up first.

"Can't wait to dig in." Mr. Adair placed his spoon for the first big scoop, placed it in his mouth and closed his eyes as if he was in heaven.

"What is this called?" he asked. "And could you please give the recipe to my wife." He smiled with a huge closed mouth grin, everyone laughed.

"Butterscotch Delight is the name of it, but it's a kind of pie really," Abigail answered. "And of course, the recipe's all yours."

"Never heard of a pie this fancy before," Mr. Adair said as he was filling his mouth with more sweetness.

"You've never heard of it? Well, I've never heard of it, and I'm married to her." Jacob laughed, grabbed Abigail's hand, and winked at her.

"Oh, stop you both," Abigail chuckled. "It's an English treat from Mama's side of the family."

"I would love to make this for Thanksgiving this year," Mrs. Adair said. "Wouldn't that be a great dessert to show your sister-in-law that I can cook?" she said to her husband, raising her left eyebrow.

"She knows you can cook," Mr. Adair assured his wife, trying not to show his humour.

"She may *know* I cook. She just doesn't think it's as good as hers." It sounded to Jacob and Abigail as if the two of them didn't get along.

"Well, I'll write you out the recipe before you go," Abigail graciously interrupted their moment of disagreement.

"And it looks like you may be here awhile," Jacob added as he stood by the window, holding the curtain back and looking out at the snow filled windows. "It's pretty mean out there."

"Maybe a game of cribbage is in order," Mr. Adair suggested as he lit his cigar and offered one to Jacob.

"No thank you, sir." He shook his head. "I never got used to smoking."

"Well, you don't know what you're missing."

"Neither do you," Mrs. Adair piped in. "That cough you have tells another story." She sternly glared at him in disapproval.

"Shall I get the cribbage board?" Jacob asked trying to change the subject.

The men enjoyed game after game of crib. The two ladies laughed and told stories in the kitchen while doing the dishes. The noise of the wind blowing against the house, along with the clatter of dishes, was all Jacob could hear while playing crib with Mr. Adair.

Once the dishes were put away, and the kitchen was tidied up, Abigail and Mrs. Adair retired to the living room to do some sewing. Abigail had been working on sewing the binding on the quilt she had just finished, while Mrs. Adair had brought her cross stitch to work on.

While the toasty warm home kept its heat, the terrific snowy wind blew hard. There were no visible lights in any windows that evening, as no one could see farther than ten feet away. This reminded Jacob of another blizzard they'd had. The one of 1908 when a surprise storm hit while they were at the Harvester's Ball at the Howards'. It also brought back more than a brief memory of the weather; it brought back Anna.

"Your go," Mr. Adair prompted Jacob. "Hello?" He waved his hand in front of his face. "Jacob?"

"Oh, sorry, sir." Jacob quickly played his turn. "You were a million miles away, lad. Where were you?"

"Nowhere." He shrugged.

"Anna, wasn't it?" Mr. Adair knew the pain Jacob endured over the loss of Anna; everyone in Abbington Pickets knew.

"There's always something that reminds me of her, and then I can't stop thinking of her." Jacob looked ashamed.

"There is no harm in that, lad. She meant a great deal to you. You'll always have those memories."

Mr. Adair's encouraging words meant a lot to Jacob. "I know, but I feel like I am betraying Abigail every time a thought of Anna pops into my head."

"It's natural, and she was a big part of your life. Abigail will understand that."

"I'll understand what?" Abigail walked into the dining room at that moment.

"That if Jacob doesn't win this hand, he has to leave Jacabig Place to me." Mr. Adair laughed at his quickly thought-up joke to cover up the situation.

"Well, that will never happen." Abigail went along with the joke, walking behind Jacob to rest her hands on his shoulders. "Jacob is an astute player, isn't that right, Mr. Hudson?" She looked amused as she watched him put down his cards carefully. "I try," Jacob said modestly with a smirk.

"I was going to make some coffee," Abigail announced. "Would you fellas like some?"

"Sounds like a great idea," Jacob and Mr. Adair both agreed.

After coffee and some leftover butterscotch delight, the storm seemed to have died down. The Adairs decided they'd better get home before another blizzard started. Jacob helped Mr. Adair with his horse and buggy, and he also wanted to check his own horses, making sure they had enough feed and bedding. The snow had blown drifts up against the door to the stable. He didn't have a barn built, so for now, the stable would have to do.

Jacob was thinking the weather might force him to build that barn a bit sooner that he had planned.

After their company had left, Abigail carried the coffee cups to the kitchen from the dining room, and they turned in for the night.

"Jacob?" Abigail quietly spoke as she lay in bed next to her husband.

"Yes, love?" Jacob answered.

"Do you think of Anna much?" Jacob was taken aback by her question. He didn't know how to answer. If he were honest, he might hurt Abigail's feelings, but he wasn't going to lie to her either.

"Why do you ask?" Jacob questioned.

"I know you and Mr. Adair were talking about her," Abigail's voice cracked as she admitted to overhearing their conversation.

"I don't know," Jacob started to explain. "I- I-" he didn't know what else to say or how to explain what he thought or how he was feeling.

"Well, you do, or you don't," Abigail's tone seemed to change. Jacob felt like he was a schoolboy being scolded by his teacher.

"Well-" again he was at a loss for words.

"Come on, Jacob. It's not a trick question."

"I know, it's just-" he stammered. "I don't-"

"Why can't you say it?" Abigail blurted out. "I know you do."

"Uh-" Jacob looked at her with surprise. "How?" He dreaded the words Abigail was about to speak. It was like he didn't want to hear the answer.

"I know you dream about her," she said.

"What?" Jacob felt the tingling of annoyance all over him like goosebumps. It was the first time he had felt angry towards Abigail. "What do you mean?"

"I know because," she paused; her face looked hurt and sympathetic at the same time. "I hear you talking in your sleep."

"What?" Jacob was surprised as ever to hear this, he hadn't dreamt a dream about Anna that he could ever recall. He hadn't had a bad dream since he quit dreaming about Lucy after his father passed away.

"You cry out in your sleep, Jacob," Abigail bluntly told him. Tears rolled down her cheeks as she spoke. "I thought it would stop, I thought because it was only your dreams, it was harmless, but then tonight, hearing you talk to Mr. Adair about her…" She put her face in her hands and began to cry.

"I don't know what you're talking about," Jacob argued. "I don't dream about her. I don't remember dreaming about her at all."

By this time, Jacob was hot under the collar. Even the sound of Abigail's sobbing wasn't making him feel like comforting her. He was unsettled by her uncompassionate disposition. They never once discussed Anna, not even after Abigail's return from England. It was like an unspoken, but forbidden memory, never to be thought of again.

Jacob didn't know what to say to Abigail. He was mad at her and angry at himself. *Why did I have to discuss Anna with Mr. Adair? Why couldn't I have kept my thoughts and feelings to myself?* Jacob didn't want to lay next to Abigail right then. He quickly rolled over in silence, keeping his body as close to the outer edge as possible, his face burned with exasperation. One thing Jacob's mother had always told him, "Never spout off when you're angry. Keeping quiet is the right thing to do; that way, you don't regret your words later."

Jacob could feel Abigail turning over on her side of the bed as well. He closed his eyes and tried to sleep. Sleep didn't find him quickly. It was almost morning when he dozed off, just in time to get up.

Jacob awoke before Abigail. He slowly climbed out of bed, as not to wake her. He folded back his share of the blankets as if to make his side of the bed. Quietly, he put on his britches, then his shirt. He left the bedroom carrying his socks, closing the door behind him. A chill was in the air, in more ways than one. Jacob was still bitter over the previous night's heated discussion; he wanted to leave the house before Abigail got up.

He stoked the stove; it was almost burnt out. In his sleepy daze, he stared at the bright red embers as he continued to stir. He added the small pieces of pine he had split the day before. At last, the fire was in full flames. He tossed in three larger logs to keep it going. Jacob could feel the heat on his hands as he rubbed them together over the stove top. Jacob poured water into the coffee pot, scooping four heaping tablespoons of coffee grounds into the basket, placing it on the stem inside the pot.

He then put the lid on, setting the pot on the stove. Hopefully, he could have coffee before he left the house.

"Good morning lad," Mr. Adair was shoveling off the wooden sidewalk of the general store. The storm had brought approximately a foot of snow, and with the wind, it appeared to have doubled in size with the way it had drifted against the doors of the buildings.

"Good morning," Jacob nodded. "Got another shovel? I'll give you a hand." Mr. Adair pointed to the shovel leaning up against the front of the building. Jacob walked over, grabbed it by the handle and started scooping snow and throwing it off the sidewalk.

"What are you doing here this early in the morning anyway?" Mr. Adair asked. "You and the Missus get into a fight?" He laughed at his own humour, not realizing the truth behind it.

Jacob laughed with him and left it as a joke.

"I was out of coffee this morning." Jacob thought it would sound better than saying he was so angry he couldn't stand to be in the same room with his own wife.

"Well, I think maybe we can help you out with that." Mr. Adair smiled. "Maybe the wife will have breakfast ready by the time we are done this job."

"Oh no, I don't want to trouble you, sir," Jacob assured him, "I only came for the coffee."

"It's no trouble lad." They both continued tossing the snow to the side of the building. With every breath, a puff of smoke like air escaped their mouths. The morning was crisp, but it was a far cry from the blizzard that had blown through the village the previous night. *Maybe winter will end soon,* Jacob thought.

Jacob had a quick breakfast with the Adairs of fried eggs, toast and another cup of coffee before heading out. He was grateful he had a bite to eat; his chores needed to be done, and he wanted to avoid the house a little while longer.

The horses were happy to get their feed for the morning. Jacob tossed hay into their stalls with the pitchfork. He walked over to the pump house out behind the shop where he had to pump hard on the water pump to retrieve water for the horses. It was a good thing that he'd dug the well when he was building their house the previous summer. It would have been such an inconvenience to have to haul water from the pump at Abbington Pickets. Jacob had another memory of Anna, her blonde hair blowing in the breeze as she took his hand while walking him across the street from the Empire Hotel to show him where the water well, used by all the locals, was located.

After watering the horses, Jacob walked over to his carpentry shop. He unlocked the door and swung it open. Brr, it was freezing inside. He hadn't lit the stove for a couple of days. Jacob picked up his axe, which was leaning against the wall inside the door, and walked out behind the shop where there was a row of pine logs stacked. He grabbed a big log, then placed it on its end on an old stump. He grasped the handle of his axe with both hands; pulling back, he swung down hard, splitting the log in two, then he split those two pieces into four. After splitting an armful of wood, he carried it into the shop and knelt down in front of the stove. He opened the door and neatly stacked the small pieces of wood inside the stove, adding crumpled up newspaper in between the pieces. Lastly, he struck a wooden match against the stove and placed it close to the paper. Within moments, flames engulfed the inside of the stove, dancing colours of red, yellow, and orange. Instantly, the stove emitted heat.

Jacob left the door open slightly to get the fire going.

It wasn't long before heat filled the arctic-like room, which made it more inviting to work in. As Jacob prepared lumber to be cut to build another six tables, he laid them out in an assembly line. The morning went by fast, and his stomach started growling. He wasn't ready to go to the house just yet. Jacob had thought more about Abigail and Anna since getting up that morning and hadn't come up with any conclusions. He was angry with Abigail for being insensitive, and he was angry at himself for not being able to control his thoughts about Anna. He knelt down, clasped his hands together, raising them up slightly, and looked up.

Lord, please help me. Please help me to understand Abigail, and forgive me for being angry with her. Ease my heart and give me peace over losing Anna. I can't do this on my own, Lord Jesus. I give this up to you. I need you, Lord... Jacob prayed hard. He hung his head down and took a deep breath. He felt a sense of peace and relief wash over him, as though a new day had begun, with a refreshing feeling. Jacob knew right then and there what he needed to do.

He grabbed his coat and hat off the hanger next to the door. Putting them on, he unlatched the door then slammed it shut behind him. He felt like running all the way to the house, which was only yards away. He grabbed the door latch, pushing the door open. Abigail was standing in the kitchen, stirring something in a pot on the stove; he startled her as he rushed over to her. He scooped his arm around her waist and nestled his face in the back of her neck just below her ear and whispered to her.

"I am sorry, love."

Abigail dropped the spoon in the pot, and slowly turned around.

Jacob held her; she put her arms around his neck, leaning her forehead against his chest. "I love you. I'll always love you."

"I know, Jacob," Abigail cried. "I was wrong; I should never have said anything about Anna. I have no right to-"

"Shhh," Jacob shook his head. "You're my wife, you have every right." He lifted Abigail's chin with his forefinger; she looked up at him with tear-filled eyes. "Anna was part of my life. I won't forget, and there will always be a special place in my heart for her. But I love you with everything I have and memories won't take that away."

"I love you, Jacob Hudson." Abigail smiled with trembling lips.

Jacob slid his finger lightly over her forehead, pushing the few strands of hair from in front of her face. He leaned down and kissed her lips, then hugged her tight.

She stood on her tiptoes to reach his six-foot frame so that her chin reached his shoulder.

He felt so warm and at peace with his wife.

The week had gone by slowly. The snow continued to come every night, but the days were filled with sunshine. Abigail was missing her family and tried to keep busy with the household chores and visiting Mrs. Adair. She began cutting out another quilt. Mrs. Adair also gave her quick lessons on crocheting doilies, which Abigail found she enjoyed doing in the evenings before bed.

It was Saturday at dinner time. Abigail had made chicken stew with dumplings. Jacob was finishing his last spoonful when he sat straight up in his chair.

"Let's go sledding." Jacob mischievously smiled at Abigail. He knew the winter felt so long and especially for Abigail to be away from her mama and papa. He wanted to do something fun for the day. He had finished his chores for the morning and could spare a few hours to spend with his wife.

"What?" Abigail looked at Jacob with surprise. "Are you joking?"

"Come on, there are so many snow drifts outside from the wind last night," Jacob continued. "It'll be fun."

"We don't have a sled," Abigail pointed out.

"Mr. Adair has one; I saw it in the back room when I worked for him a while ago," Jacob said. "I'm sure he would let us use it."

"I don't know, Jacob. We're not kids anymore."

"When did you lose your sense of adventure?"

"You are not funny, Mr. Hudson," Abigail tried to remain the adult. "Besides, I have all these dishes to do." She looked around the room.

"I'll help you do them when we get back," Jacob promised.

"Oh, alright." Abigail laughed. "It *will* be fun."

Jacob filled the wood stove to keep the house warm while they were gone. Abigail put the food away from dinner and went into the bedroom to get dressed in warmer clothes.

"I love it when you wear those britches," Jacob teased. "Oh, Jacob." Abigail blushed as she put on her boots and tied them up.

Jacob was already suited up, waiting at the door for Abigail.

Jacob and Abigail walked over to the general store to borrow Mr. Adair's sled. He was more than happy to let them use it and have a little well-deserved fun for the afternoon. Jacob pulled the wooden sled behind them as they trudged through the fresh snow. The curved runners under the wooden frame made it slide smoothly on the hard-blown snow. It was an antique, homemade sled, but in excellent condition. Jacob hadn't sledded down a hill since he was a boy with his siblings; it was silly fun, but they both could use the day together. The snow crunched in rhythm under their boots with every step. The sun was shining brightly, reflecting off the snow, making it difficult to see in the distance. Abigail squinted, holding her hand level with her eyebrows to protect her eyes.

"Over there." Jacob pointed to the hill that was northeast of Jacabig Place. The closer they got to the hill, the faster and faster they walked with anticipation, much like two children running to see what was under the Christmas tree on Christmas morning.

Jacob grabbed Abigail's hand as they trekked up the hill, dragging the sled behind them. They finally reached the top; it had seemed like they would never get there.

"Alright. Ready?" Jacob motioned Abigail to climb on the front of the sled. He had placed it on the edge of the hill, which tipped slightly forward, waiting for the moment that gravity would let go. Jacob straddled the sled behind her, still holding the rope; he wrapped his arms around to the front of Abigail and held her tight. Using his right leg, he kicked off, and with a big gush, the sled quickly sent them to the bottom of the hill in a matter of seconds with both of them thrown from the sled.

Jacob laughed loudly as he laid in the fluffy snow, staring at the clear blue sky above. He thought that this was the most fun he had in a long time, feeling like a free little child again. He rolled on his side, looking around for Abigail. He saw her, lying to his left, but she wasn't moving.

"Abigail?" he called out to her. "Wasn't that fun?" She still didn't move. Jacob jumped to his feet and ran over to her, sliding down on his knees beside her.

"Abigail! Abigail!" Jacob cried out as he bent down over her limp body. "Are you alright?" Jacob's heart was pounding with fear.

Jacob stared down at her smooth ivory face with rosy cheeks and dark eyebrows that outlined her eyes. At that moment, her red lips began to slowly curve. Jacob raised his left eyebrow with curiosity, then at once her brown eyes quickly opened, and Abigail burst out laughing.

"Gotcha!" She laughed at Jacob. "You should have seen your face."

"That was NOT funny!" Jacob sternly said to her. "Not funny at all." His heart was still trying to slow down with the rest of his body. Jacob sat there, catching his breath; Abigail sat up and saw the fear in his eyes.

"I'm sorry, Jacob," Abigail sincerely said. "I was only joking with you."

Jacob hopped to his feet and jumped back, bent down, and scooped up a handful of snow in his gloved hand. He placed his other hand over it and pressed the snow together tightly to form a ball. He started to step back even farther, then reached his right hand back and threw the snowball at Abigail.

It smacked right into Abigail's leg. She looked up at Jacob with surprise. "Oh? So that's how you want to play it?" Abigail reached down beside her and scooped up a handful of snow as well and made a snowball and quickly threw it at Jacob. He ducked as the snow flew past him. The two of them were in the middle of a full-fledged snowball fight.

"Alright, alright, alright!" Abigail yelled, covering her head from all the snowballs Jacob was throwing; he was faster than she was. "I give up."

Jacob tossed aside the snowball he was holding and ran over to Abigail, who was laying in the snow. He dropped down and started tickling her ribs.

Abigail giggled, rolling from side to side as Jacob persisted tickling her.

Jacob finally gave up and laid down next to her. They both laid still staring up at the sky above, without a cloud in the sky. The air was crisp, and they could see their breath puffing from their lips like smoke as they breathed.

"Let's make a snow angel," Abigail suggested with delight. "I haven't made one since I was a little girl." She spread her arms up above her head to create the wings, and her legs to make the dress of the angel. She jumped up, trying not to step on it as she looked at her creation.

"Come on, Jacob. Look at my masterpiece," she encouraged him.

Jacob was reluctantly laying on the snow, giving Abigail a run for her money. Jacob loved to tease his Girlie, just to get her riled up.

"Jac-ooob," she insisted.

She picked up his hand and pulled his arms, but Jacob pulled her down with him. He held her in his arms and drew her closer to him.

Abigail smiled as she looked into Jacob's eyes. Something caught her attention, and her smiling face turned to fright.

"Jacob, the house is on fire!" Abigail screamed as she pointed towards Jacabig Place.

"Oh no, not again," Jacob laughed. He wasn't going to fall for her joke again.

"I am not fooling," Abigail insisted frantically. She stood up and started running.

Jacob knew then she wasn't playing around. He immediately turned around and saw the smoke for himself. Both of them were running as fast as their legs could carry them.

Jacob and Abigail reached Jacabig in a matter of minutes. When they reached the door, it was open, and Mr. and Mrs. Adair were both inside with buckets of water. Both of them coughing and holding tea towels over their mouths and noses. They saw that Jacob and Abigail were in the house with them. Mr. Adair ran outside, while the three of them followed suit. Each one of them were coughing and sputtering from the pouring smoke that came from the stove. Once everyone caught their breath, Mr. Adair explained what he'd seen.

"I was outside getting the horses ready for a delivery when I noticed the smoke pouring out of your chimney," he started to explain, "I ran up closer and saw the flames coming out the top."

"Good thing he called out to me," Mrs. Adair said between coughs. "I grabbed the pails, and we ran to the water pump."

"Oh my Lord," Abigail gasped. "We could have lost our home."

Jacob held Abigail close as he listened to the details the Adairs were telling them.

"I ran into the house and closed the damper, but then smoke was coming out from around the door and the pipe joints. The chimney was glowing red."

Jacob had never seen Mr. Adair with such a scared look on his face.

"We are so relieved you and Abigail weren't in the house," Mrs. Adair said to Jacob. "I was so worried," she walked over to the two of them and hugged each of them.

"I shouldn't have filled it so full when we left today." Jacob shook his head with regret. "I haven't had any trouble with that stove before. I'll have to be more careful." Jacob was remembering the fire that had taken Anna's life. *I have to be more careful*, he repeated over and over in his head. *What if we had been sleeping? What if Abigail had been alone?* Jacob couldn't stop thinking of the terrible things that *could* have happened.

Mr. Adair wiped his forehead with his handkerchief. His face was black with smoke.

"It was a good thing you were outside when you were," Jacob said. "Thank you, sir."

"It was a very good thing you weren't too far from home either," Mr. Adair added.

"I'll open all the windows in the house and air it out," Jacob told him as he walked towards the doorway. The smoke had subsided, but was still lingering in the air.

"Let me help you." Mr. Adair followed Jacob.

"Come on honey," Mrs. Adair put her arm around Abigail, pulling her gently away. "Come over to the store. I'll make some tea while we wait for the house to clear out." Abigail and Mrs. Adair slowly walked together towards the store.

The men followed the women once they'd opened every door and window to the house. The four of them had a small lunch to go with their tea, consisting of pork sandwiches, slices of cheddar cheese, and bread pudding. They had a good visit in between customers at the general store. Jacob assisted Mr.

Adair with loading some crates for a customer, and Abigail helped Mrs. Adair do the dishes.

"Well, love," Jacob looked at Abigail. "I am sure the house has been aired out enough."

"And freezing cold," Abigail added with a slight smile, not looking forward to the job of cleaning.

Jacob helped her on with her coat, and both stood at the door. "Thank you so much for all you have done, sir," Jacob shook Mr. Adair's hand and tipped his hat to Mrs. Adair.

"We are so grateful you were not hurt, and the house is alright," Mr. Adair smiled. Abigail and Mrs. Adair hugged, and then they left, closing the door behind them.

Jacob and Abigail reached Jacabig Place and entered their home, expecting the worst. The aroma that met them at the door was of soot and smoke; it nearly took their breaths away. Abigail covered her mouth while crunching up her face with a disapproving look as they walked into the kitchen. The room was cold and dark with a hue of grey to all the curtains, furniture, and walls.

Abigail wiped her finger along the top of the table and looked at the thick black soot that gathered; it was filthy.

"I guess I know what I'm doing tonight," Abigail said with a dreadful sigh.

"I know I'll be looking at that stove and trying to figure out what went wrong."

Both Abigail and Jacob got busy. Jacob hauled water into his shop to heat it on the stove for Abigail. He didn't want to use the stove in the house until he'd had a look at it. While she was washing walls, pulling down curtains, and mopping floors, Jacob tinkered with the stove.

"Uh huh!" Jacob exclaimed. "The damper got stuck open. Mr. Adair was able to close it completely, but then when you open it, it stays open," Jacob explained to Abigail as if she knew what he was talking about. She listened with interest.

"Are you going to be able to fix it?" She asked.

"Yep, it's almost done now," Jacob said as he tinkered some more with the damper. "There. We'll see if that works."

"I sure hope so. I'm freezing and the only thing keeping me warm is the water I'm washing the walls with!"

"Alright, Girlie. I'm hurrying," Jacob went outside to retrieve some kindling to start the fire. He came back with an arm full of wood.

"I'll get this place warmed up in no time." Jacob winked at Abigail.

Abigail had every candle and oil lamp lit in the house as it was getting darker. She thought maybe that would even bring heat into the rooms.

Jacob was correct, and the stove heated up like it was supposed to. The damper fluctuated as it should, and the heat radiating from it warmed the room quickly. It was almost midnight when Abigail stopped cleaning. Jacob helped her after he fed the horses and brought in wood for the night.

As they lay in bed, staring at the ceiling in the darkness, the moon shone through the window, giving a little light. Jacob could see Abigail's tired face; they both were exhausted from the eventful day.

"Good night, my love." Jacob rolled over, kissed his wife, and closed his eyes.

Jacob awoke to the sound of knocking. Still half asleep, it didn't register in his mind what the noise was. *What was that?* He asked himself. There was it was again, knock, knock, knock. Jacob jumped out of bed and started to get his britches on.

"What's wrong?" Abigail asked sleepily, as she squinted her eyes, looking at Jacob in the sunlit room.

"Someone's at the door." Jacob hopped from one side to the other, putting his socks on. He grabbed his shirt, sliding his hands through one arm and then the other, quickly leaving the room as he was buttoning up his shirt.

"Coming," he called out to whoever was on the other side of the door.

"Sorry, lad. I didn't mean to wake you."

Jacob obviously looked like he was still half asleep.

"I wanted to make sure you and the Missus were all right," said Mr. Adair. He was holding a basket in one hand.

Jacob motioned him to come inside, they both stood inside the door.

"Boy it sure looks good in here after all that smoke damage from yesterday," Mr. Adair said as he looked about the room.

"It sure does, thanks to Abigail staying up half the night cleaning," Jacob said as he yawned. "What time is it anyway?" he asked his neighbour.

"It's nine o'clock."

"Oh wow, we did sleep in. The day is almost gone." Jacob grinned. "Bet the horses are a little cranky with me this morning," he added.

"I am sure they'll live," Mr. Adair laughed. "I also wanted to tell you about the terrible news from abroad."

"What is it?" Jacob asked. "What's happened?"

"The *Titanic* sank," Mr. Adair point blankly said.

"What?" Jacob asked. "The unsinkable ship?" The whole village had been hearing about the ship for a few years through The Leader, a newspaper that came from Regina. It was supposed to be an unsinkable ship, built for speed, and the largest vessel ever manufactured, able to hold thousands of people. Construction of the luxurious ship had begun in Belfast, Ireland in 1909.

"That's what the paper says," Mr. Adair concurred. "Over fifteen hundred people died."

"That's awful," Jacob couldn't believe the news. "What's awful?" Abigail entered the room.

"The Titanic went down." Jacob turned to her.

"Oh, dear Lord!" Abigail couldn't believe what she was hearing. "But it was unsinkable?"

"I guess not," Jacob added.

"This is from the Missus." Mr. Adair handed the basket to Jacob. On the top was a rolled up newspaper.

"Thank you, but won't you stay for coffee?"

"Sorry, I'm doing my deliveries." Mr. Adair put his hat back on and turned to leave.

Jacob watched him walk down the steps and climb onto his wagon. "Can you believe it?" He turned back to Abigail opening the paper and reading the headlines. "What a tragedy, what a loss."

Abigail was still looking stunned by the news. "Jacob," she stared at him, "Claude's mama was on that ship."

"What?"

"He told me he was waiting to go back to Quebec in the summer because his mama would be back from England. She was helping take care of a sick aunt, and she was going to be coming home on the *Titanic*. He was quite excited she was going to be making history by being on the maiden voyage of the unsinkable ship."

"Are you sure?"

"Sure that she was travelling on the *Titanic*?" Abigail asked.

"No, sure that he was excited? He doesn't get excited about anything." Jacob slightly grinned at his little joke.

"This is no time to be laughing, Jacob," Abigail scolded him.

"I'm not laughing."

"Well, whatever you're doing, stop it." She gave him a disapproving look.

"We need to go to Goldenrod and tell him," Abigail stated. Jacob was not heartless, he knew it was serious, and he knew that they needed to deliver the news as soon as they could.

"I'll go feed the horses and get them ready to ride. Horseback will be faster than driving the wagon." Jacob got his boots and took his hat and coat off the hook by the door.

"I'll make coffee. we need to have a bite to eat before we leave," Abigail added. "Mrs. Adair sent some lovely buns."

Within an hour they were en route to Goldenrod. The snow drifts were high in some places, but it was hard, and the horses swiftly galloped over it with ease.

When they raced into the yard, Claude was the first person they saw. It was dinner time, so he was walking towards the house.

"Whoa," Jacob said as he pulled on the reins. He climbed off, helping Abigail as well. He nodded to Claude; he didn't know what they were going to say to him or how to do it.

"Good day, Claude," Abigail spoke up.

"Bonjour," he looked up at Jacob and Abigail with a look on his face that couldn't really explain what he was really thinking.

Abigail walked over to meet him before he reached the door. "Good to see you," Abigail said to him.

By that time Mr. and Mrs. Rodgers were standing at the open door with smiles as wide as the sunrise. "Abigail! Jacob!" Mama exclaimed as she held her arms out for a hug.

"Mama," Abigail ran into her arms. Then she hugged her father.

"Hello, Mama, Papa," Jacob said, still finding it awkward to call them that. He noticed Mr. Rodgers was looking well, but

Mrs. Rodgers was pale and still getting thinner. He could feel it as well when he embraced her.

"What a surprise this is," Mama gushed. "We weren't expecting to see you for another couple of weeks."

"Come in, come in." Papa turned around and slowly walked with his cane to make room for everyone to get into the door. "Dinner's almost ready." Aunt Gladys was standing in the kitchen smiling. "Glad to see you, folks."

Abigail hugged her aunt, then asked, "What can I do to help?" She walked over to the pantry door to retrieve an apron. "Mama, you sit. I'll do it."

Jacob sensed that Abigail knew exactly what he was thinking. Her Mama was sick.

Everyone sat down at the table, said Grace, and started passing the food around. Claude sat quietly in his usual spot. Jacob thought they should eat before they delivered the bad news.

Abigail got up and put the kettle on for a new pot of tea for after dinner.

"Claude, Abigail tells me your mother is in England."

"Oui," he answered plainly.

"She was visiting your aunt?" Jacob was trying to get to what he wanted to tell him.

"What of it?" Claude seemed impatient with what Jacob was getting at. "She should be home soon. She was coming back on the *Titanic*," he said matter-of-factly.

"Claude," Abigail interrupted before Jacob got out his words. Claude looked at Abigail with curiosity. "I am afraid we have some bad news." she handed him the newspaper. Claude unfolded it. Everyone could see the headline that read: TITANIC SINKS! Fifteen hundred and three passengers dead!

Claude's face turned pale.

For once, Jacob actually felt sorry for him. Jacob knew that Claude needed to be knocked down a peg or two, but not that way. No man deserves to be told their mama or papa has died. He knew the feeling all too well and wouldn't want to share with anyone, not even with his worst enemy. "I'm so sorry," Jacob looked at Claude. "If there is–"

With that, Claude stood up and threw his napkin down on his plate. He grabbed his hat and coat, put on his boots, and left the house, slamming the door behind him. Everyone in the room was quiet for quite some time, not knowing what to say.

"That poor boy." Mama broke the silence. "What is he going to do?" She sighed with sorrow for Claude.

"I don't know." Jacob shook his head. "I'll go talk to him," He got up from the table.

"Maybe you should give him some time," Abigail suggested, grabbing hold of his hand. "He has to figure out what's happening here. He doesn't even know if his mother was for sure on board.

Possibly she wasn't."

"I guess that is a possibility," Jacob agreed as he sat back down.

Jacob and Abigail spent the afternoon doing small chores for Mama and Aunt Gladys. Things like reaching up high to retrieve a box from the top cupboard, or getting on a ladder to take down the curtains to be washed. Claude never came back into the house; he did his chores before supper and then retired to his house without eating. Jacob wanted to go talk to him before they left for home.

Jacob walked down the familiar path to the bunk house. He knocked on the door.

"Oui?" A gruff French-accented voice came from the other side of the door.

"It's Jacob. Can we talk?"

"I don't really feel like talking."

"I know what you must be going through," Jacob said through the door.

"How could you possibly know?" Claude snarled back. "Believe me, I know," Jacob assured him, not wanting to go into details.

"Leave me alone," Claude barked.

"You don't have to do this alone," Jacob continued. "We're all family here," he tried to encourage him.

"Just go." Claude's voice softened a little.

"You really need a friend right now," Jacob persisted. "I know that more than anyone here." Jacob knew Claude's disposition was harsh, but there had to be a reason for the way he acted. The door unlatched and slowly opened. Jacob pushed on it gently and walked through. He didn't really know what he was going to say.

Claude walked away from the door and sat on the chair by the table. Jacob felt a nostalgic sense of déjà vu. It brought him back to the time when his good friend Bert was trying to get through to him in his darkest hour. Jacob sat down in the chair across from Claude.

"I know we haven't been really friends, Claude," Jacob started, "I don't really know the reason why. In any case, I believe you have been hurt so badly you put up a wall around you and won't let anyone else in."

"You wouldn't understand," Claude point blankly said. His face was tear-stained, with puffy red eyes.

"Try me," Jacob answered quickly. "Besides, you don't know for sure if your mama was on that ship, do you?"

"She sent a letter the day she bought the ticket to say she was definitely going to be on that ship." He put his head down. A single tear fell on the wood floor.

"Well, she could be safe and sound," Jacob tried to reassure him, but knowing that only over eight hundred had lived out of over twenty-four hundred passengers. Jacob knew how he would feel in Claude's shoes. He had an unusual sense of compassion for the Frenchman right then. "Let me go with you to inquire about the list of survivors."

"It's alright," Claude quietly said. "I'll wait for the notification. I'm her next of kin. They'll be notifying me."

"Are you sure? Because I don't mind," Jacob repeated.

"I am sure."

"If there's anything I can do for you," Jacob told Claude. "Just let me know."

"Merci," Claude said without lifting his head. Jacob felt maybe he had got through to Claude. Lord knows he needed a friend right now.

Jacob and Abigail rode home before dark. The previous few days had been scary and stressful, to say the least, but as always, God saw them through it.

chapter eleven

WHEN THE SNOW melted, it finally felt like it was really spring. Jacob helped put the crop in as usual; Bert also came to help, even though he had his other job, working for the Canadian Pacific Railway. Mr. Rodgers was able to delegate the process, a change from the previous year. When Jacob was working alone; he thanked the Lord for his many blessings. A beautiful wife, a nice house, a wonderful family that loved him.

Claude received a remorseful letter informing him that his mama had indeed gone down with the *Titanic*. King George V gave a message in the British newspaper, giving his and the Queen's sympathies to all the families who lost their loved ones, which of course didn't make Claude feel any better. He was now homeless; he didn't have a family to go back to. He'd lived only for his mama, and going away to school to become a lawyer to support the two of them had been his lifetime goal. Now that was gone.

Jacob felt sorry for Claude more than ever and wanted to help him in any way he could. He had been praying for Claude. Jacob knew knowing God was the only way for Claude to be truly happy.

It was the end of June. Jacob and Abigail planned to spend Saturday at Goldenrod. Jacob, Bert, Ernest, and Claude were going to spend the day cutting wood in the bush, while Abigail was going to help her mama and Aunt Gladys weed the garden and get some yard work done. Abigail had her own little vegetable garden at Jacabig Place, but she didn't have as many flowers as they did at Goldenrod and she did love to tend the flowers.

The day was an exceptionally hot one. Summertime had definitely begun. Jacob and Abigail rose at five o'clock that morning so they could be at Goldenrod early. The two of them had just driven into the yard with their horse and wagon when Bert, Ernest, and Alice, along with little Gracie, drove in as well.

"Good morning, lad." Bert waved to Jacob as he helped Abigail off the wagon.

"Good morning." Jacob waved back, smiling. Abigail walked over to their wagon to help Alice carry the items she had brought with them. Ernest carried little Grace to the house as he followed the women.

"Come in for some breakfast." Mrs. Rodgers waved them in while standing at the door. Her hair was pinned up neatly. She reached into the pocket of her apron, pulling out a hanky.

"Thank you, Mrs. Rodgers, we'll be right in," Jacob said.

"Jacob, didn't we discuss that you would call me 'Mama' now too?" Abigail's mama said sternly as she coughed into her hanky.

"Yes, Mama," Jacob agreed, although he felt rather awkward, as he hadn't called anyone that since his own Mama.

"You'd better take care of that cough," Jacob said with sincere concern.

"That's what I have been telling her as well," Aunt Gladys piped up stepping behind Mrs. Rodgers. "But you know how she doesn't listen?" She winked at Jacob with a smile.

"Oh you two, stop worrying." Mrs. Rodgers smiled. "You sound like two little old ladies."

Jacob laughed but didn't really think it was funny.

"I am a little old lady." Aunt Gladys grinned mischievously at her sister.

They were all headed into the house when Jacob noticed Claude yawning as he strolled his way to the door.

"Too early for you?" Jacob asked with a little sarcasm.

"Just didn't get a good sleep," Claude responded, shuffling along.

Mr. Rodgers was already sitting at the head of the table when everyone got inside.

"Good morning, how's the two love birds?" Mr. Rodgers asked with a smile.

"We're great, Papa." Abigail walked over and kissed his cheek.

"Well, I finally taught your daughter how to crack an egg without breaking the yolks," Jacob added as he put his arm around Abigail's shoulders. Abigail blushed.

"You never mind, I don't see you baking bread, Mr. Hudson," Abigail told Jacob sternly. Jacob and Mr. Rodgers laughed.

"How are you feeling?" Jacob asked Abigail's father.

"Feeling pretty darn good," Mr. Rodgers said. "That's good to hear, sir," Jacob added.

"It's 'Pa' now." Mr. Rodgers grinned.

"Alright," Jacob agreed.

"I am going to come out with you lads, only to navigate,"

"Are you sure that's a good idea … ah … Pa?" Jacob apprehensively asked. He didn't want to offend his new father-in-law by telling him he shouldn't be coming because he wasn't up to it.

"Maybe you should wait until noon," suggested Bert.

"No, I need to get back into the swing of things." Mr. Rodgers' British accent sounded more stern than usual.

"Alright, but if you get tired, one of us can bring you back to the house," Jacob agreed. Jacob knew full well they would be slowed down with Mr. Rodgers going along, but he respected his wishes. He wanted Mr. Rodgers back to the way he was, and it was a true miracle that he'd made it this far, considering it had looked very grim over a year ago.

Breakfast was a quick one. The men were anxious to get into the bush, and the women were itching to get the dishes done up so they could get started in the garden.

Claude hitched Myrt and Gert to the stone-boat and pulled it to the front of the barn. Jacob handed Bert the two-man crosscut saw and the two-headed axe to put in the back of his wagon. Then they helped Mr. Rodgers in, and Bert climbed on with Mr. Rodgers. Ernest jumped in the back of the wagon, while Jacob drove the stone-boat with Claude. It was barely eight o'clock when he led the way into the bush, and it was already getting warm out. They travelled a quarter of a mile north of the house to find a grove with fallen trees that were perfect for burning. They would also be cutting down green wood for longer burning, but the old dry wood made it easier for starting the fire.

Mr. Rodgers sat in the wagon while the young lads worked.

They had a good system going. Jacob and Claude used the crosscut saw to cut down a tree, and Bert used the axe to cut off branches, and Ernest gathered the branches, stacking them in a separate pile for kindling. They each took turns at different jobs. After cutting for a couple of hours, they stopped to load the logs onto the stone-boat. Once it was loaded, they started filling Bert's wagon.

It was just past noon when the men pulled up to the barn with a healthy first load of wood. The women had dinner ready when they walked in the door. They had half the garden weeded when they stopped to prepare dinner. The men still had at least two more loads they wanted to haul in before they called it a day.

Dinner was over, and everyone was back to work. Mr. Rodgers was still hanging in there and was being stubborn about staying back at the house. He wanted to be a part of it all; he was tired of feeling useless.

Another load of trees was lying on the ground and ready for loading. The wind was really starting to blow. It was blowing so much, it made it difficult for them to carry the logs. After an hour of struggling with the wind, Jacob noticed the dark cloud that was coming their way.

"Wow, that came up fast," Jacob observed. "I think we'd better pack it in boys."

"I think you're right Jacob," Bert agreed as he picked up his axe and put it in the back of the wagon.

"We should try to load the last two logs," Jacob suggested. "I think we should leave them," Claude argued.

"Jacob's right," Mr. Rodgers agreed.

With that, a gust of wind came up fast. It almost knocked Mr. Rodgers over, but he caught himself by grasping the side of the wagon. Bert, Ernest, and Jacob attempted to carry one of the logs when another gust of wind took them by surprise and knocked the three of them down to the ground, almost landing the poplar log on them. Trees were bent over, the tips of their branches almost touching the ground. Leaves were blowing in the air, and small twigs were flying. It felt like small pins were slapping them in the face.

Jacob never thought he would ever agree with Claude. "I guess we better get going. We'll come back another day," Jacob said, as he started to worry about Mr. Rodgers.

"Come on, Pa. Let's get you in the wagon." Bert and Claude both helped lift Mr. Rodgers, but the wind was so strong, it knocked them back. The three of them tried again to get Mr. Rodgers into the wagon, to no avail. The sky had turned so dark, almost as if it was evening; it also looked as if it could rain.

"Look! Over there!" Claude pointed towards the west, where there was a long skinny funnel.

"Tornado!" Jacob yelled. *Abigail. I have to get to her.*

"Quick, unhitch the stone-boat," he ordered Claude and Bert. "Do you think you could ride a horse, Mr. Rodgers?" Jacob asked.

"I think so," Mr. Rodgers hesitated.

"Stay here," he yelled, the wind was so loud, it was hard to hear what the others were saying. Jacob unhitched the horses from Bert's wagon.

"Help me!" Jacob hollered and waved at Bert and Ernest as they pushed Mr. Rodgers onto the horse. It was going to be a hard ride in that wind and without a saddle.

"Lean forward," Jacob ordered Mr. Rodgers. "And stay down," Jacob climbed on behind Mr. Rodgers, holding the reins on either side of him.

"Grab a horse," he yelled at Claude, Ernest, and Bert. They each climbed on a horse, Bert leading the way, then Claude, followed by Jacob as Ernest rode behind him and Mr. Rodgers to make sure they didn't have any trouble. The wind was bearing down hard on them as Jacob kept his upper body hunched over and his head down, only looking up to see where he was going. He could still see the murky green sky washed with charcoal grey and the twister swiftly moving towards them. Claude and Bert were quite a bit ahead of them; Jacob was secretly wishing Mr. Rodgers had stayed home for the afternoon. All he could think about was whether or not the women were safe at the house.

The wind tore limbs from trees. Leaves and straw swirled around with acceleration. Debris from buildings flew through the air. It sounded like there was a train going through the yard as the four horses galloped to the barn. Bert approached the barn first, quickly jumping off his horse to open the barn door. He stood hunched over trying to keep his hat on his head and his coat over his shoulders as he balanced himself to slide the door open for each of them to run their horses through. Jacob quickly jumped off his horse to help Mr. Rogers get off. With Bert and Jacob on either side of his father-in-law, they walked steadily and as quickly as they could to the house. Their coats were almost blown off their bodies as the tornado moved a little northwest of them.

Claude forced his body against the front door, shoving it open. Bert and Jacob walked Mr. Rodgers through the door and Claude closed it behind them. The wind shook the windows in the house and whistling came from every room. There was no sign of the women; the dishes were only half done and still sitting on the table.

"Abigail!" Jacob hollered as he ran from the porch to the kitchen. "Abigail!"

"Son!" Mr. Rodgers called out to Jacob. "They're probably in the basement."

Jacob headed towards the hallway to the basement stairs.

Bert and Claude helped Mr. Rodgers follow.

"Jacob."

It was the sweetest sound Jacob had ever heard. "Abigail! Are you alright?" Jacob asked as he pulled Abigail to his chest and held her tightly. He didn't want to let her go. The helpless feeling he had when she fell from the tree at Appleton's Haven and the terrifying pain of Anna's death crept up on him. Jacob didn't want to go through that again, ever.

"Yes, we heard the wind, and it sounded as though the house was going to come crashing down on us," Abigail explained. "We came to the basement and crouched here," she gestured to the cold storage room.

Mrs. Rodgers was happy to see her husband; she kissed him on the cheek as he hobbled towards her, collapsing in her arms.

"We were so worried about you boys." Aunt Gladys stood beside her sister rubbing her shoulder while she supported her husband. "It was a frightening experience, that's for sure," she added. "I'll take cold, damp, rainy ole England any day of the week after that."

Bert hugged his beloved Alice and baby Grace. Ernest stood with his hat in his dirty, calloused hands, smiling, grateful for the safety of his kin.

For an hour, they waited out the wind storm. Jacob hadn't seen anything like it in his twenty-two years on the prairies. He'd heard stories of it happening, but had never experienced a tornado. It was cool in the cold storage room; everyone huddled close together, covered with quilts the woman had brought from upstairs. Jacob worried about the horses, praying they'll be alright and withstand the storm. Baby Grace cried most of the time, feeling the uneasiness of her parents and the howling of the wind.

Suddenly, the noise stopped. It was as if everything in the world stood still.

"Do you hear anything?" Abigail asked.

"I think it's over." Jacob looked around the room, as he listened to the silence in the air.

"You're right. I think the wind is gone," Mr. Rodgers said, speaking of the monster that came through to ravage their ranch.

"Let's go," Jacob hopped up, helping Abigail and Mrs. Rodgers to their feet.

Everyone single-filed out the door and down the hallway and up the stairs, Jacob leading the way. He was anxious to see what there was to find outside. As they reached the outdoors, there didn't seem to be any damage to the huge fieldstone home that had kept them safe. The barn appeared to be intact, as well as the other buildings. Jacob ran to the barn door to check Myrt and Gert, as well as Bert's horses. Everything appeared to be well.

Claude went to the bunk house to make sure it was in good shape. In fact, other than a few trees blown down, and the extra leaves and twigs in the grass, the ranch had faired very well during the tornado.

"We'd better go fetch Bert's wagon and the stone-boat," Jacob suggested to the men.

"You bet," Bert agreed. "Then we need to head out to the farm to see if we have any damage."

"And check the cattle," Ernest added. Ernest was such a quiet soul. He was a very nice-looking young man, but his eyes were full of sadness. Not long after Ernest came to Canada, he sent money for his love to come and join him, just as Bert had. They were to be married and build a life in Canada. One rainy day, all that came from overseas was a letter from his fair lady, explaining that she was marrying another. She never did send the money back.

The four men climbed on horses and headed to the bush where they had been cutting wood. Mr. Rodgers stayed back at the house. Once they were hitched, Myrt and Gert pulled the stone-boat, and Bert's horses pulled the other wagon to the yard. It wasn't long, and the Hibbert's were on their way back home.

"Everything appears to be alright here at the ranch," Jacob told Mr. Rodgers as he stood at the door. Jacob wiped his forehead with the back of his hand, while still holding his hat. "Claude and I looked in every building. Nothing but fallen branches."

"Thank you, lad, for checking," Mr. Rodgers said gratefully. "I'm sorry I slowed everyone down today. I didn't think things through, and I know that." He looked down with a shameful look on his face, shaking his head. "I am sorry, lad," he repeated.

"Nonsense, Pa." Jacob patted him on the back as his father-in-law stood leaning on his cane. "I would have done the same thing." He smiled to cheer him up. "We're men, aren't we?" They both had a light-hearted laugh. The truth was, everyone was exhausted; hard work and stress made for achy, tired bones.

"Well, Girlie, I don't like to hurry things, but I really think we should get back to Abbington Pickets," Jacob told Abigail.

"Yes, you're right, Jacob," Abigail said, hugging and kissing her ma, pa, and aunt goodbye. She knew it would be time to leave as soon as the men made it back from the bush. The women finished doing the dishes and got the kitchen a little more organized than it was before the storm hit.

"I'm so glad the wind didn't do any damage at Goldenrod," Abigail said to Jacob on the ride home. "Ma and Pa don't need another thing more to worry about."

"It's a good thing," Jacob agreed. He steered the horses westward, towards the village. As they travelled, many of the trees that were close to their path were torn out of the ground, their roots still attached.

"Jacob! Look at that!" Abigail pointed in amazement. "I can't believe it."

"Wow, I've never seen anything like it," Jacob agreed. "I didn't realize the wind could be that strong."

As they drove nearer to Abbington Pickets, the sun was going down, which made it harder to see. The closer they got, the more damage they witnessed. Poplar trees were lying down on the ground; pieces of lumber were lying in the grass along their path. Jacob stopped the horses; there was a granary door lying on the path. Jacob picked it up and put it in the back of the wagon.

Jacob was beginning to get concerned. Finding pieces off buildings a mile from where they stood was not a good sign. But he didn't want to alarm Abigail until there was something to worry about.

The closer to Abbington Pickets they travelled, the more damage there appeared to be. The debris from buildings, wagons, broken tree limbs, roots, and stones was a sight like no other. Abigail sensed Jacob's apprehension.

"Dear Lord," was all Jacob could say when they came across an upside down wagon with two horses still attached. The horses were lying still, as though they were sleeping. It was plain to see they were in no pain. On the far side of the wreck, Jacob noticed a person's foot sticking out from under the wagon. His heart skipped a beat.

"Whoa," Jacob pulled on the reins of his own horses and stopped the wagon. "Stay here," Jacob told Abigail. He jumped off and headed towards the wreck. It was hard to recognize whose wagon it was, but in a small community like theirs, Jacob knew he would know who it was.

Jacob reached the box of the wagon with the person lying underneath. He put his fingers between the ground and the rough wood and tried to lift it upwards. The frame was heavy and appeared to be restrained by the horses. Jacob swiftly moved to the horses and detached the tug buckles on their harnesses. He then ran back to see if the wagon was released enough to move it off the person. He again gripped the underside of the wagon and lifted with everything he had in him.

"Jacob, please be careful," Abigail yelled. "Let me help you."

"NO, stay there," Jacob said through his clenched teeth as he grunted, lifting the wagon. Still not far enough. He didn't want Abigail to see what could be beneath it. Jacob ran to the back of his own wagon and jumped in, grabbing the hack saw he always carried with him. Abigail turned around as she watched him hurry about, a desperate look on her face, wanting to do something for him. Jacob scurried as fast as his legs would allow.

"Don't worry. Simply hold the horses," Jacob instructed her. "It'll be alright," he reassured Abigail, not knowing himself what he was about to find.

Jacob crouched down on his knees where the tongue was attached to the horses. As the saw's teeth ate through the wood, Jacob hoped that would keep the weight off the wagon so he could lift it up, praying that it was going to work this time. Jacob dropped the saw, and jumped up, dashing to the box, lifting with all his might one more time. This time, it moved easier. Jacob groaned loudly as he lifted, but again it wasn't enough.

Running back to the wagon, he grasped the handle of his axe and ran to the tree a few yards from the wreck. He swung the axe hard. With four big swings, the tree fell down with a loud thud. Jacob picked up one end of the tree, dragging it to the upside down wagon. Picking up a large rock, he placed it a foot from the wagon box, sticking the smallest end of the tree under the box.

He leaned the tree against the rock, using it as a fulcrum, then he pulled down hard on the larger end of the timber. With a long, painful heave that required everything he had in him, he hoisted the wagon up higher than before.

"Watch out!" Jacob hollered at Abigail as he used the tree as a lever under the wagon, and forced it downward with all his strength, pushing the wagon over on its side. He shoved it under the wagon again and strained until the wagon was right side up. He let go of the tree and ran towards the person laying face down in the grass. He noticed there was also a woman who had been right under the wagon; she too wasn't moving. As he turned over the body of the well-dressed gentleman, he jumped back in horror.

"Oh dear Lord, no!" Jacob gasped as the blood drained from his face.

"What is it, Jacob?" Abigail ran over to see what was wrong. Jacob turned to her.

"I told you to stay there," he firmly said to her, not wanting her to see the two bodies of Mr. and Mrs. Adair.

Abigail covered her mouth with her hands and gasped loudly. Jacob jumped up to reach her; he pulled her towards him and held her. Jacob was in shock to see one of his father figures, a man he respected, a man whom he could never thank enough, dead from the terror of the wind. Abigail was sobbing on Jacob's shoulder, both of them in disbelief.

"I didn't even know her first name," Abigail whispered, tears running down her cheeks.

Jacob, hardly listening, held her close. He wasn't sure what he should do next. They needed to get to Abbington Pickets to get help. Jacob didn't want Abigail to have to help with the mess.

Why were they travelling out this way anyway? Jacob wondered.

"Josephine," Jacob said in a daze.

"What a beautiful name," Abigail commented as she picked up Jacob's hand and held it in hers. "Jacob, you're bleeding." She pulled her white hanky from her apron pocket, softly dabbing it over the wound on his cut-up hand. Jacob didn't feel anything. The hurt in his hand was nothing compared to the pain in his heart.

In the distance, Jacob could see the church. Relief swept through him. When he looked towards the north, he wasn't seeing the usual sights. There weren't as many buildings or trees, in that direction, as usual. The sun had almost been swallowed up by night, but there was enough light to see the silhouette of every structure.

Worry came to him. There was something missing, something he couldn't see. Where was their house? Where was their shop?

As they got closer, Abigail gasped. "Jacob!" Still holding his hand, she quickly brought it up to her chest, holding onto it as tight was she could. "Where is our home? It's not there."

Jacob knew it too. His heart sank; he felt all his hard work and love for craftsmanship had been crushed. Jacob stopped the horses in front of the rubble that used to be their round house, Jacabig Place.

"Why is this happening to us?" Abigail cried. "Does God not love us?"

"God loves us, Abigail," Jacob whispered as he held her gently. "Were we not saved by not being here during the storm?"

Abigail sobbed in his arms for the loss of their friends and their new home. The two sat there in awe of the devastation.

Jacob knew he had to find help to retrieve Mr. and Mrs. Adair. His home was destroyed by the storm, but their lives had been taken; there was no comparison.

chapter twelve

THE LEADER HAD been delivered, broadcasting the news about the tornado. It had come from the west, forming eleven miles south of Regina, then plowed through the city, demolishing hundreds of buildings, leaving thousands of residents homeless, and killing twenty-eight people.

Abbington Pickets had been favoured that warm summer day when the funnel tore in from the southwest, sidelining south of Abbington Pickets, moving northeast, ravaging Jacabig Place, and persisting northward. Many trees were plucked from the soil with their roots still attached. Each tree lying down parallel, facing the same direction, caused a railroad effect. Many buildings were consumed by the wicked storm outside of Abbington Pickets that day.

The next few weeks were a blur to Jacob and Abigail. Mr. and Mrs. Adair's funeral, helping at the general store, and cleaning up their home site, so they could start rebuilding as soon as they could, consumed their time. Jacob's workshop had minimum damage, which was a blessing as they would be living there during the rebuilding. Abigail wanted to build their home exactly as it had been, round and perfect. Jacob was content to do it for her.

Jacob wanted to help keep the general store open a couple days a week to help the community. There wasn't anywhere near Abbington Pickets that they could get supplies as easily. Jacob didn't want to let Mr. Adair down or the people of Abbington Pickets. He had told David, Mr. Adair's brother from Kingston, that he would help with the store until he could figure out what he was going to do.

Jacob and Abigail seemed to be burning the candle at both ends. There was no time to go to Goldenrod to help there or visit. In fact, Mama, Papa, Aunt Gladys, Claude, Bert, Alice, and Ernest all came to pitch in for a few days. Everyone was outside picking up debris and going through the fallen structure of the round house, taking out what was still useable and putting it in one pile for later, and stacking anything that was burnable for winter. Jacob's brothers, Andrew and Peter, pitched in, as well, and of course, Charles was available. It gave Jacob a reprieve when he had to go help with the general store.

The villagers of Abbington Picket were a wonderful help as well. Mrs. Smyth and a few other ladies brought meals every day since the storm; each of their husbands offered help every afternoon. Reverend Young came for prayer and to give a helping hand where he could. Anna's father had volunteered to make deliveries for the store.

"Look at what I found, Girlie." Jacob handed her the black mantel clock he had given her before they got married. It had a few scratches, and one of the legs were bent; it was a miracle that it was in that great of shape considering what it had gone through. There were a few things in the house that were saved like the new cook stove. The chair from Goldenrod, besides needing a good cleaning and the back leg needed to be glued, it was in great shape. Of course, the bed frame was still intact as it was made of metal.

Abigail found clothes, and linens, tablecloths, and even the quilt she had made. All were filthy but washable.

At times, it was exasperating for both of them. Sometimes Jacob would find Abigail sobbing somewhere by herself. It was a difficult time. It wasn't just the loss of their home and their belongings; it was the loss of two great friends who had meant a lot to both of them, especially Jacob. Just when they felt ready to give up, another miracle was found.

"Jacob!" Abigail went running towards him. "Look what I found," she was carrying a rectangular metal box in her arms.

"My tool box." Jacob's heart smiled. It was the small tool box Abigail had given him for Christmas two years previously. It had his name printed on the side of it. It was beaten up, and the handle was broken off, but that was something Jacob could fix. "That's wonderful, Girlie." Jacob's tired grin was sincere. He took the box from Abigail, opened it up and went looking through the three compartments. Of course, the tools he'd put in it were still inside. Jacob gave Abigail a hug.

"There's light at the end of the tunnel," Jacob encouraged his exhausted wife. "God is reminding us of how blessed we are."

"Well, at the moment I don't feel very blessed, Jacob," Abigail looked at him with tired red eyes. He knew she didn't mean it. They were both plain exhausted.

"God has a plan for us, we have to be patient." Jacob didn't want to admit that he was a little discouraged himself, but he knew his God, and He was faithful. Abigail began to weep in his arms as Jacob held her. He stroked her once neatly combed hair.

Exhaustion had a way of taking away all a person's pride and dignity, stripping them to the core.

"I miss our friends, our life, like it was before," Abigail sobbed.

"I miss them too, Girlie," Jacob soothed. "But they're in heaven. We'll see them again one day."

"We have no home, hardly any possessions; our things have been broken or carried away by the storm. Our beautiful house, which you poured your heart and soul into, is gone."

"Abigail. That's only stuff, earthly possessions. Jacabig Place can be rebuilt. Things can be made again," he consoled her. "We have each other," Jacob said quietly as they sat together, holding each other.

It seemed like it took an eternity to finish cleaning up the remains of the round house and the yard. When it was finally done, Jacob told Abigail that Charles said he would help rebuild Jacabig Place, even if he had to do it himself. He said that he'd done it once so he could do it again blindfolded. He was such a character. It was an early morning near the beginning of September, a special day. Jacob had a surprise for his Girlie. The birds were singing, the sky was blue and white, while the sun was beginning to come up in the southeast. Abigail walked into the kitchen part of the shop while tying a ribbon in her hair, to begin making breakfast. She was wearing her light grey dress, her waist was wrapped with a burgundy belt, and her long sleeves were trimmed in the same colour of lace. The front bodice had three pin-tucks on each side of her breast, from the shoulder seam to the waist.

Jacob quietly walked up behind her, placing his hands over her eyes.

Quickly, Abigail brought her hands up to grab his. "Hey, what–"

"Keep your eyes closed, Girlie," Jacob whispered in her ear. "Come with me."

"But I can't see, silly." Abigail laughed.

"I'll guide you," Jacob reassured her. "Simply follow my lead," He gently walked her forward towards the door.

"Don't peek!" he told her as he let go of one of her eyes to open the door in front of them. "Alright, keep walking."

Abigail walked slowly with hesitation about where she was headed.

As they walked through the doorway and onto the step, Jacob stopped and let go of her. "You can open your eyes now." He smiled as they both stood staring at two horses.

"What's this?" Abigail looked over at Jacob with a confused expression.

"Don't think I forgot," Jacob began, "because I know most men would forget, but I didn't."

"What are you talking about, Mr. Hudson?" Abigail took delight in being formal when she didn't understand her husband's ways. "Forget what?"

"Our first anniversary." Jacob smiled with pride in his almost good britches and brown plaid button-up shirt, sporting a newsboy hat. He knew Abigail was only playing with him. What woman would forget an anniversary, especially their first one?

Abigail smiled bashfully and shook her head. "What are you up to?"

"Well, my beautiful, we're going for a ride," Jacob informed her. "I know we have a lot of work to do, but this is our day.

We're going to have some fun for a change. I want to see my Girlie happy again."

"Oh Jacob, you're such a sweetheart." Abigail turned to him and kissed his cheek. "You always have such great ideas."

"Nonsense, you deserve everything and then some." Jacob grinned. "Now, let's get on these beautiful creatures and go for a ride."

Jacob helped Abigail as she put her foot in the stirrup and pulled herself up onto the horse. Jacob handed her the reins and climbed up on his own horse. He'd no sooner got his bearings when Abigail's horse started to run.

"Race you," she yelled as she took off on her horse, leaning forward to gain acceleration.

Jacob quickly dug his heels into his horse's sides. It jumped into a gallop behind Abigail as Rusty took her to top speed.

"But you don't know where we are goi-" Jacob yelled after Abigail as he raced to catch up to her. It was obvious where Abigail was headed. Appleton's. *How did she know that's where we were going to ride?* Jacob asked himself.

The wind blew Abigail's hair loose from the ribbon she had put in it. It draped in the back like a rippling cape, flowing behind her. Jacob barely caught up to her before they both reached the historic tree. The autumn colours were beautiful this time of year, as the leaves were starting to fall. With every step of the horses' feet, there was a familiar rhythmic crunching.

Abigail reached Appleton's five seconds before Jacob. She quickly jumped off her horse and began to tie it to a small tree. Jacob followed suit.

"What a ride!" Abigail exclaimed out loud. Somehow the rushing breeze blowing past her face, through her hair, had left Abigail invigorated.

Jacob beamed as he watched his love smile with blushing cheeks.

"This is just what we needed, Jacob." Abigail stretched her arms out to the great open sky. "Breathe in that fresh air and soak up the sun."

"Ah, well, I soak up the sun every day, love." Jacob laughed at her.

"You know what I mean, Jacob," Abigail scolded him as she wrinkled up her nose. "Let me be poetic, would you?"

"I'm only teasing." he smiled. "You can do or say anything you want." Jacob took Abigail by the hand as she twirled around. "This is your day."

"It's our day," she corrected him.

Jacob untied the bag he had fastened on his horse. He carried it to the tree, knelt, and proceeded to empty the leather pouch.

"What do you have there, Mr. Hudson?" Curiously Abigail came over to the tree to see what Jacob had up his sleeve.

"Well, I thought maybe you would like to have a little breakfast, maybe a cup of coffee…" Jacob grinned as he took the jar of coffee out of his bag and set it on the ground. He reached for something else. "…and possibly, and now this is if you are really good," Jacob teased, "you could read this new book I bought you." Jacob hid the book behind his back to tantalize his wife. He knew how much she loved to read and Jacob hadn't seen her read in a very long time.

"Oh Jacob, stop teasing." Abigail tried to reach the book from behind his back. He then raised it above his head. Abigail jumped up to grasp the book out of his hand, but Jacob was too tall for her to even get close enough. She began to tickle Jacob under his arms. He quickly dropped his arms to make her stop, so she stretched out to grab the book out of his hand, but he put his arm in the air again. Again she began to tickle him. That time, Jacob ran to the bottom of the tree and began to climb the huge-limbed beast of a tree.

"Oh, no you don't," Abigail cautioned him as she followed, but Jacob was too swift for her. He was up the tree and sitting on the large horizontal limb, dangling his legs down, teasing Abigail with the book in his hand and a big grin on his face.

Jacob's tanned face, shadowed by the umbrella of leaves above him, made his teeth appear even whiter than usual.

Abigail wasn't as quick as her long-legged husband, and her dress was a bit of a disadvantage to her climbing the tree.

"If you don't come down here, Mr. Hudson," Abigail grabbed his boots, "I will just have to pull you down." Jacob knew she was only fooling, but he loved to tease her anyway.

"I'm too quick for you, Girlie." Jacob waved the book around again. Abigail reached quickly for his boots. As fast as she did, Jacob jumped to his feet and looked down at her like the cat that ate the canary. Abigail pretended not to care anymore. She sat down on the ground below the tree.

"The coffee's getting cold," she said. Jacob had packed two cups, so she proceeded to pour the coffee. "I guess you can stay up there all day if you like," she pouted. At that second, a swish from behind alarmed her and Jacob crouched behind her, putting his arms around her, placing the book in her lap. Abigail smiled. "You are such a tease."

"I know, but you love me this way." Jacob smiled.

"Indeed I do, Mr. Hudson," Abigail concurred.

Jacob served the fried egg sandwiches he had made for breakfast, along with cold cooked bacon and of course coffee. Jacob hadn't seen Abigail that happy in a while. He was praying for continued strength because he knew the road ahead still wasn't going to be easy, but if they could have one day to forget their troubles and count their blessings, it would be a gift from God.

The rest of the day was spent with continued laughter, lying in the sun, watching the clouds float by.

"This has been one of my favourite days." Abigail looked up at Jacob. She was resting her head on his lap as he leaned against the tree while she read aloud to him.

"Mine too, Girlie," Jacob agreed. They were in peace with the presence of each other and with the Lord. Neither wanted to ride back to reality and head for Abbington Pickets, not yet anyway.

"This has been one of my favourite days." - Abigail

chapter thirteen

OVER THREE MONTHS had passed since the storm had hit. Those weeks were difficult and hard and included finishing harvest at Goldenrod. As if there wasn't enough to do, there always was more to be done. Jacob's hands blistered and bled from hammering, pitching hay. There was ten times the workload than he had been doing. Abigail wrapped his hands every night with salve and bandages. During the day he wore gloves to prevent infection, and to be honest, he didn't want anyone to know about it.

Jacob was finding it hard to keep up with the work that paid the bills. Their savings were dwindling fast. It was a good thing that David Adair had let him order lumber on credit to start the new house. Eventually, it would need to be paid, and that didn't sit well with Jacob, but he didn't want to disappoint Abigail.

It was the beginning of October, and the rebuilding of the round house had begun. It had been a long, painful, and hard-working summer, and fall was no exception. The house was coming along. The walls were constructed and erect. The work went by faster than before with all the extra help Jacob had been receiving. Andrew, Peter, Charles, Bert, and Ernest pitched in. They worked hard to get as much done as they could. Jacob's goal was to get the roof finished, and all the windows and doors in before snow fell. Abigail was working at the general store and making meals for the men. The workload was a lot for Abigail's ma, pa, and Aunt Gladys, who were back at Goldenrod. It was a blessing that Aunt Gladys was there. She had been a big help and had decided to stay as long as she was needed.

"Dinner's ready," Abigail called up to the men working on the rafters. She looked up while holding her hand over her eyebrows to shield her eyes from the sun. She had prepared mashed potatoes, carrots, buns, and fried chicken with gravy. She was hoping if she cooked enough, that there would be leftovers for supper time.

"Smells good, Girlie," Jacob hollered from above as the aroma rose and tantalized his taste buds. Abigail set up a picnic-style seating arrangement on the ground beside Jacabig. The men climbed down the ladder in single file.

"I am so glad dinner is ready. My stomach was starting to complain." Charles laughed as he rubbed his belly.

"You're always hungry, Charles," Jacob added as he gave him a friendly shove. "Your stomach's been talking for years." Everyone laughed.

"I don't know how you stay so thin," Peter added as he looked down at his own waist, patting his stomach. "I can't seem to keep this under control." Peter wasn't fat by any means, in fact, he was slim like his brothers.

"Oh and you're so fat," spoke up Andrew. Everyone laughed at the contradiction.

"Well, lads, enjoy it while it lasts," Bert spoke up. "My dad's friend was a skinny, gangly sort of lad, but when he got older, he weighed three hundred pounds." At first, everyone stared at him in disbelief, then they all burst out laughing. Bert shrugged his shoulders and said. "Wait and see." Ernest grinned and shook his head at his brother-in-law's tall tale.

"Oh all you boys are all slim and trim," Abigail interrupted. "You don't have anything to worry about, so eat up. You need your strength to get that roof finished." She grinned at Jacob, and he gave her a wink.

"Come, sit down, Girlie." Jacob looked up at Abigail as he patted the grass beside him as if it was a chair meant for royalty.

"Let's say Grace," Jacob piped up as if everyone had forgotten about giving thanks for the meal they are about to eat. "Bert, would you?" Jacob looked over at his friend.

After Bert had said the blessing, everyone filled their plates with delicious food, and for a few minutes, no one said a word, all that could be heard was the clattering of forks touching the plates.

"You boys *were* hungry." Abigail smiled. It was the first time Jacob saw her smile that way, back the way she used to. It made his heart sing.

Dinner was over, and the men scurried back up the ladder to continue working. Abigail picked up the dishes, and all the leftovers and hauled them to the shop. She began to heat water to do the dishes. Hammers were swinging; the echo of constant banging was heard all around Abbington Pickets.

Jacob sat up on a rafter, balancing himself as he hammered nails into the fresh lumber. At that instant, he saw a flash of movement from the corner of his eye, followed by a loud shriek.

Jacob quickly turned his head to see what it was. Nothing prepared him for the horror of what he saw below. He heard gasping all around him as everyone witnessed what had happened. He lifted his leg over the rafter, rapidly making his way to the ladder as fast as he could go without falling. The other men followed suit.

Jacob jumped the last five steps, running his fastest. Inside the house, on the floor, he slid to his knees before his brother's body, laying so still. He put his head on Andrew's chest to listen for a heartbeat. He could barely hear one. He scooped Andrew's head up and held it in his lap. A few minutes later, Andrew opened his eyes, squinting at the light. He slowly gazed all around him with a confused look.

"What happened?" He looked up at Jacob, "And why are you holding my head?" He half grinned. Everyone laughed lightly, looking at each other and sighing in relief.

"Brother. You're alright!" Jacob smiled as he helped Andrew sit up.

"Oh, that kind of hurts." Andrew rubbed the back of his head. "What did I do? What happened?"

"You fell from the roof," Jacob informed him "Don't you remember?"

"Not really."

"I found Doc." Bert rushed through the doorway with Doc Johnson in tow.

"Bert told me what happened." Both Doc and Bert looked surprised when they saw Andrew sitting up.

"You're a-" Doc stuttered and stammered, not wanting to say "alive." "You're sitting up. Well, that's a good sign, but maybe you better lay down again while I have a look at you," Doc continued as he began to examine Andrew. "Could everyone wait outside and give us some room to breathe," Doc said gruffly. The men walked out of the house.

"What happened?" Abigail ran in, almost running into Bert as he was leaving. She shielded herself behind him, holding onto his shirt sleeve, carefully looking at Jacob. She saw Andrew laying on the floor and Jacob sitting over him. "Tell me, what happened."

"The lad had a bit of a fall from the roof," Bert told Abigail.

"Oh my Lord," Abigail said under her breath as she slowly covered her mouth with her hand.

Bert patted her on the back. "I think he's alright now," he reassured her. "Doc wants us to wait outside."

"I think you may have a concussion," Doc said to Andrew as he packed up his equipment. "Keep an eye on him, Jacob." He looked at Jacob then back to Andrew, "and you take it easy. No more heights for you for a couple of days."

"Thank you for coming so quickly." Jacob shook Doc's hand and walked him outside to inform everyone that Andrew was going to be alright.

"Come on, Andrew." Abigail put her arm around him. "Come to the shop, and I will make you some tea."

"No, no," Andrew argued. "I'd better keep an eye on these men, make sure they do it right." He grinned.

"Are you sure?" Abigail persisted.

"Abigail's right." Jacob walked up behind her. "You should go in the shop and take it easy."

"No, I feel fine, really," Andrew assured both of them. "A little sore, that's all." He rubbed his back with his right hand.

"Alright," Jacob gave in, "but you're not climbing on the roof again today." Jacob pointed his finger up in the air as he spoke.

"That's right," Peter concurred as he slapped Jacob on the back. "You sure gave us a scare, brother." Both Peter and Jacob's eyes filled with tears, each of them trying not to show their emotion.

"Glad you're alright." Bert shook Andrew's hand.

"Thank you for your help," Andrew said to Bert. "I heard you ran for Doc."

"Not a problem, lad," Bert said. "I am glad you're alright."

"Good to see you upright," Ernest said quietly, then he turned around and went back to work. Ernest, the man of few words, had more feelings than anyone knew.

"Well, you sure gave Jacob a heart attack," piped up Charles. There wasn't much Charles took seriously, and he would hate to admit when he was really scared or having any sort of emotion besides humour.

The men worked the rest of the day on the roof. Andrew delegated, supporting them from the ground. The afternoon wasn't as productive as it could have been and it wasn't long before Abigail called them in for supper.

"Hope you don't mind," Abigail said flustered. "Well, I mean I didn't have time to cook the roast I was going to."

She placed the plate of leftovers from dinner on the table. "Oh … well." Charles threw his hands in the air, getting up from the table and backing away. "I guess I'm not eating." Everyone looked at him with surprise as he burst out laughing. "I'm fooling," he said as he sat back down. Everyone laughed with him.

"Oh, Charles." Abigail laughed. "You're such a card."

"You should have known he was joking." Jacob jabbed Charles in the ribs. "He loves to eat, remember."

"You all love to eat, remember?" Abigail reminded them of their dinner conversation. "But I did make dessert." She grinned, holding the dish up.

"Is that bread pudding?" asked Bert.

"It is," Abigail answered. "Alice gave me the recipe."

"Thought it looked familiar." Bert smiled.

"Well, it's the first time I've made it," Abigail admitted. "I hope it tastes as good as hers."

"I am sure it will." Bert smiled.

"Well, let's have dessert first," Charles piped up, holding his spoon in the air.

"I don't think so," Abigail scolded him like a child. "Wait for Jacob to say Grace and eat your supper, mister. Then you can have dessert." Everyone in the room laughed.

After supper, everyone packed up and headed home. It had been a hard day, and the ride was going to be a long one. The next day, Bert and Ernest were cleaning their barn, Peter had wood to cut, and Charles was returning in the morning to help Jacob.

"Boy, your brother sure startled us all today," Abigail said as she dried the dishes.

"I know," Jacob agreed as he placed a piece of wood inside the stove. "He's sure going to be sore in the morning."

Abigail set the last plate in the cupboard, folded the tea towel in half, and hung it on the hook on the wall.

"I'm headed for bed." Abigail kissed Jacob.

"I'm going to go feed the horses. I'll be right back." Jacob put on his coat and boots, grabbed his hat off the hook by the door and placed it on his head. He picked up the lantern by the door, lit it, unlatched the door, and walked outside, heading towards the stable. He hung the lantern up on the nail beside the door where It shone enough so he could see what he was doing.

Jacob pitched enough hay into the horses' stalls to feed them for the night.

Jacob then grabbed the lantern and started walking back towards the shop when he heard a noise from afar. He stopped to listen but couldn't make out what it was; the longer he stood there, the closer the noise got.

"Jacob!" It was a voice and the familiar sound of horses pulling a wagon, galloping at full speed.

"Peter?" Jacob yelled towards the noise, holding the lantern up in the air, trying to see who was coming.

"Jacob," the voice repeated as it almost reached him.

"Peter," Jacob knew for sure this time that that's who it was. "What are you doing back here?"

"It's Andrew." Peter tried to catch his breath. "Something's wrong."

"Jacob?" Jacob heard Abigail's voice. "What are you doing?" She ran outside to see what was happening.

"We need Doc," Peter yelled. "NOW!"

Jacob helped Abigail onto Peter's wagon, then jumped into the back where Andrew lay. Peter continued to drive the horses towards Doc's house.

"Andrew," Jacob spoke to his brother. "Are you alright?" Andrew was lethargic; he could barely keep his eyes open.

The ride was rough and bumpy, Abigail held on to the back of the seat of the wagon as she turned around to watch Jacob and Andrew.

Peter stopped in front of Doc's house.

"Don't move him," Abigail warned Jacob and Peter as she jumped off, running to the front door and knocking with panic.

"Doc, Doc, Doc!" She pounded on the door.

The door opened, and Doc stood there, holding it open. "Abigail, what's the matter?"

"It's Andrew," Abigail told him. "He's in the wagon. Come quickly."

Doc ran back into the house, coming out with his black leather bag. He climbed up into the wagon. Peter and Jacob were on either side of Andrew. Andrew's breathing was laboured and he was unconscious.

"He just fell asleep," Jacob told Doc as he made his way to where Andrew was laying. Jacob still had his lantern in his hand,

and he held it up over Andrew. Doc lifted Andrew's eyelids to look at his pupils.

"I think we should carry him into the house," Doc instructed, "It's getting cold out, and I don't think we can do any more damage by moving him."

"What are you saying?" Jacob asked defensively.

"Carry him in, and we'll go from there."

Doc climbed off the back of the wagon as Jacob and Peter lifted Andrew simultaneously. They carried him carefully to the end of the wagon, then hopped off and picked him up again. Jacob lifted under Andrew's arms, and Peter straddled each of his legs, shuffling as the two of them walked towards Doc's house.

Abigail held the door open as the men brought Andrew in. "Bring him over here," Mrs. Johnson directed them to the bed where Doc examined his patients. Jacob and Peter laid Andrew down.

"Come, dear, let's wait over here." She showed Abigail the kitchen table of the one-room house.

Jacob watched Doc's wrinkled, tanned hands as he opened his bag, digging out his stethoscope, putting the ear tips in each ear, placing the chest piece on Andrew's chest. Seconds went by as he listened. Slowly putting his head down, he pulled the earpieces out, shaking his head slowly.

"I am so sorry, boys."

"What? Are you sure?" Jacob questioned Doc as he looked down in disbelief at his brother's face.

"Yes, I am sure." Doc looked at Jacob sadly.

"The fall was earlier today. He was fine," Jacob argued, "You said it yourself. He was fine."

Abigail stepped cautiously behind Jacob. She put her arms around his waist as he held his brother's hand. Peter stood there without saying a word. He was in complete shock. Everyone was.

"No, please God, not my brother," Jacob whispered over and over. "Please no … you can't take my brother too."

Jacob wasn't a little child anymore, like when he saw Lucy, die; he wasn't that young man who had cried out when he lost Anna. Jacob was a mature, God-fearing, loving man, with not a bit of hate in his heart. At this moment, he didn't cry, he didn't shed one tear; he stared at Andrew's pale face, feeling numb, motionless, and absolutely alone.

"Why did this happen?" Peter finally spoke. "Why was he fine one minute and on the ground the next?" He raised his voice.

"Peter," Jacob said calmly.

"Why?" Peter repeated loudly.

"Peter!" Jacob said again as a reference to be quiet.

"There must have been internal damage," Doc began to explain. "He was bleeding on the inside; there was no way of knowing." Doc shook his head. He had compassion for their family. He felt sorry that he couldn't have foreseen Andrew's fate and that he couldn't have done more.

"I am sorry I couldn't do anything." Doc left them alone to be with their brother to say goodbye.

The next few days went by in slow motion for Jacob. He spent two days building the coffin for Andrew's final resting place. He wanted it to be perfect, just as his Mama's and Lucy's were.

Constructing such a personal, delicate piece was like therapy for Jacob. He worked and prayed for peace and understanding. It was the one last thing he could do for his brother, while he spent time with God and worked through his own feelings.

"Does it get easier? Does it ever end?" Jacob asked himself.

The day of the funeral was overcast with misty rain; a dreary day, suitable for the occasion. Everyone's hearts ached for the loss of this young man's life. Jane, Peter, and Missy, and Sarah and her family, were brought together to mourn the loss of their brother. Jane didn't take his passing as well as the others. The no-nonsense, plain-Jane girl, was having a hard time letting go. She had lived on Crocus Flats alone since their pa's death; Andrew and Peter worked the land, but Andrew was the one who helped her every day with the chores and the upkeep of the house. The two of them had a special bond, and now she would be really alone.

As she threw her body over the wooden frame, crying out his name, Jacob pulled her away from their brother's casket.

He held her back, whispering in her ear. "Jane, please, you have to let go."

Jane sobbed quietly, backing away from the coffin, covering her face with her hands, not wanting to be watched by the community onlookers. She ran from the churchyard and towards Jacob's shop. Her hair fell loose from its tight bun, draping down her back, soaking up the rain. The sky opened, and it began to downpour, followed by the startling sound of thunder and a flash of lightning.

"Go after her, Jacob," Abigail encouraged him as she stood beside Mr. and Mrs. Rodgers, holding an umbrella Claude was kind enough to bring them in the rain. Most of Abbington Pickets' residents were able to fit in the All Saints Anglican Church to support the Hudson family. Bert, Alice, Grace, and Ernest had come from their farm. Charles, his mama, and his pa were there. Anna's father was also present.

"Jane! Jane!" Jacob called out to his big sister as he ran, pulling his coat up over his head. The rain was coming down even harder by the time he reached the shop to find Jane inside.

"Jacob, I am so sick of all this tragedy," Jane cried out as Jacob got inside the door, closing it behind him. "I am tired of all the death! I don't think I can stand it anymore!" She collapsed on the chair beside the table.

Jacob knelt down beside her. "It's going to be alright, Jane," Jacob soothed.

"Of course it will be for you," Jane said sharply.

Confused by her comment, Jacob shook it off. She was too upset to question.

"You have someone," she cried. "You have Abigail. I have no one."

"I know it's hard when you're alone," Jacob tried to make her feel better. "But God has a plan for you. He has a plan for all of us."

"Easy for you to say," Jane retorted. "You're a man."

"What does that have to do with anything?" Jacob asked, handing her his hanky.

"Everything," Jane stated plainly as she blew her nose. "You can work harder, people respect you, heck they sit up and listen when you talk. Not me, I am only a woman."

"That isn't so," Jacob reassured her, confused by where her thoughts were coming from.

"Jacob, let's face it. I can't run Crocus Flats myself. I can't hire anyone. Who would do what I told them to do?"

"This isn't the time to worry about that," Jacob said quietly. "We've just buried our brother." He looked down at the floor in sadness. He was beginning to understand exactly what Jane meant. He knew it wasn't going to be easy for her. It hadn't been easy for her since Mama died, but she had always managed.

Jane had every right to be worried, every right to be so upset. Everyone had a breaking point, and Andrew's death was hers.

Peter was married, had started his own family, and had his own work to do, along with helping to farm Crocus Flats. With Andrew gone, he would be doing Andrew's and his own work. He would be doing it alone.

Does it get easier? Does it ever end? Jacob asked himself. He felt ashamed about the doubt he had in his heart right then. "I promise you, Jane," Jacob informed his sister, "I will do everything in my power to make this easier for you."

Jane looked at Jacob with swollen red eyes, tear-stained cheeks, and wet stringy hair falling in front of her face. There was a glimmer of hope in her eyes. "We may have to sell Crocus Flats," she said.

"Not if I can help it," Jacob firmly said.

The door burst open with the sound of rain and footsteps. Abigail stepped in. Peter, Missy, Sarah, and her family. Mr. and Mrs. Rodgers, Claude, Bert, Alice, Grace, and Ernest all followed her.

"It's raining too hard," Abigail announced, as she put her umbrella in the basket by the door. "No one's going home until this passes."

"Well, come on in and make yourselves at home." Jacob gave a faint smile. He was grateful for his family, but couldn't stop thinking about the dilemma he was discussing with Jane.

"Here let me take your coats." Abigail held her arms out for all the coats they gave her. "I know it'll be crowded. Just find a place to sit." Of course, there weren't enough chairs, but everyone seemed to manage and find something to sit on.

Abigail put the coats in a pile on their bed. Jacob added more wood to the stove. The rain pounded down on the roof with a song to sing.

"I'll make tea," Abigail said.

"I'll help you." Alice gave Grace to Bert, and she walked over to the table to help Abigail.

The night was spent reminiscing about Andrew and the good times they had had with him. Each sibling told a story as they sat around the table, drinking hot tea.

"Do you remember when Andrew climbed the house to the roof?" Peter laughed.

"I do," Jane and Sarah both looked at each other in amusement. "Jacob was only a baby."

Jacob's ears perked up. He'd never heard this before.

"Well, anyhow, one summer day Andrew got mad at Pa, and of course Pa yelled and sent Andrew running."

"It wasn't really funny at the time," added Jane.

"Well, it is now." Peter gave her a look as he continued to tell the story. "He climbed up the back side of the house and shimmied over the roof until he got to the bell tower, where he sat until dark."

"Papa, Mama, and we children all called and called him that evening before supper," Sarah piped in.

"If you think Pa was angry before, he was extremely cross when he saw him up there." Jane frowned.

"Especially because he refused to come down," added Sarah.

"But then the cat climbed up there with him, and he was worried the cat would fall down the bell tower," Peter said.

"The cat almost did fall down," Jane corrected Peter.

"Pa told him if he was silly enough to get up there, he could figure out a way to get himself down," Peter continued. "Andrew was getting scared by that time. He didn't want to come down because of the wrath of Pa, and he was also scared to come down because once he got up there, he realized he was terrified of heights." Everyone in the room laughed.

"How did he get down?" asked Jacob. "What happened to the cat?"

"Hold your horses, brother." Peter grinned as if he withheld a secret. "Well, the cat was walking along the top of the bell tower and slipped inside. Fortunately for the cat, his front claws caught the edge and held on until Andrew reached for him and pulled him out."

"Poor little kitty," Alice sympathized.

"Well, that wasn't all." Peter smiled. "The cat was so scared that when Andrew placed him back on the roof, he slid down and fell onto Pa's head. At least he landed on top of his hat."

"Mama was so amused, she couldn't stop laughing," Jane said. "Of course, everyone was laughing but Pa. He threw his hands in the air, telling Andrew to get down himself, and stormed off to the barn."

"How did Andrew get down?" Alice and Mrs. Rodgers asked simultaneously with worried faces.

"What about the kitty?" Missy frowned with sadness for the life of a cat. "Did he live?"

"Of course the cat lived," Peter added, "and Andrew found a way down."

"I can't remember how," Jane hesitated, "I only remember that he got down safe and sound."

"And Pa didn't talk to Mama for at least three days for laughing at him," Peter remembered.

Everyone was silent for a few minutes, reflecting on their own memories of Andrew.

Mrs. Rodgers, Alice, and Abigail made beds on the floor for everyone. Good thing each had packed a quilt in their wagon before coming to Abbington Pickets.

The silence of slumber filled the shop as everyone lay sleeping in their beds. Jacob lay wide awake. He couldn't stop thinking about Crocus Flats, Jane, and what they'd talked about. He had promised her he would take care of it. What was he going to do? He had his house to finish, the general store to keep going, and the ongoing help his in-laws required.

"God, please tell me what to do," Jacob prayed to the Lord. "Please, in all of this, give me the strength for what needs to be done. In Jesus' name. Amen."

chapter fourteen

THE MORNING BEGAN with rays of sunshine, and not a cloud in the sky. The rain had stopped halfway through the night, leaving everything with a shiny appearance of clean air. Everyone was up by daybreak. Jacob had already gone out and fed the horses before anyone else had stirred.

Abigail, Mrs. Rodgers, and Jane began to make breakfast in the small makeshift kitchen. The two small children were crying in their mothers' arms as they waited for the milk to warm over the stove. Abigail had asked Peter to get water from the well. Bert and Ernest chopped and carried in wood for the stove, piling it in the wooden box close by.

Jacob was walking back from checking the general store. It had rained quite hard; he wanted to make sure there were no leaks or broken windows.

"Everything alright?" sounded a voice from behind him, "I mean the general store?" It was Peter, carrying a pail of water.

"Yep, things seem to be alright there," Jacob confirmed.

"What's wrong brother?" Peter asked with concern. "I know that look."

"What look?" Jacob smiled faintly. "There's nothing wrong."

"Come on," Peter insisted as they both slowly stepped along the muddy path towards Jacabig Place.

"I think we should sell Crocus Flats," Peter blurted out to Jacob's surprise. "I know that's what's troubling you."

Jacob stopped walking and turned to his brother. "NO," Jacob stated. "Absolutely not."

"We have to. Jane barely could pay the taxes last year," Peter insisted. "If it hadn't been for Andrew, she would have never done it."

"Why didn't anyone tell me?" Jacob questioned. "No one said a word." Jacob's forehead wrinkled as he stared at his brother.

"Jacob," Peter began. "You had enough on your plate."

"No one even told me!" Jacob retorted. "I could have helped."

"Your father-in-law, your wedding," Peter started listing. "Jacabig, and the Adairs. Did I miss anything?"

"I would have helped her," Jacob stated. "I can help her."

"You have enough to do. Be reasonable." Peter's voice was sharp.

"I can do it."

"No, you can't," Peter yelled. "You can't always do everything."

"Think about Jane," Jacob pointed out. "What will this do to her?"

"She'll be fine. She can come and live with Missy and me," Peter concluded.

"I am sure she would love that. Crocus Flats is the last thing she has of Ma and Pa," Jacob pleaded. "I'll help her out."

"Jacob, there isn't enough of you to go around. You have the house to build, the General Store to look after, table orders to finish, not to mention your in-laws to look out for," Peter argued. "Jacob, you have enough!"

"Mr. Rodgers is getting back on his feet, and with Claude's help, he's been doing quite well," Jacob retorted.

"It's impossible. You can't be at Abbington Pickets and at Crocus Flats at the same time." Peter raised his voice again. "Don't be foolish."

"You don't know that!" Jacob bellowed.

"Stop it!" Abigail was standing right beside them. "Look at you two. Since when do you fight?"

Peter shook his head in annoyance. Jacob could tell Abigail was worried about him. He always got along with his siblings, but this was a different matter, and obviously, the two of them didn't see eye to eye on the subject.

"It's a little argument." Jacob smiled at Abigail.

"A little argument? Everyone in the shop can hear you." She sternly looked at the both of them as if she were a scolding mother.

"Jacob's right, Abigail," Peter piped up. "It's only a disagreement."

"Well, it's time to eat," she said sharply, then she turned around and headed back to the shop.

Jacob turned to Peter. Neither was happy with the other. "I don't want to fight with you," Jacob said.

"I don't want to either, but you can't do everything," Peter lowered his voice.

"Think about it. We can decide when we're in a better frame of mind."

"You aren't going to change my mind," Peter said firmly.

"You may be older, brother, but you can't make all the decisions." Jacob left it at that. Both of them went into the shop, but neither felt like eating.

After breakfast, Mr. and Mrs. Rodgers and Claude were the first to leave, followed soon after by the Hibberts. Sarah and her husband and little Megan were stopping at Peter and Missy's before they left for Kingston. Jacob had a few tables to send to Mr. Adair in Kingston, and as they loaded the wagon, no one hardly said a word. Jacob knew it would be quite a while before he would see Sarah again, as winter was soon upon them. Jane was the last one to climb into the wagon. Jacob helped her up and told her he would come out and see her soon. Abigail and Jacob stood waving as the wagon slowly moved westward.

Jacob's heart was heavy. The thought of selling Crocus Flats broke his heart not to mention Jane being alone. Even if they didn't sell it, there was a big workload before him. Costs were adding up, income wasn't coming in as it should, and savings were dwindling. What was in store for him? What was he going to do? The dilemma he felt the previous night seemed to get bigger. What did God have in store for him? For his wife? For his family? Jacob turned to his wife.

"We need to pray together." The sadness in Jacob's eyes told his story.

Abigail didn't say a word; she slipped her hand in his and gave it a squeeze. They went inside to pray.

chapter fifteen

"CLAUDE, I HAVE another proposition for you," Jacob got to the point as he stood at Claude's doorstep. It was the day after Peter and Jacob's heated discussion. Jacob had ridden out to Goldenrod to talk to his least favourite person. Claude wasn't too thrilled by Jacob's surprise visit; nonetheless, he gave Jacob his time.

"My father-in-law seems to be doing much better," Jacob continued. "It's been a year and a half since you started working for him."

"Your point being?" Claude rudely asked.

His tone made it even harder for Jacob to say what he was about to. "Well, I need another hired hand."

"Well, find one." Claude hardly seemed interested in what Jacob had to tell him.

"I want you to be that person."

"Why me?" Claude asked. "We don't even like one another."

"Because you know how we do things," Jacob admitted. "You know how *I* do things."

"I'm sure you can find someone as good as yourself," Claude said sarcastically.

"Will you at least hear what I have to offer?" Jacob suggested.

Claude reluctantly nodded and invited Jacob inside his quarters.

"My sister needs help at Crocus Flats." Jacob cut to the chase. "Now that my brother…" Jacob hesitated, closing his eyes. He took a deep breath as he looked down, clenching his teeth and trying to get a hold of his emotions. He looked back up at Claude. "Since he passed, she has no one to help her with the chores, upkeep of the house and whatnot; you know, for the heavy work." Jacob thought his request was quite self-explanatory.

"Does Mr. Rodgers know you're asking this?" Claude questioned with some interest.

"Not yet, but I'll talk to him of course," Jacob said. "Goldenrod is closer to Abbington Pickets than Crocus Flats. I'll be able to help Mr. Rodgers when it's needed." Claude's left eyebrow raised as Jacob explained.

"Your quarters will be in the barn, the pay would be five dollars more a month than here and, of course, Jane will feed you three meals a day, and do your laundry."

"I'll think about it," Claude spoke as though Jacob wasn't offering him anything spectacular. Claude then walked past Jacob, put his hat on his head, unlatched the door, and headed in the direction of the barn.

Jacob turned around and watched him as he got farther away.

"Alright then," Jacob called after him. "We'll talk again. Perhaps tea next time?" he teased. He shook his head at Claude's candour as he closed the door behind him. He still didn't understand Claude's way of thinking, nor would he ever.

Jacob wanted to give his horse a drink at the barn before going to the house to see his in-laws. When he got there, he didn't see any sign of Claude. *Guess he had other work to do,* Jacob thought. He pumped water into the water trough, then stood holding her reins petting her back as she drank. He led her to the house, tied her to the hitching post, and headed to the door of the stone building to talk to his father-in-law.

"Jacob," exclaimed Mrs. Rodgers. "What a lovely surprise." She rushed over towards Jacob, who was standing in the doorway. He took his hat off as she put her arms around him.

"Son, good to see you." Mr. Rodgers smiled as he looked up from his newspaper. He was sitting at the kitchen table with a cup of coffee in front of him.

"Good morning." Jacob was still feeling uncomfortable about calling his in-laws "Ma and Pa."

"Come," Mrs. Rodgers said. She pulled on his arm. "Have a cup of coffee." Jacob smiled as he took his coat off and hung it on the hook by the door. Mrs. Rodgers had scurried back to the kitchen to pour Jacob his cup of coffee.

Jacob pulled the curved-back wooden chair away from the table and sat down across from Mr. Rodgers.

"Have you eaten?" Mrs. Rodgers asked, "I can make you some pancakes."

"No, no thank you." Jacob grinned. "Your daughter fed me quite well this morning."

"That's my girl." Mr. Rodgers smiled.

"How have you been doing with the chores?" Jacob asked Mr. Rodgers.

"Well, you know son," Mr. Rodgers began as he took off his glasses off. "I'm doing much better now."

"Good to hear, sir." Jacob continued to struggle with the right words to say.

"Would you say you could do the chores on your own?" Jacob asked, tilting his head down slightly, and raised his eyebrows to see the expression on his father-in-law's face.

"Well, I'm sure we could get along without Claude if we had to," he said with a confused look on his face.

"Claude is handy to have around, that's for certain," Mrs. Rodgers contributed.

"Why are you asking?" Mr. Rodgers said.

"Well, sir," Jacob started to explain when his father-in-law gave him that familiar look again about not calling him "Pa." "Pa. Jane needs help at Crocus Flats, and as you both know, I am a bit fixed for time. I wanted to hire Claude to help her out,"

Jacob said it almost all in one breath as if he thought they would say, "No, absolutely not!"

"Of course, lad." Mr. Rodgers sat back in his chair; he had a look of relief on his face. "Be glad to help out."

"Is that all?" Mrs. Rodgers said as she dried her hands on the towel and sat at the table as well. It was as though they were expecting terrible news for some reason. "Well, Claude came in just before you and said that you had something to say." She looked at her husband then back to Jacob.

"Oh." Jacob was surprised Claude would say anything about it. "I see." *I think he likes to cause trouble,* Jacob told himself.

"We want to help, Jacob," Mr. Rodgers said. "You have done, and are still doing so much for us. I don't know how we'll ever repay you."

"Not necessary." Jacob shook his head firmly. "You're family; there isn't anything I wouldn't do for you."

"Well, I plan to pay you back…" Mr. Rodgers cleared his throat, trying not to get emotional. "You know … for all the … well, you know." He looked away and could barely speak.

"There's no need," Jacob persisted. "I insist."

"We'll talk about this another time," Mrs. Rodgers interrupted both of them. "Right, dear?" She looked at Mr. Rodgers.

"Claude's all yours if he wants to go," Mr. Rodgers said.

"Thank you … Ma, Pa." Jacob kissed Mrs. Rodgers on the cheek and hugged her. He shook Mr. Rodgers' hand. "I have to get back to Abbington Pickets; I'm expecting a shipment from Kingston. I'll wait to hear from Claude."

"You bet." Mr. and Mrs. Rodgers walked Jacob to the door and stood in the doorway as they watched him climb on his horse and ride away.

Jacob waved as he rode down the lane, his mind full as his horse followed the familiar path alone. He kept mulling it over and over in his head as the wind blew his hair back and cooled his sweaty forehead. He had so many things to think about. Before long, winter would be upon them, the house wasn't as far along as he would have liked. He prayed that Claude would take his offer so Peter wouldn't insist on selling Crocus Flats. He wondered how his sister was doing since Andrew had passed. Jane always had a rough exterior, but really she was a softie.

"How were Ma and Pa?" Abigail greeted her husband at the front door. She was wearing a dark blue pin-striped skirt with a white blouse; the long sleeves and collar were trimmed with white flat lace. Jacob took his hat off and kissed her lips without saying a word; he hugged her tight, holding her for several minutes. Abigail embraced him back.

"Is everything alright?" Abigail looked at Jacob with concern.

"Have I told you lately how much I love you?" Jacob whispered. "You're so beautiful and thoughtful; I'm truly blessed to have you as my wife."

"I love you too, Jacob." Abigail blushed. "Is everything alright?" she repeated hesitantly. Abigail knew Jacob was an affectionate man, but it seemed to her as if he was about to lose something, or someone very dear to him.

"Of course," Jacob said, still standing adjacent to Abigail. He stared into her big brown eyes, feeling his whole heart loving this woman. The confidence in her eyes, the gentleness in her smile and the love in her heart kept him strong, determined, and ready to take on anything. He pushed the hair from her forehead with his muscular, tanned hand. Jacob smiled.

"Did Claude accept your offer?"

"Not yet, but he will." Jacob was confident that he would. Claude was a man who was in it for himself. He would take it, if not for the money, maybe for the laundry. Jacob was certain.

"Charles is meeting me over at Jacabig." Jacob gave Abigail another quick kiss. "I'll see you at lunch."

"I am going to the general store." Abigail smiled. "See you later."

Abigail swung her black crocheted shawl over her shoulders. Jacob saddled up Rusty and brought him to the house for her. He helped Abigail onto her horse, and he watched her trot away towards the general store.

Jacob picked up his tool box, along with some other tools, placing them in the wooden wheelbarrow that leaned up against the back of the shop. He lifted the wooden handles to bring the legs up off the ground and pushed it. The wooden wheel wobbled as it rolled along the uneven ground. Jacob could see Charles's horse tied up in front of the round house.

"Well, it's about time." Charles grinned as he sat on the rooftop. It made Jacob a little uneasy to see him up there. They hadn't worked on the roof since Andrew fell. "Thought you would never stop kissing that girl of yours." Jacob blushed at the thought of Charles watching them.

"You just never mind." Jacob grinned. "Jealousy will get you nowhere." He chuckled.

"Oh, don't think I need to be jealous," Charles said matter-of-factly. "I have lots of women."

"Oh, really?" Jacob laughed. "Lots of women, huh?"

"Yep," Charles said. "You wouldn't believe it until you see it."

"I guess you'd better introduce us to these fine young ladies," Jacob stated, knowing that Abbington Pickets wasn't filled with many available young ladies, but he went along with Charles' story anyway.

"Nope, sorry." Charles shook his head with a frown. "Can't do it."

"Alright then," Jacob humoured him. "It can be your little secret." He unloaded the wheelbarrow, put on his carpenter's apron, and began to climb the ladder.

"Thought you would have had this roof done by now," Jacob teased.

"Well, I guess you should have been up here sooner," Charles smiled.

"I guess you're right."

The day went by fast, as Jacob and Charles worked tirelessly trying to close in the cylinder-shaped house. There was one quarter left when darkness fell. Charles went home after a late supper, which Abigail had prepared.

"If only we could've finished the roof," Jacob told Abigail as they got ready for bed. Jacob sat on the edge of the bed, taking off his socks, neatly placing them on the back of the chair.

"You can finish tomorrow." Abigail climbed in between the crisp white cotton sheets. She fluffed her pillow, as well as Jacob's, while he was still sitting on the edge of the bed contemplating the day's progress.

"I know, but we were so close." Jacob slid his legs in between the clean fabric. He leaned over and kissed Abigail.

"You can finish tomorrow," Abigail repeated with a smile.

"Good night, Girlie." Jacob quickly flicked the end of Abigail's nose.

"Stop that." Abigail wrinkled up her nose at Jacob. He knew she secretly loved to be teased.

Jacob reached over to the clear glass oil lamp on his night table beside the bed, turned the knob down, and blew it out. He pulled the covers up as Abigail snuggled in beside him. Her head was leaning against his chest, and he put his arm around her. He could smell the fragrance of her hair as he dozed off.

Jacob sat up in bed like a spring, wondering what had made him jump awake that way. He then heard a loud bang like a shotgun had gone off. He listened intently, only to hear it again. Abigail heard it too. As they both sat in bed, Jacob realized what it was.

"Oh, no!" Jacob hopped out of bed, stumbling to reach his clothes in the dark. "It's pouring outside."

"The roof," Abigail whispered slowly, in a daze, realizing then why Jacob had wanted to have it closed in.

Jacob struck a match and lit the lamp. He finished getting dressed as he raced towards the door.

"There's nothing you can do now, Jacob," Abigail yelled after him as she put her arm in the sleeve of her housecoat, trying to keep up with him.

"I can get a tarp and climb up there and…" Jacob shook his head as he opened the door and looked into the darkness.

"You will not, Jacob," Abigail said sternly, standing beside him and holding onto his arm.

"If only I could see out there…"

"Jacob, it's darker than a black hole out. You're not going out there."

"I think I can get the tarp out of the general store." Jacob began to put on his coat, not hearing a word she was saying.

"NO!" Abigail pleaded. "And fall off the roof like Andrew?"

Jacob stopped where he stood; it was like someone had hit him hard enough to knock him down.

Abigail's voice got quieter. "Not to mention the lightning out there. You could get killed."

"I'm sorry, Girlie." Jacob was discouraged. He knew it couldn't be done in the dark, in the wind, with the rain pouring down in buckets. He knew Abigail was right; he resigned himself to the fact he wasn't going to get outside and do anything until morning, which of course would be too late.

Jacob didn't sleep much during the night, and morning came quickly. He was up and dressed before daybreak and feeding the horses. He came back in for breakfast because it was still raining. It wasn't thundering and lightning anymore, but it was a steady rain, and enough to prevent him from doing anything for their house.

While Abigail was putting the eggs on the table, there was a knock at the door. Jacob got up from his chair, walked over, and unlatched the door.

"Charles, get in here." Jacob held the door open, greeting his friend. "Don't you know it's raining outside?" Jacob laughed as he stood back to let Charles in.

"Oh really?" Charles chuckled as he walked through the door, taking his hat off quickly, along with his dripping coat. "I hadn't noticed."

"What are you doing out in the rain?" Abigail grinned at the water trickling down his face, while the rain dripped from his soaked auburn hair.

"Well I thought we could get a lot done on the house today," Charles joked.

"You're funny." Jacob smiled, trying not to show his disappointment.

"We are just about to have breakfast," Abigail said, "come sit, have some eggs and toast."

"Yes, come on in," Jacob agreed. Charles sat down at the table with Jacob. Jacob said Grace then Abigail began to fry more eggs.

"So tell me," Jacob looked confused. "What are you doing here?"

"No, seriously," Charles began, "I came over to see what we can do with the house in spite of the rain."

"I guess we'll have to wait until the rain is done," Jacob added.

"I suppose. Now let's eat some eggs." Charles grinned as he scooped up a fork full of eggs, stuffing it into his mouth.

Abigail poured each of them a cup of freshly perked coffee. She sat down at the table with the men and began to eat as well.

"Mmmm, that coffee is good." Charles looked at Abigail, "but it has a different taste."

"That would be the spices I perked it with." Abigail giggled as she wiped her mouth with a napkin. "It's an old family recipe, or should I say secret." She winked at Jacob. He knew what she meant, ginger settled the stomach, and cinnamon made it taste better, along with a couple secret ingredients. Abigail made the coffee to calm Jacob through his sleepless night. Her mama and her grandmother would make this fancy coffee every time someone got upset. They weren't expecting company, so she didn't think anyone else would be tasting it.

"Well, it has zing, that's for sure." Charles held the cup up as if to say cheers and took another mouthful of the hot and spicy liquid.

The rain had subsided to a light mist. After breakfast, Jacob and Charles gathered a tarp from the general store, some nails, and a couple of hammers. While Abigail worked at the general store, they worked at covering the hole in the roof.

"Bonjour, Abigail," a voice came from the doorway. Abigail was putting away the tins of coffee that had come in, and she turned her head to see who was there.

"Claude." Abigail smiled. "What brings you to town today?"

"I came to see Jacob…" Claude started to explain as Abigail set the last can on the shelf. She started to turn around, and at the same time, she noticed the edge of her apron was caught under a tin of coffee. Before she knew it, at least six tins of coffee fell to the floor with a loud bang.

"Let me help you." Claude crouched down and picked up a tin of coffee and looked at her embarrassed face.

"It's alright," Abigail said quickly, picking up one tin, and placing it in her other arm, then picking up another. "I can manage, thanks." As she grabbed one more tin, the first one fell from her grasp, landed back on the floor, and then rolled away.

Abigail was even more embarrassed by the incident.

Claude gently grasped both of Abigail's arms in an attempt to help her up. "Here, I can help you," he repeated.

"No, it's fine. Really." A flustered Abigail crawled on her knees closer to where the tin had rolled, then reached forward to take it in her hand as Claude continued to try to help her get up.

"What are you doing?" Jacob's voice came from the doorway. "Could you kindly not touch my wife?" he added, firmly.

Charles was standing right behind him with a mischievous look on his face. He tried to hide it by turning away and letting out a gasp, which almost turned into laughter.

Realizing how compromising it must look to Jacob, Abigail remembered the incident at Goldenrod in Robin's Roost and thought Jacob might not be so nice to Claude this time.

"I dropped a bunch of coffee," Abigail said, still on her hands and knees. She was looking up at him while holding a tin in her left hand, using her other hand to balance herself.

Claude jumped to his feet, holding his hand out for her to help herself up.

Abigail didn't want Jacob to think that it was more than what it really looked like. She had nothing to feel guilty about, but somehow she couldn't help it.

Jacob lunged forward to reach Abigail, putting his hand around her waist, and reaching for her other hand with his. "Did you hurt yourself?" he asked Abigail.

"No, silly me." Abigail blushed. "I pulled the tins of coffee down with my apron," she tried to explain. "Claude just got here," she added quickly.

"I can see that." Jacob's jaw clenched tightly as he looked over at him.

"I know how funny this looks," Abigail felt the need to expand on the situation. Even though her heart was all Jacob's, she didn't want Jacob to think otherwise. "But-"

"I came to see you, Jacob," Claude interrupted, looking at him. "Let's talk business."

Jacob was so irritated by Claude's presence he wished he hadn't even asked him to work at Crocus Flats, but he was desperate. He didn't have much choice. Farm hands were hard to find in Abbington Pickets.

"Come to the shop, and we'll talk," Jacob suggested, wanting him to get away from Abigail.

"No time," Claude argued. "I'll get to the point and be on my way."

"Alright." Jacob anxiously awaited what Claude had to say.

"I'll take the job," Claude said abruptly, "on one condition."

"What's that?"

"I get every Monday off."

"Done," Jacob agreed, not knowing why he would want that particular day off every week, but he guessed it was a small price to pay for the help he needed.

"I'll start next week."

Jacob reached his hand out to shake on it; Claude quickly shook it, put on his hat, and left the store.

"Do you need a hand with mov-" Jacob called after him, but Claude kept walking towards his horse. "I guess he doesn't need help moving his belongings." Jacob shook his head at Claude's rude disposition.

"Maybe you can offer him a tin of coffee." Charles laughed.

Jacob glared at Charles for suggesting it, not feeling the humour in the whole situation.

"Couldn't resist! But seriously, he is a different sort." Charles tried to be more serious. "Why didn't you ask me to work at Crocus Flats? I would've helped you out."

"I guess I figured you had enough to do," Jacob explained.

He didn't want to admit the real reason. Charles was a great friend, and a big help, but he liked to drink, and Jacob didn't want Jane exposed to that kind of behaviour. Charles was a friend, but not the kind of friend anyone would want to their sister. "Besides, you're helping me." Jacob gave him a playful punch in the arm.

"Did you get the roof done?" Abigail asked. "I mean the tarp put on?"

"We sure did." Jacob put his arm around Abigail and kissed the top of her head. "I have some tables to finish before tomorrow."

"Yep, and I have to go too," said Charles but the only place he had to go was across the street to the Empire Hotel.

Jacob kissed Abigail goodbye. She proceeded to finish putting the cans of coffee back on the shelf and the two men put on their hats and walked outside.

"You could join me." Charles smiled at Jacob.

"No thanks." Jacob was surprised by his friend's request. He knew what that place did to Jacob. "I don't go there anymore. You know that, Charles."

"I thought you might've changed your mind."

"Nope, not going to happen." Jacob held his ground. "That's a dark place, Charles. I've learned my lesson, and you shouldn't be hanging around there either."

"What? Are you my mother?" Charles joked. "Talk to you tomorrow." Charles stepped off the wooden sidewalk and headed towards the Empire Hotel. Jacob could hear the all too familiar noise as he watched Charles open the door and disappear inside.

Jacob didn't need that kind of temptation in his life; he had all he needed with his wife. Life wasn't always perfect, but he had God and his family, and that was all that mattered. Jacob was relieved that Claude was working for Jane, but worried at the same time. God would see him through, he knew that.

chapter sixteen

THE WEEK WENT by quickly. The rain had kept Jacob from working on the house, so he did his other chores as well as constructed his tea tables to send to Kingston. Abigail worked at the store, which was busy most days. The floor of the house had gotten so wet that it had to be re-floored, which put Jacob even further behind. He had to order more lumber, yet another cost he could barely afford. Charles came to work on the roof that day as the days were cooler, and they could tell winter was coming soon.

"Looks like Claude's coming through town." Charles perched up on the rafters of the house, watching as he pointed towards a horse and wagon packed high with crates. Since Jacabig Place was built on a slight hill, it made the view as far as the eye could see, especially from the roof. Claude's wagon was going down Main Street, past the church, and appeared to be stopping at the general store.

"This should be good for a laugh." Charles chuckled quietly to himself, knowing what would happen if the wagon stayed at the store too long.

"That guy never ceases to amaze me." Jacob cringed as he hammered even harder.

"Well, he never seemed to have any tact." Charles laughed. He watched Jacob clench his teeth, swinging his arm hard as the head of the hammer hit the square-headed nail.

"I guess I'll go to the store and talk to Claude before he heads to Crocus Flats." Jacob made his way to the ladder.

"There's no need," Charles pointed out. "He's coming to you." Claude was halfway between the general store and the round house.

"I'll keep on working," Charles spoke, "unless you need a hand with something?" He smiled mischievously, thinking he could say or do a few things to that lad if given the chance.

Jacob quickly climbed down the ladder to the ground as Claude drove up.

"That's quite the load you've got there," Jacob spoke first, trying to set aside their differences.

"Oui," was all Claude said, not bothering to get off the wagon.

"You get settled at Crocus Flats, then Jane will let you know what needs to be done," Jacob said clearly.

"Alright," Claude nodded.

"I'll come by on the weekend and see how things are going."

"I don't need a chaperone," Claude retorted. "I know the drill."

Jacob ignored his comment, hoping he had made the right decision. "Alright then, see you in six days." He turned and walked back to the ladder as Claude drove away, then he climbed back up to the roof as Charles watched him.

"Everything good?" Charles asked.

"Everything's good," Jacob concurred without looking at Charles.

He began swinging his hammer, not wanting to discuss it. He knew how much he didn't care for Claude, not really knowing why. Perhaps it was Claude's attitude. He had proven himself through his work, and Jacob was fairly certain he could trust Claude with Jane. That was Jacob's only comfort.

Bang! Suddenly pain pierced through Jacob's hand and radiated up his arm. Jacob yelled under his breath as he brought his throbbing hand to his chest and cradled it with the other. He felt like screaming at the top of his lungs, but instead he clenched his teeth while scrunching up his face. Charles knew immediately how much pain he was in.

"Are you alright?" Charles tried to shuffle his way closer to Jacob to have a look.

"No, I'm fine."

"That didn't sound fine, that didn't look fine." Charles shimmied right beside him, trying to see.

"I said it's fine," Jacob raised his voice sharply. The pain pulsed throughout his whole hand. *Great, on top of everything else the last thing I need is to be injured.* Jacob was really resenting Claude at that moment, and he knew Charles was only trying to help.

"Sorry, I didn't mean to bark at you," Jacob apologized to his friend.

"Don't worry about it." Charles smiled his goofy grin. "You have a lot to deal with right now. I don't know how you cope as well as you do."

"I have friends like you." Jacob half-smiled as he tightly wrapped his hand with his red and white handkerchief. He took a deep breath and tried to shake off the pain.

"I think we should take a break," Charles suggested.

"I can't afford to take a break."

"Well, if you don't, you won't be doing anything," Charles argued, "especially if that hand of yours is broke."

Jacob tried to prove he could still work. He held a nail with his wounded hand while swinging with his other one. The pain was overwhelming, and he couldn't keep his fingers closed to hold the nail. The nail fell to the floor of the house with a ping.

"Alright, we'll stop for some lunch," Jacob reluctantly said as he held his red and swollen hand for a minute before climbing down and heading to the shop.

"Soaking it in some nice cold well water will do it some good," Charles called after him. "I'll go get you some."

After Charles climbed down, he followed Jacob to the shop for a pail and headed towards the well in Abbington Pickets, which was past the general store.

"I have a well out behind the shop!" Jacob called out after him, but Charles was too far away to hear.

Charles had other ideas; he thought maybe, just maybe, he might mention it to Abigail on the way. Then she could talk some sense into him.

"He did what?" Abigail didn't take very long to grab her shawl, lock the door, and ride her horse back to see Jacob.

"Ahh, I should have known Charles would tell you." Jacob shook his head. "That's what I get for trusting him to help." Jacob smiled slightly at his little bit of humour. "That's why he went for water in Abbington Pickets in the first place."

"I'm glad he did." Abigail gently took Jacob's hand in hers, carefully unwrapping it, exposing a swollen, bruised mess. "Jacob." She looked at him with disapproval.

"It's not as bad as it looks," Jacob stretched the truth.

"Of course it is." Abigail shook her head.

"How's the hand?" Charles walked through the door, carrying a pail of water.

"Oh sure, you had to get the water," Jacob sarcastically said to Charles, "and just happened to run into Abigail."

"Of course," Charles confidently answered. "She happened to be on the way." Charles winked at Abigail as he set the pail on the floor in front of where Jacob was sitting.

"Of course." Jacob didn't like Charles' sense of humour sometimes.

"I am glad he did," Abigail argued. "Your hand looks awful. Doc should have a look at it."

"NO," Jacob argued. "I'm fine. My hand is fine." He put his hand in the ice cold water. It stung as though needles were piercing his skin. Jacob closed his eyes, breathing deep through his nose, trying to get a hold of the pain.

"I made sure I pumped enough to make it nice and cold," Charles said, proud of his quick thinking.

"That was so nice of you," Jacob said under his breath, still holding his hand under the ice cold water.

"I'll fix us some sandwiches." Abigail got up and started cutting slices of bread and preparing lunch. Charles stoked the stove and added more pieces of wood. Abigail put the kettle on top to make tea.

"Alright," Jacob said, looking unhappy. "I'm feeling really useless right now."

"Don't worry about it," Charles said. "We have it under control. Besides, if you use your hand and it's broken, you'll be useless for months."

"So behave for at least one day," Abigail interrupted as she placed the plate of sandwiches on the table. She walked over to the boiling kettle then poured it into the teapot. She carried it over to the table. As she placed the cups down, she waited for the tea to steep before pouring.

"I still think Doc should come and have a look at your hand," Abigail persisted. "What could it hurt?"

"It's fine," Jacob insisted.

"You tell him, Charles." Abigail looked at Charles. "It's not fine, is it?"

"I am sure Jacob knows what he's doing." Charles knew enough to stick up for his friend.

"The swelling is already going down," Jacob pointed out as he pulled his hand out of the water.

"I will take a look at that," a new voice came from the doorway. It was Doc.

"Are you fooling me?" Jacob glared at Charles.

"What?" Charles turned a little red, knowing Jacob was going to be mad. "He happened to be riding by the well when I was getting water."

"Of course he was," Jacob stated.

"I was," Doc agreed. "Now let's see what you've done to yourself." Doc sat on the chair across from Jacob. Doc held Jacob's beaten hand in his, looking it over, moving it from side to side, pulling each finger gently. Jacob held his breath each time as the pain got worse with every movement. He knew deep down it wasn't good news, but he didn't have time for this.

"I think you broke a couple bones in your hand," Doc said grimly.

"Are you certain?" Jacob asked. "I haven't got time for this." Abigail stood behind Jacob with her hands on his shoulders for reassurance.

"You'll have to make time Jacob," Doc gruffly told him. "It's a fact, and you'll have to deal with it properly, or you won't have any use of it."

Jacob didn't want to hear that news. He didn't want to face the fact that he couldn't use his hand for a while; there was so much work to be done, so many things to think of.

"Abigail, make sure he does what he is told." Doc looked at her, giving her complete control. She nodded.

Doc wrapped Jacob's hand tightly with cotton strips of fabric and a splint to keep him from bending his fingers.

"Keep this on for at least four weeks, maybe six. It depends on you," Doc ordered Jacob as he closed his black leather bag, got up from his chair, and stood at the door. "I am very serious, Jacob." Doc knew Jacob well. "Do *not* use that hand at all, or you'll find out what it's like to be a one-handed man." He put his hat on and left.

"Don't worry," Charles told Jacob. "I'll keep working." Jacob was so disgusted with himself. How foolish he'd been to let himself get distracted that way. How could he have let Claude get to him? The more he thought about it, the more it made him angry.

"Thanks, Charles." Jacob tried not to show his irritation.

"You can still help with your other hand," Charles suggested. "It may slow us down a little, but I'm your right-hand man," Charles encouraged him. "We'll get it done."

"Yes, I'm sure we will." Jacob didn't sound as enthusiastic as Charles.

Abigail didn't say much. She knew how disappointed Jacob was and how painful this was for him, in more ways than one. He won't be able to make tea tables for David in Kingston, he won't be able to pitch hay to the horses or split wood for the fire; there will be many things he won't be able to do. Abigail shared his disappointment, as she wanted the house finished as fast as he did, but she couldn't show her discouragement, not to him or anyone.

"It could be worse," Abigail said bluntly. "Now let's make the best of it." She began to clear the table. "You two go out and see what can be done." She knew Jacob all too well, almost as much as he knew himself. He wasn't going to sit in the house all day and mope about his pain. He would do things, whether she wanted him to or not.

"You bet," Charles agreed. "That roof isn't getting done on its own."

"You're right, for a change. You're right," Jacob agreed, not because he was happy about the situation, but because he wanted things done, one-handed or not.

Abigail returned to the general store while the men went back over to Jacabig Place to continue working. She appreciated her time at the store. Just as Mrs. Adair had done, she enjoyed the people she visited with while they bought their goods. Abigail did, however, love to bake at home and tend to her gardening, but she liked the feeling of being a working woman.

"I'll get up there and start banging on the roof. You can see what tools we need and bring them up as I need them," Charles suggested.

"Sounds good." Jacob watched Charles climb the ladder. "I'm going to see if I can start doing anything with the floor before the lumber arrives," Jacob yelled up to him.

He looked at the floorboards, the water damage was as bad as he remembered it. The lumber was swollen, soaked, and turning black in some places. Jacob was able to use the crowbar with his right hand and began pulling up the discoloured boards, throwing them in a pile.

The day seemed to drag on, as did the rest of the week. Not as much was accomplished as should have been with two working men, especially with one of them using only one hand. The roof still wasn't complete, and it was Saturday, time to visit Crocus Flats. Charles offered to work on the roof by himself, but Jacob didn't feel comfortable with him doing it alone and told him to take the day off for a change.

Abigail packed some things in the wagon to give to Jane. She tried to take the load off of Jacob, so he would follow the doctors orders to not use his hand.

"Is everything ready to go?" Jacob asked.

"I think … I remembered … everything." Abigail looked around the room slowly, hoping she hadn't forgotten anything. Jane had a grocery list for Abigail, since it was perfect timing that they would be visiting.

"Hee-yaw," Jacob told the horses as he flicked the reins lightly to get them going.

Jacob hadn't made this journey in a while, and the scenery was all too familiar. Many flashbacks came to mind as they drove the horses down the dusty road. Jacob remembered running his horse as fast as its legs would take him when his Mama died. That wasn't a memory he wanted to relive. He also remembered the ride back to Crocus Flats when his father had his accident; as reluctant as he had been to go, it had changed his life forever.

"How are you feeling?" Abigail placed her hand gently on his knee.

"I would feel better if I could do something more." Jacob grinned faintly. "But I'm alright."

"It'll heal faster than you think," Abigail encouraged. "Especially if you take it easy." Usually, it was Jacob doing the encouraging. "This time next year, you won't even remember it." She smiled.

"You think so?" Jacob didn't want to show his true feelings.

He was thinking about Claude and Jane, and praying that all was well there.

He also remembered the ride back to Crocus Flats
when his father had his accident; as reluctant as he
had been to go, it had changed his life forever.

They drove into Crocus Flats' lane as a black Labrador Retriever came running down the road to greet them.

"When did Jane get a dog?" Jacob looked at Abigail.

"I don't know." She looked back at Jacob. "She never said anything to me about it."

"We always wanted a dog when we were young," Jacob explained, "but Pa never wanted one. He said we would never look after it."

Jane was standing in the doorway when they reached the house.

"Whoa." Jacob pulled on the reins to stop the horses. "It's good to see you."

Jane walked to the wagon to greet them, the black dog followed her. Jacob stood up and carefully jumped from the wagon. "What happened to you?" Jane looked at Jacob's hand.

"Oh nothing," Jacob said, as he reached for the crates in the back of the wagon.

"I'll tell you later," whispered Abigail. Jane nodded.

"You shouldn't be doing that," Abigail pointed out.

"Let me get Claude. He can carry those crates for you," Jane said as she hollered towards the barn for Claude to come.

"I can manage. It's fine," Jacob said even more determined to do it himself.

"No, really he can help," Jane persisted, as Claude walked, still in his usual, no-hurry saunter.

"You could move a little faster," Jane told him.

Oh here we go, Jacob thought to himself, he won't be working here long.

"Sorry," Claude apologized as he increased his pace, hopped up into the wagon, and reached for the other crates without a word.

Jacob couldn't believe his eyes. *What? Who is this? No sarcasm? Where is the real Claude?* "How are you doing?" he asked.

"Fine," Claude said plainly, continuing to do his work without interruption.

There, that's the Claude I know. Jacob told himself. "Where did you get the dog?" Jacob asked Jane as they carried the groceries into the house with the dog following close behind Jane.

"The MacDonalds," Jane said. "It was Claude's idea," she explained. "He thought it would help make me feel safer, especially at night." Jane set the box down on the floor, and her furry friend walked up to her as she petted its head. "And he's absolutely right," she said as the dog licked her face.

"Well, he seems friendly." Abigail smiled. "What's his name?"

"She," Jane corrected, "her name is Daisy."

"Aww, that's a sweet name." Abigail joined Jane in petting the black beauty.

Claude went back to the barn to continue his work. "How's it working out with Claude?" Jacob asked Jane as she poured a cup of tea for everyone at the kitchen table.

"You know," Jane started, "I think he's going to work out just fine."

"That's great." Jacob felt relief. "He does what you ask? He's respectful of you?"

"Yes." Jane nodded her head. "It was awkward for me at first, but he really does have a soft spot, you know."

"Really?" Jacob was curious about that, since Claude never seemed to have any tact or regard for anyone.

"Yes," Jane said. "Let's just say we have an understanding."

"You do?" Jacob was really interested now.

"We do, so simply leave it at that." Jane took a sip of her tea. "Besides his accent is divine." She gave Abigail a quick smile.

Jacob couldn't pinpoint it, but there was something definitely different about his sister. It hadn't even been a week, and already things are going very well. It was an answer to prayer, that was for sure.

"Good to hear." Jacob got up from the table, putting on his hat. "You two beautiful ladies have a nice visit, and I'll go out and talk to the lad."

"Jacob, don't be too bossy," Jane said with a concerned look on her face. "He's doing well, really."

"Don't worry, Claude can take care of himself." Jacob walked out the door and towards the barn. Daisy happily ran beside him with her tongue hanging out. Jacob hadn't been to the barn since he left for good. It was where his father had been trampled by his own horses.

Jacob reached the barn to find Claude cutting wood and stacking it inside the lean-to that was attached to the east side of the barn. The yard was looking in pretty good shape. It still needed quite a bit of work, but Claude had only been there a week, so that was understandable.

"Tell me," Jacob began, "how's it really going?"

"I already told you," Claude said. "It's fine."

"Are you quite certain?" Jacob wanted to be sure.

"Yes." Claude snapped.

"Alright, I believe you," Jacob said apologetically.

"Well, why do you keep asking?"

"I only want everything to work out," Jacob explained.

"Well, it is." Claude continued to stack the wood.

"I am happy to hear it." Jacob was truly impressed. "Jane seems to be happy with you here."

"Well, I said I would do the work, didn't I?" Claude scowled, not stopping for a second.

"Yes, you did." Jacob backed down. "As long as my sister is happy, I'm happy." Jacob was beginning to believe this arrangement was going to work out. He bent down and picked up a log with his good hand, then threw it on top of Claude's pile.

"Well then, I guess we agree on something for a change," Claude said.

"I guess you're right," Jacob agreed. "Well, Jane will have dinner ready, and we don't want to be late for that." Jacob decided there had been enough small talk, and that Claude was working out better than expected, and all was well.

Jacob and Abigail stayed for dinner. Claude was quiet through most of the meal, except when Jane spoke to him. It was clear the two had a working agreement. Jacob was surprised, realizing that Claude actually respected another human being. He respected Jane. That pleased Jacob, and he felt he could handle all Claude's rudeness, selfishness, and arrogance as long as he valued Jane.

It was about one o'clock that afternoon when Jacob and Abigail said their goodbyes and rode back to Abbington Pickets. Jacob wanted to get some extra chores done before dark, and Abigail wanted to make a chocolate cake for the church dinner the next day.

chapter seventeen

"JACOB, YOU'VE BEEN using your hand too much." Doc's eyes looked over his glasses to see Jacob's face as he held Jacob's bruised and swollen hand.

"Why do you say that?" Jacob asked the doctor.

"Because your hand should be healed more than this."

"I told you to take it easy," Abigail scolded Jacob as she poured tea for everyone.

"I didn't ask for a house call either," Jacob pointed out.

"I know you Jacob." Doc smiled. "You work too hard."

"I have work to do," Jacob insisted. "It's got to get done sooner rather than later."

"Like I told you before," Doc reminded him, "if you don't take it easy, you won't have to worry because you won't have any use of it."

"It isn't that bad," Jacob argued. "I just hit it with a hammer."

"Yes, but you broke some bones in your hand," Doc explained.

Doc left Jacob with a world full of worry. It had been two weeks since Jacob had wounded his hand. Jacabig wasn't finished enough to move in before winter.

"Give your hand a break," Abigail encouraged. "I can help you the best I can."

"You can't build tables. You can't finish the house," Jacob said sharply.

"Jacob." Abigail looked hurt by his comment. "I can do what I can. Maybe I am not a carpenter, maybe I can't make your tables, but I can do what I can."

"Right, and tables are what pays the bills," Jacob said heartlessly. For the first time, he showed his frustration during the difficult time. "We don't have the money to pay for the lumber that came in for the floor, let alone the manpower to do the work to replace it."

"I know you're hurting, Jacob," Abigail said, tears stinging her eyes. "But we will get through this. So the house doesn't get finished until next year. It's not the end of the world."

Abigail put the situation into perspective and when Jacob realized the truth, it made him feel ashamed. He had no right to speak that way to his wife. Girlie was the one person who stood by him through good and bad, the one that loved him unconditionally, who was his best friend.

"Abigail, I'm so sorry." Jacob grabbed Abigail's hand as she turned to walk away, pulling her close in front of him. He put his arms around her waist.

Abigail put her arms around Jacob's neck and nestled her head on his chest.

"I'm so selfish and heartless," Jacob whispered.

"The one thing you are not is selfish. Or heartless," Abigail informed him as Jacob kissed her lips. "You're a proud, honest, hard-working, selfless man, and I love you."

"I love you too, Girlie. I'm so sorry," Jacob repeated, feeling his first apology wasn't enough.

Abigail knew that Jacob always wanted to fix everything, and he would do everything in his power to do so. His broken hand was the last straw; he couldn't repair what needed to be done, and it broke her heart to see him struggle like he was.

"God will see us through," Abigail told him. "Isn't that what you're always telling me," she smiled.

"Yes, you're right, love." Jacob held Abigail, feeling blessed to have his wife standing by his side.

Saturday morning came with a hard frost. Fortunately, there had been no snow yet. Jacob and Abigail were sitting at the table, having breakfast when there was a knock at the door. Jacob got up and answered the door to find Charles and ten other men, along with their wives, standing on and around his doorstep.

"Good … morning …" Jacob hesitantly said, a confused look on his face.

"Good morning, Jacob, Abigail," Charles answered as he took his hat off and held it in front of him.

"What are all you guys doing here?" Jacob asked with surprise.

"We," Charles pointed to himself and then the rest of the men behind him, "are at your service today. We're going to work on Jacabig Place, and we're going to get it finished by the end of the day.

"What?" Jacob was taken aback. "Are you fooling?"

"Nope," his red-headed freckle-faced friend proudly confirmed. "There's no one who works harder than you, my friend, and we're here to help you."

"Lad," Bert piped up. "You helped us when little Grace was brought into this world."

"You were there when my farm almost burnt down," one man said. "If it weren't for you, we would've lost everything."

"You helped me when my wife was sick," another fellow said. "You brought supplies to the house when I couldn't leave her side."

"You helped with our threshing," another farmer shouted.

"Don't forget the time my horse got away, and you found her and brought her back," Mr. Patterson said.

Everyone had a remembrance of one time or another that Jacob had helped them out over years he'd lived in Abbington Pickets.

Jacob was overwhelmed by the men who came to help. He was touched, and it almost brought him to tears that these neighbours and friends would come and help him out in his time of need. Abigail stood beside him, tears welling up in her eyes. Their dream home was really going to happen sooner rather than later.

"Well, alright then." Jacob smiled from ear to ear. "Let's get it done." Jacob reached for his hat and coat by the door.

"Oh, no you don't mister," Charles said. "Doc said no using your hand. You won't be doing a thing."

"But you'll need a supervisor, won't you?" Jacob laughed.

"That we will!" Charles and all the men and women standing behind him laughed and then cheered, their tools ready in their hands. The men headed to Jacabig as the women came in the house carrying baskets of prepared food.

"Hello, Abigail." Alice's kind face lit up as smiled at Abigail, Grace on one hip and a basket in her other hand. Grace was growing like a weed. She was already almost eighteen months old, and her curly brown locks, the same colour as her mother's were hiding under her bonnet. "Good to see you." Alice leaned towards Abigail to give her a bit of a hug. Abigail reached out and hugged them both. Alice had a glow about her, her face was full, and she beamed. She was going to have another baby in a couple more months.

"Here, let me help you." Abigail took the basket from Alice. "Come on in, ladies." Abigail greeted each one as they came through the door, taking their coats and draping them over her arm.

"I brought carrots to cook and a loaf of bread," Mrs. Patterson told Abigail.

"I brought mustard bean pickles and banana loaf." Mrs. Young held up her basket.

"I made scalloped potatoes," Mrs. Johnson added. "They're Doc's favourite."

"And I cooked ham," another lady said, smiling as she set it on the table, knowing that Doc's wife was bringing the potatoes.

"Apple crisp," Charles' mom proudly told Abigail. "It's Charles' favourite." She beamed.

"I made stuffed green peppers," Mrs. Thomas announced. "Here's chicken and dumplings!" exclaimed another lady.

"I brought beef stew and biscuits," Alice told Abigail. "We can heat it up closer to dinner time, but it's all cooked."

"Wonderful, I love stew." Abigail smiled at her friend. She and Alice didn't get a lot of time together because of the distance between them, but they made use of the time they did have. Alice was a great baker and wonderful cook as well. Abigail liked to collect all of her recipes when she could.

"It's Bert's favourite." Alice grinned. "I think Ernest's too, but then again, he likes everything." She chuckled.

"We sure have a variety of food," Abigail said cheerfully. All the women got settled in with their contributions for dinner and supper as Abigail made them all feel at home, finding them each a chair and making fresh coffee. Each lady had brought something to do: sewing, knitting, crocheting, and embroidery.

"I brought mud cookies," Mrs. Smyth announced, "and for us, not the men." Everyone in the room giggled as she passed them around. The ladies began to do their handiwork and visit before preparing for the first meal.

Over at Jacabig Place, eleven men pounded nails, sawed lumber, and replaced the floor. It was a steady hum as Jacob walked around, asking each one if they needed any help, always getting the same response. "No, thank you. Strict orders from Doc." Jacob finally gave up and resorted to going back to the shop for a cup of coffee. Maybe the women had something he could do.

"Well, what are you ladies doing?" Jacob smiled as he entered the shop, taking off his hat. It was humming with chitter-chatter; each one was busy with their own thing while talking to the woman next to them. When they saw Jacob, they stopped talking for a moment and stared.

"Well, Mr. Hudson, if you must know, we're visiting." Abigail laughed as she walked up to her husband, giving him a kiss. "Would you like some coffee?" The ladies went back to their work.

"I sure would," Jacob told her. "Those men won't let me do anything to help," he complained.

"You're not supposed to be doing anything. At all." Abigail reminded him. "That's why you're in this fix in the first place. Remember what Doc said?"

"Oh, not you too?" Jacob was feeling slightly betrayed and gave her a scowling look as he sat at the table. Abigail set the cup of coffee in front of Jacob and sat down across from him.

Jacob took a sip of coffee, and Abigail secretly gave him a one of Mrs. Smyth's "women only" cookies.

It was a long day for Jacob, but it was also a good day.

Jacabig Place was getting finished before snowfall, and that was really important to him and Abigail. They could move into the house, and once his hand was healed, he could do the carpentry work for the inside as they lived there. It was bigger than the shop, and both he and Abigail would be able to work at it and have it finished by spring if everything went as planned.

"Wow, the house looks wonderful," Jacob exclaimed as he walked through the round house, looking at all the things that had been done that day. Jacob couldn't have even begun to imagine that it would all get finished, but he was glad he was being proven wrong.

The men all beamed with pride as each of them showed Jacob what they had accomplished. Each window was in place. The door, which had already been put in but not secured, was steady as a rock. The flooring was replaced with new lumber, which only needed a coat of linseed oil. The men had placed the wet wood in the rafters of the stable to let it dry so the lumber could be re-purposed the following summer. The roof was completed, and the shingles were in place.

"Oh, my." Abigail was astonished at what she saw as she and the other ladies came out to see the finished product. Her eyes filled with tears as she stood beside Jacob. He put his arm around her. They both stood in awe.

"I can't tell you how much this means to us," Jacob said to all of them. "God has blessed us, and we can't thank you all enough." Jacob was busting at the seams with pride to know these neighbours he called friends. How one can be so selfless and help another fellow man out. He was overwhelmed with gratitude and love for each and every one of them. Abigail was at a loss for words and humbled as she stood by her husband.

All the women and their husbands walked through the house and admired it as well. Each husband told his wife what he had done. It was a moment that all of them shared, a time where they put aside their own problems, their own lives, and did what they could to help another. They each felt a sense of pride about their own handiwork as well.

"It's a dandy house, Jacob." Doc slapped him on the back as he walked up beside him. "We wish you both the best in your new home."

"Thank you, Doc." Jacob smiled. He hadn't ever seen Doc dirty, like he was today, in a worn-out shirt and a pair of britches with patches over the knees. He still had the same gruff look on his face, though. He knew Doc wasn't that mean on the inside. He cared a great deal; he just didn't like to show it.

"Well, lad." Bert shook Jacob's hand. "You've got a great house."

"Thank you, Bert," Jacob said, "You've been a good friend, you and Alice."

"You two are special people to us both," Bert said. "You saved my life. I'm forever grateful."

"You saved mine in return," Jacob reminded him. "I think we're even." He grinned. Bert nodded in agreement.

"Well, Jacob, Abigail," said Charles' father. "You've come a long way, and I know you'll be happy in your new home."

"Supper will be getting cold," Mrs. Smyth declared as everyone was still looking around.

"Well, that's why my stomach's been talking to me," Charles announced for all to hear. Everyone laughed.

"Alright everyone, let me say a prayer of blessing for this young couple and their new home," Reverend Young announced, "and of course for our supper," he added.

Everyone held hands as Reverend Young prayed.

It was the last meal of the day. Whatever was left from dinner was served for supper. It was a wonderful array of food, much like a church potluck. The men were in their glory to get such a variety.

The shop was maybe a little small for this many people, but it held all the love and friendship that was inside. It was something each of them would remember.

"I'll come back tomorrow and help you move in," Charles offered as he was leaving.

"Thank you, Charles." Jacob shook his friend's hand.

"I can come over tomorrow too," Doc said also. "Won't be long now and the snow will start to fly."

"We better get you two moved in as soon as we can," added another.

"Alright, tomorrow's moving day." Jacob smiled at Abigail as he held her hand. They were finally going to be in their new home, once again.

chapter eighteen

JACOB AND ABIGAIL were in their rebuilt home and already making use of the bigger space. At Goldenrod, Mr. and Mrs. Rodgers were managing pretty well without Claude. The chores took Abigail's pa longer than Claude, but he got them done. Anything that was beyond what he could do would have to wait for when Jacob could do it. Fortunately for Jacob, the snow fell in late November. It gave him more time for his hand to heal before the weather made it more difficult to do the chores. Once winter came, it wasn't long before Christmas was there and gone as fast as it had come.

Jacob began building walls for the kitchen and their bedroom as soon as his hand was mended. Abigail helped him as much as she could, and they both took turns working at the general store.

Jacob constructed tea tables in the evenings, and by February he had enough ready to send a shipment to David Adair in Kingston.

Jacob built the interior of the house exactly the same as the first round house. For a few finishing touches, Abigail had sewn curtains for the windows on her ma's sewing machine.

The last Sunday in March, Jacob and Abigail rode out to Goldenrod for dinner after church.

Jacob noticed that Abigail's ma was looking better. She had gained back some of the weight she'd lost and she didn't appear to be coughing as much. Having Aunt Gladys there was such a relief for her. It took a lot of the stress off Mrs. Rodgers, knowing she had someone else to help her. Jacob was relieved.

"We want to have a special first Easter at Jacabig Place this year," announced Abigail to her ma and pa. "We've had such turmoil this year, and we want to celebrate our blessings and have a big Easter."

"We have a big house here," Mama tried to intervene. "I mean we could do it as well."

"Mama," Abigail interjected, "you don't understand what I'm saying."

"We want to celebrate the resurrection of our Lord and Saviour in our new home with all our family and friends," Jacob pointed out.

"We want to start our own traditions," Abigail added. "Oh, of course," Mrs. Rodgers replied. "We know what you mean. It's hard for us old birds to let go." She smiled faintly, but she seemed disheartened.

"Mama," Abigail said. "It's only for this year. You and Pa and Aunt Gladys are coming, and we are going to invite all of Jacob's family, as well as Bert, Alice, Grace, and Ernest," Abigail told her mother excitedly.

"Sounds like a really big Easter." Pa grinned. He seemed to be thrilled with the idea, more so than Ma.

"As long as we don't get that surprise blizzard that likes to arrive in the middle of April," Jacob added. "That'll be a factor, of course."

"Of course," Pa repeated. "By the way, I have been meaning to ask you, how's Claude doing at your sister's?"

"He's doing alright." Jacob rubbed the back of his neck with his hand, trying not to show his smiling face.

"Good to hear, son," Pa said. "But by the look on your face, maybe he's doing more than alright?"

"Uh, well I think Jane's happy with his work." Jacob stuck with his story.

"Jane's more than happy with Claude." Abigail laughed, joining in the conversation.

"Well, Pa," Jacob embarrassedly explained, "we," he gestured to himself and Abigail, "think that Jane likes him."

"Well, of course, she should like him if he's working for her," Mama commented.

"No, no, she *likes* him," Jacob repeated raising his left eyebrow.

"Ahhh." Pa understood completely and grinned.

"I guess you'll see for yourself in a couple of weeks." Jacob winked at Abigail, knowing everyone will be coming for Easter.

After dinner, Jacob helped Mr. Rodgers in the barn with a few chores. Once they were finished, Jacob and Abigail rode back to Abbington Pickets. As they neared the village, Jacob could see their house.

"Doesn't that look like the most amazing house you've ever seen?" Jacob teased Abigail.

"Why, yes Mr. Hudson." Abigail looked over at Jacob. "You're absolutely right."

"I bet the guy that built that house is pretty amazing," Jacob continued to joke around.

Jacob continued in the direction of Jacabig when he noticed a horse and carriage coming towards them.

"Wonder who that is?" Jacob said to Abigail. "Are you expecting company?" he asked.

"No, but whoever it is, they sure look fancy."

Jacob agreed with Abigail. There wasn't a carriage that elaborate in the whole village of Abbington Pickets. Even the white horses looked wealthy. The carriage was black with a thin white pinstripe around the edges as well as around the door, which had silver handles. As the carriage got closer, Jacob recognized David Adair as one of the occupants.

"Mr. Adair didn't say anything about coming to see us," Jacob stated as they neared the round house. Jacob and Abigail climbed off their wagon as they watched the carriage get closer.

"Good afternoon, Mr. Adair," Jacob greeted his guests as they pulled up beside where Jacob and Abigail were standing. "What brings you to Abbington Pickets?" He hadn't seen David Adair since the funeral in the summer.

"Good morning, lad, Abigail." David smiled and tipped his hat. The stern fellow who sat next to him sported an expensive black suit with matching top hat. His white shirt was neatly pressed, with a bow tie that nestled below his neck between the turned down collar points. There was a folded white hanky in his breast pocket. He had dark brown hair and a moustache that joined up to his sideburns.

The driver stepped off the carriage. He wore a black uniform with matching cap. His white-gloved hand opened the door to let the two men step out of the carriage. Jacob shook Mr. Adair's hand as he stepped down to the ground.

"This is Mr. Langley," Mr. Adair introduced them. "This is Jacob and Abigail Hudson." Jacob reached out and shook the sophisticated gentleman's hand. The stranger stood slightly shorter than Jacob and smiled with pearly white teeth.

"Mr. Langley is a solicitor from Kingston," David began to explain. "Would it be alright if we went to the general store to talk?" he asked.

"Sure," Jacob replied. He looked over at Abigail.

"I can make some tea," Abigail suggested.

"No, thank you," Mr. Adair shook his head. "I'd really like you present when we talk."

Jacob was beginning to think there was something wrong. "We can all go together," Mr. Adair said.

"Hop in," Mr. Langley said as his driver held the door for all four of them to climb inside. The driver drove the carriage to the front of the general store where they all stepped out and went inside.

"You've been keeping the store in good shape." David looked around and noticed everything was clean, in place, and well stocked.

"You're quite the businessman," Mr. Langley commented.

"I can't take all of the credit." Jacob blushed a little, looking over at his wife. "Abigail works hard here every chance she gets."

"That's impressive." David smiled. "Brings to mind why we're here to speak with you."

Jacob's curiosity grew stronger with every second.

"Is there anywhere to sit down?" Asked Mr. Langley as he looked around in the room for an area to talk.

"Right over here." Jacob pointed to the office in the back of the store. "After you." He held his hand out as David and Mr. Langley walked past Jacob towards the office. There were two chairs in front and one chair behind the desk. David and Mr. Langley took the two; Jacob held the chair for Abigail to sit behind the desk, then he stood beside her, waiting to hear what the men had to say.

Mr. Langley took a folder out of his brown leather briefcase and placed it on the desk. He took his eyeglasses out of his breast pocket, put them on, and fixed the arms of the glasses behind his ears. He opened the file and looked up at Jacob and Abigail, peering over his glasses.

"I'll let Mr. Adair tell you about why we're here, and then I'll explain the legal points."

Jacob was extremely anxious to find out what this was all about.

"Jacob, my brother loved you like a father," David began. "You were the son he never had."

"Thank you, sir." Jacob felt a sense of pride to be told that. It was a compliment. Mr. Adair was a good friend and mentor to him. He knew they had a bond.

"With that being said," David continued. "It's taken us some time, I admit, but Michael's will has been found, and you're in it, Jacob."

Jacob was taken aback upon hearing this information. He knew Mr. Adair was important to him, but he had only known him since he moved to Abbington Pickets. It wasn't like he was a relative who had known him all his life.

"Jacob, my brother has left you everything that belonged to him and Josephine," David point blankly stated. "The general store, their personal belongings, and their money. Everything."

"Pardon me?" Was all that came out of Jacob's mouth as he raised both his eyebrows in disbelief. He put his hands on his forehead, pushing his hair back over his head. Jacob looked at Abigail, astonished, and she was staring back at him in amazement.

"Does this mean…" Jacob's eyes widened, looking at Mr. Adair.

"Yes, you are now the proud new owner of a general store," David finished Jacob's sentence with a big smile on his face. "It couldn't have happened to a better couple." He looked at Jacob and Abigail with respect and admiration.

"Thank you, sir." Jacob stood up, walked up to David, and extended his hand. Mr. Adair stood up and firmly shook his hand in return. Abigail beamed as she watched the two men. Jacob backed up, turning around to Abigail; he put his arms around her, hugging her tightly. Tears of joy rolled down her cheeks.

"God answers prayers," Jacob whispered. Abigail nodded.

"All you have to do now is sign the papers," Mr. Langley said, interrupting their moment.

Jacob signed all the necessary papers, along with Mr. Langley and David. Everything was happening so quickly. Jacob felt like he was in the middle of a dream.

"Alright, Mr. Hudson." Mr. Langley looked at Jacob. Creases rippled across his forehead, appearing in all seriousness. "The general store and all its contents are now yours. That means everything in the home part as well. All moneys, meaning cash in the house or General Store and bank accounts that belonged to Mr. and Mrs. Adair belong to you."

"You'll need to come to Kingston to finalize the accounts at the bank, and put them in your name," David added.

"How soon can you come?

"Umm," Jacob glanced at Abigail at a loss for words. "Uh … I could probably plan a trip next week. Is that soon enough?"

"Yes, lad that would be fine." David shook Jacob's hand again; he put his hat on and opened the door to leave. Mr. Langley turned around and shook Jacob's hand as they stood outside the general store.

"Thank you, sir."

Mr. Langley's driver was waiting for them. He opened the carriage door as he stood with his left hand behind his back, holding onto the door with his right.

"Shall we take you both home?" Mr. Langley asked.

"Thank you, no." Jacob, still overwhelmed, looked at Abigail. "We'll enjoy the walk back."

"Suit yourselves," Mr. Langley told him. Then both men stepped up into the carriage, and the driver closed the door and climbed up into the carriage himself.

"We shall see you next week, Jacob." David smiled, tipping his hat to Abigail.

"You will." Jacob and Abigail waved as the carriage drove off. They both watched for several minutes as the carriage got farther away. Neither had anything to say. It was a bittersweet moment for both of them.

Jacob and Abigail walked back into the general store. Jacob felt overwhelmed. He missed Mr. Adair, wishing he was still alive, feeling guilty because the death of a very good friend made it possible for him to receive such a blessing.

chapter nineteen

"WHY DON'T YOU like me?" Jacob asked bluntly.

"Why don't you like me?" Claude repeated his question. Jacob and Abigail had come to Crocus Flats to tell Jane the good news about the general store. Claude was in the barn feeding the horses when Jacob got there. Claude was his usual happy self.

"You want to know why?" Jacob asked. "Do you really want to know why?"

"Enlighten me," Claude retorted.

"Ever since you came to Abbington Pickets, you have been, rude, mean, sarcastic, unfeeling, distant, ahh." Jacob counted on his fingers the reasons he found it hard to like Claude. "Am I missing anything?" Jacob asked sharply.

"Really?" Claude raised his voice. "That's all you've got to say?" he added with sarcasm. "Because I don't think I have NOT done my job with all of those terrible traits you speak of."

"I'm not saying you aren't doing your job," Jacob argued. "Do you think I would have asked you to come to Crocus Flats if I didn't think you could do the work?"

"Well, what are you saying?"

"You asked a question," Jacob stated. "I'm simply answering it."

"Do you want to know why I don't like you?" Claude asked.

"Of course I do."

"Because, look at your life," Claude started. "How can you be so damned happy?"

"What?" Jacob was now really confused. "What about my life?" He was really curious.

"Well, let's see," Claude began. "Your father was a tyrant, didn't respect you, even disowned you. Your girlfriend ran off to England to marry another man. Meanwhile, your mother was killed in a freak accident, not to mention your wife-to-be was burned to death in a fire."

"Claude," Jacob started, "that's in the past. God has healed my heart."

"What kind of God allows things like that to happen?" Claude questioned.

"God doesn't give you more than you can handle." Jacob tried to be encouraging.

"Well then, let's talk about the more recent, your father-in-law almost dies, let's not forget your best friends were murdered by a wagon, the house you built from the ground up was destroyed, and then while rebuilding it your brother is killed. What in God's name do you have to be so happy about?"

"I don't know how you know so much about me." Jacob was shocked by the fact Claude knew all that information and was amazed that Claude even cared or thought about it.

"People talk, you know," Claude said bluntly. "I did live at the Empire Hotel, let's not forget."

Of course, let's not forget, Jacob repeated to himself. It all made sense. It was a small town, and yes people loved to talk, especially if it wasn't about themselves. Jacob looked up at God and silently asked for help, help to know what words to use.

"I'm asking God to tell me what to say right now," Jacob admitted. "Because, to be honest, I don't know."

"God? How can you even say there is a God," Claude yelled back at him. The angrier he got, the thicker his accent became. His face was red, and sweat trickled down his forehead.

"Claude–"

"How can a God, especially a good God, the one you speak of, do such things!" Tears welled up in Claude's eyes.

"I don't always understand it either, but I have faith," Jacob tried to explain.

"My father left when I was five years old, leaving my mother penniless with my little brother and me," Claude retorted. "We never had any money. We were homeless sometimes. No other man would look at a woman who already had children." Tears were now streaming down his face, years of anger and pain poured out of him.

Jacob reached out to touch Claude's back. Claude abruptly backed away.

"Don't you touch me," Claude yelled. "I don't need your sympathy."

Jacob backed away to give him space. He realized how Bert must have felt when Jacob had been in his dark place after Anna died. *How did he do it?* Jacob asked himself. *Thank God he didn't give up.*

"My little brother died because my mother didn't have the money for the medicine he needed," Claude shouted in anguish.

"Claude, it's alright to be mad at God. He understands," Jacob tried to explain.

"Stop it! There is no such thing as God," Claude cried. "If there were, he wouldn't have taken away my brother and my mother! The only family I had."

"Your mother and brother are still with you, and they're in heaven with our Heavenly Father."

"Stop saying that. You don't know what you're talking about." Claude stepped forward, pulling his arm back, making a fist and throwing a punch at Jacob.

Jacob stepped to the side, missing the force of Claude's hand in his face.

Claude fell to his knees and began to cry, head in his hands. "I should never have come here," he sobbed loudly.

"You can go on," Jacob began to tell him. "Jesus is your Saviour; He will give you the strength to go on."

"Stop it," Claude said quietly. "I don't want to hear any more." He shook his head.

"Clau-"

"Don't say any more. Go away."

Again, Jacob reached out to Claude. Claude pulled away from him abruptly.

"Just go!" Claude shouted, looking up at him with anguish in his eyes. Sweat beaded on his forehead and his hair fell down to one side from his usually neat part.

Jacob stood up slowly, walking backwards, watching Claude sitting on his knees. He knew how he must be feeling, how helpless he felt. Jacob wanted Claude to know what it was like to have Jesus in his heart and on his side, to have everlasting joy. Today was not that day, Jacob realized that. Jacob continued to pray for Claude silently.

"What is going on here?" Jane asked with a worried look on her face as she and Abigail stood in the doorway of the barn.

"Did you hurt Claude?" Jane looked at Jacob with scowling eyes.

"No," Jacob said. "Of course not." Jacob realized how the situation must have looked from their perspective. But he knew they had to trust him. "Go back to the house," Jacob pointed towards the stone building, "both of you." Jacob didn't want to be rude, but he knew the condition Claude was in and knew how he felt.

Claude was still sitting on his knees sobbing. Both the women looked concerned, but Abigail knew her Jacob and put her arm around her sister-in-law.

"Let's go," Abigail told her. "They'll be fine."

"Are you sure Jacob?" Asked Jane.

"Please go," whispered Claude from the floor.

Both of them, as well as Daisy, walked slowly to the house. Jacob crouched down to Claude's level, bending over to look at his face.

"I'll be here if you want to talk," Jacob told Claude. "Any time. Remember that."

Jacob stood up and started to walk slowly back to the house. He felt helpless, knowing what Claude was going through, knowing that unless he asked God for help, he would never have peace.

Suddenly Jacob heard a voice screaming ahead of him. He looked up immediately. Claude also heard it, he began to stand.

They both saw Abigail running towards them.

"What's wrong?" Jacob ran towards her, seeing the terror in her eyes. Abigail, panting from running hard, reached Jacob with her arms out to touch him.

"Quick. It's Jane." That got Claude's attention. Abigail was almost in tears. "Daisy ran into the trees. We followed her. Right before our eyes, she fell through the ice. Jacob, I didn't know there was a slough there."

Jacob's eyes widened with fear. "It's not your fault," he told her, knowing that Abigail wasn't familiar with the farm. "Where's Jane now?"

"She wanted to go in after the dog," Abigail gasped as she told the events quickly. "I begged her not to do anything. That I would be back with your help."

"Claude-" Jacob turned to see that Claude was running back towards the barn, only taking a few minutes and returning with a long rope looped over his shoulder.

"Oh! We have to hurry," Abigail cried out. "I'm afraid Jane will jump in after Daisy."

Claude ran past Jacob and Abigail. They followed, Abigail yelling after him with directions to find Jane. They raced by the house, down the lane, and towards the bush northeast of the house. As they ran, Jacob prayed to God for speed and strength.

"Over there." Abigail pointed. They could see Jane. She was holding onto the edge of the snow-covered ice, where she had fallen in. Her lips were blue, and she was shivering uncontrollably. There was no sign of Daisy. Jane's hands kept slipping as the snow gave way and she lifted her arm to grab hold of something, anything. Then she slipped under the water.

Claude reached the slough's edge first. Jacob didn't get a word out of his mouth before he saw Claude wrapping the rope around his waist, tying it with a square knot. He then tied the other end of the rope to the nearest tree. Moving fast, he jumped into the icy water. He ducked under the water and a minute later he emerged holding Jane by her waist. He lifted her head above the slushy water.

Jacob grabbed hold of the rope, hoping the knot Claude had tied was going to hold them both.

"Grab the rope and pull hard," Jacob instructed Abigail. He pulled with all his might. Abigail stood behind him, pulling along with him. Claude was able to hold onto Jane as they were both being dragged towards the edge. Their water-soaked clothes made it extremely hard, but once they were on the snow, Jacob continued to pull them to solid ground. In a blink of an eye, Claude jumped back in.

"Claude no…" Jacob yelled after him. He immediately took his coat off placing it over Jane to get her warm. He continued to pray.

"Keep her covered," Jacob told Abigail. "Please don't move." He reached for the rope again and began to yank on it. Claude's head appeared out of the water, one arm reaching high above the cold water as he gasped for breath. Jacob heaved, pulling hard, placing one hand in front of the other, drawing in the rope as Claude's whole body came out of the water. Claude was holding as tightly as he could onto a soaked black dog who resembled a drowned rat.

"He got the dog," Abigail yelled.

Jacob wasn't as thrilled, knowing how long the dog had been under the ice-covered water. The chances of Daisy surviving weren't good.

Once Claude was pulled to the edge, he crawled until he reached Jane. His black hair was dripping wet, and his water soaked clothes made it hard for him to maneuver. He lifted his arm to touch Jane's face.

"Is … she … alright?" His blue lips quivered as he spoke and his whole body shook with cold and fear.

"We have to get you both to the house," Jacob ordered them. "Or you'll die of hypothermia." He lifted Jane with both of his arms and carried her.

Jane whispered over and over. "Did you get Daisy?"

"Everything's going to be alright," Jacob reassured her. He didn't want to mention Daisy, in case she didn't make it. The rescue would have all been for nothing.

Abigail helped Claude, placing her coat over his shoulders.

Claude bent down and scooped Daisy up with both his hands, holding her like a little child. Everyone walked as quickly as they could towards the house.

"You could've died," Jacob scolded his older sister. "What were you thinking?" He paced the floor in front of the bed Jane laid in. She was in dry clothes with a foot warmer and quite a few blankets. Daisy laid at the end of the bed with a blanket wrapped around her. It was a miracle all three of them were still alive. Not only could they have been trapped under the ice and drowned, but they could also have frozen to death or died of hypothermia.

"Oui. For once I have to agree with your brother," Claude added. "What were you thinking?" He gently scolded her as he sat in a chair with his bare feet in a pail of hot water. He was wearing dry clothes and had a blanket around his shoulders.

"Daisy's a great dog, but not worth your life." Jacob was still scared about what had happened.

Jane sobbed quietly. "I'm sorry," she whispered, "I couldn't lose her too."

"Leave her alone," Abigail spoke quietly. "I think she knows."

"But..." Jacob began to say.

"Shhh." Abigail put her finger to her lips, shaking her head. "Let her get some rest."

Jacob left the room, still feeling the adrenaline it had taken to pull his sister and Claude out of the water. He looked down at his hands, turning them palm side up. The rope burn was deep, but at the time he hadn't felt anything. His hands throbbed in pain now as he looked at the bloody open wounds.

"Let's get your hands fixed up." Abigail sympathized with her husband. Jacob sat at the kitchen table. Abigail brought a bowl of warm water and soap, setting it on the table in front of him. She took hold of his right hand, placing it in the warm bath. It hurt like bees stinging every inch of his hand. Jacob breathed in deep through his nose then held his breath. It hurt. There was no doubt about it.

Once both his hands were clean and dry, Abigail put salve on each palm, wrapping his hands with torn strips of cotton fabric.

"Doesn't this look familiar." Jacob smiled lightly, looking up at Abigail.

"At least it'll heal faster." Abigail smiled at him. She put away the medicine and the bowl of water, then put the kettle on the stove and made tea. She placed a cup on the table for Jacob.

"I'm going to go check on Jane." Abigail kissed Jacob's forehead then walked up the kitchen stairs to her room.

Jacob sat slowly sipping his tea, thinking about the day's events and how God had saved his family. He heard someone enter the room. It was Claude.

"Can I … um … talk to you?" asked Claude as he looked down at the floor, unable to look at Jacob. He still had the blanket wrapped around his shoulders. He wasn't shivering anymore, and his lips were back to their normal colour.

"Of course," Jacob got up and pulled out a chair for Claude to sit in. "I would get you a cup of tea but-" He held his wrapped hands up.

"It's alright," Claude said. "I don't need any." He grinned lightly. "I've had quite a few cups already."

The two of them sat in silence for some time, making it feel a little awkward, but Jacob knew that Claude obviously wanted to talk or he wouldn't be sitting there right then.

"I was there," Jacob broke the silence. He knew what was still on Claude's mind. "I was exactly where you are right now. Right after Anna was killed. I didn't care about anyone or anything."

Claude looked up at Jacob in surprise.

"If it wouldn't have been for God and good friends, I don't know where I would be. I sure wouldn't have the good life I have right now, especially with Abigail."

"You call losing everything you've lost a good life?" Claude faced Jacob with no understanding of what Jacob was telling him. His eyes welled up with tears, which he tried to hold back.

"I will see my loved ones again." Jacob didn't know what he was going to say until he said it. God led him in the right direction. "As for our house, our belongings, that can all be replaced."

Claude started to sob, putting his hand over his eyes in shame. "I don't know a day that I haven't felt so angry and bitter," he cried. "Then my mother died." He sobbed louder. "I went numb."

Jacob leaned over and put his hand on Claude's shoulder. He understood.

"You can be happy, you can have the peace you've never known," Jacob assured him.

Claude shook his head in disagreement. "No, I can't."

"Yes, you can. Give your life to The Lord," Jacob continued to encourage him. "He loves you."

"It's too late," Claude disagreed. "I've been a hateful person."

"After today, I don't believe that you're a hateful person," Jacob stated. "You're a good person."

"I thought I'd lost Jane." Claude shook his head. "That God was punishing me. That it was too late."

"It's never too late," Jacob said. "God loves you. He forgives you."

"I don't know." Claude shook his head and wept in his hands.

"I can see you care for my sister," Jacob said. "Am I right?"

Claude looked at Jacob and nodded.

"I don't know why God allows some things to happen and some things not to happen," Jacob began. "But I do know one thing. God is a faithful God."

"I don't know." Claude was still unsure.

"Do you want to be happy?" Jacob asked. "Do you want to be at peace?"

Claude nodded, wiping his eyes with the back of his hands. "If you give your life to the Lord, you will always have peace," Jacob explained. "I'm not saying it'll always be easy, but you'll have the strength for anything."

"I want what you have, Jacob," Claude spoke shyly.

"You do?" Jacob asked.

"I really do," Claude agreed.

"Say this prayer after me." Jacob put his hand on Claude's shoulder, they both bowed their heads, and Jacob prayed out loud. "Dear Jesus, thank you for dying on the cross. Please forgive my sins. I give my life to you. Please help me find peace. In Jesus' name, amen."

Claude repeated every word of the prayer of salvation after Jacob, then smiled a joyful smile for the first time.

Jacob had never seen that side of him before. He felt at peace and thanked The Lord for giving him the strength and words to say at the right moment. It had been a terrifying, yet miraculous day, but God saw them through, and now Claude was saved, and that made Jacob's heart smile.

"Now let's go see my sister." Jacob smiled. "I am sure she would be happy to see you and hear your good news."

chapter twenty

THE FOLLOWING WEEK Jacob travelled to Kingston to sign the legal papers. He met David Adair and Mr. Langley at the Bank of Kingston. It wasn't a long procedure for the lengthy trip, but it was necessary. The weather stayed nice for the days he was away, and that made for a quick trip. Abigail stayed home to work at the general store while keeping the home fires burning.

Jacob had asked Claude to go with him for two reasons. One was that he needed help to load the lumber he was bringing back, and secondly to cover up the fact that Jacob wanted to buy a special gift for Abigail on the way back home. Jacob was looking forward to spending some one on one time with Claude so he could finally get to know the "real" Claude.

Jacob learned that Claude really didn't want to be a lawyer, that he was doing it to make his mother proud. The money was a bit of a factor as well, but it wasn't something he looked forward to doing, even though he had the right temperament. He was now planning to stay in Abbington Pickets area and put down roots since he didn't have family anywhere else in Canada. His mother was English, and his father was French, but he had no relatives left in Canada that he knew of. Jacob informed him that his family was Claude's new family and he would always be welcome.

Jacob was blessed to learn that Mr. MacDonald's brother was trying to sell their piano for a good price. Jacob took the opportunity to make a trade for a surprise birthday gift for Abigail. He knew how much she'd enjoyed her first piano, which had been demolished in the tornado. Even though Abigail never complained, Jacob knew she really missed it.

On the way home from Kingston, Jacob and Claude stopped at the MacDonalds' and picked it up. Jacob and Claude, along with the help of three other strong men, were able to lift the piano into the wagon. The last six miles took a little longer to travel, due to the weight of the load.

Jacob and Claude returned home the following Saturday.

"You're home." Abigail waved, beaming as she stood outside Jacabig Place watching her husband steer the horses close to the house. The sun was shining brightly from the west as it was nearing the end of the day. Abigail held her hand over her eyebrows to shield her eyes from the light.

Jacob never tired of Abigail's smile nor her angelic British accent. Even though it had only been five days, Jacob missed his Girlie.

"It's good to have you home." Abigail watched Jacob jump off the wagon and run towards her.

He wrapped his strong arms around her and twirled her around. "It's good to be home, I sure missed you." He kissed her quickly not really wanting to embarrass Claude. "We have to go into Abbington and find Charles and a couple of other lads before Claude can go home," he announced.

"Whatever for?" Abigail questioned.

"It's a surprise, Girlie." Jacob flicked the end of Abigail's nose before he hopped back up on the wagon. "We'll be right back."

"But you just got home," Abigail shouted back after him. She stood with her hands on her hips, shaking her head and watching the wagon.

"Well, of all the nerve," she said out loud with a smile. It wasn't too long before Jacob and Claude returned with three other men, Charles and two of his next door neighbour's sons. The three extra men were riding in the back of the wagon with the lumber. They jumped off after reaching the house.

Abigail came back out of the house, this time with a black crocheted shawl wrapped around her shoulders.

"Now what are you guys up to?" She lifted her eyebrows with suspicion.

Jacob ran up to Abigail. "Close your eyes." He grabbed her hands placing them over her eyes. "Don't look until I tell you. Promise?"

"But..." Abigail tried to object.

"Promise?" Jacob insisted.

"Alright, alright, I promise." She wrinkled up her nose as she held her hands over her closed eyes.

Jacob pulled the wagon as close to the house as he could get. The back of the wagon was adjacent to the door. He kept glancing at Abigail to see if she was looking.

"No peeking," Jacob warned.

"I'm not," she stated impatiently.

Jacob and the other men worked fast, first untying the rope that held the piano in place as well as the canvas that was covering it. Jacob placed a wide board on the end gate of the wagon and set the other end on the ground. Jacob and Charles' friends pushed the end of the piano as Claude and Charles pulled the other end and guided it down the board. The boards creaked and cracked as the heavy piece of furniture rolled down and reached the ground.

"Alright lads, we're going to have to put our backs into it," Jacob encouraged. "On the count of three: one, two, three." Each of the men lifted the piano over the steps, carrying it halfway into the doorway. The weight was so great they had to set it down for a moment.

"Almost there," Charles said.

Jacob looked at the other shaking his head, holding his finger to his mouth, hushing them. He didn't want anyone ruining the surprise.

"I would sure like to know what you boys are up to." Abigail could hardly contain her curiosity, especially with hearing all the noise they were making.

This pleased Jacob, who liked keeping her in suspense. "You'll see. No peeking!" Jacob looked over at Abigail as he was holding onto one end of the piano.

"I'm not," Abigail repeated with annoyance.

"One more time, lads," Jacob instructed. This time they only lifted the end of the piano that was still outside. They pushed it as they lifted until the big beast was all the way in the door.

"Can I look yet?" Abigail stood in the same spot, anxiously shifting from one foot to the other.

"Not yet," Jacob repeated. He walked up to Abigail. "Wait here a few minutes longer, please." He kissed her forehead and quickly went inside with the other men, closing the door behind them.

"Alright, we have to be quick. She's getting impatient." Jacob chuckled. "Let's push it over here," he said, showing them to the dining room. The wall across from the dining room table, which was the east wall, was where he wanted it. It was the same place the first piano had sat. Jacob was so thrilled to bring this special gift to Abigail; he couldn't wait to see the look on her face when she saw it.

"Thank you, lads," Jacob told his helpers. "Abigail is going to be thrilled." Each of them wanted to see the big moment, so they stood around, looking at each other with wondrous looks on their faces.

"Ah, sorry, lads." Jacob realized why they were all still in the room. "I want to be alone with my wife for this one."

"Ahhhh," they all simultaneously groaned.

"Well, if we would have known that…" Charles teased. They all laughed as they walked outside.

"Well, I best be getting home anyway," Claude stated, "before it starts getting too dark."

"It was good to have you come with me to Kingston." Jacob shook his hand. "Thank you."

"Merci, it was a nice break from the usual work. I'm happy to get back to it." Claude grinned as he walked towards the stable to saddle his horse. "I'm anxious to see Jane," he shyly admitted.

"She'll be happy you're home as well, I'm sure," Jacob added.

"Well, I have to be at the hotel." Charles smiled as he left with his two neighbours.

Jacob watched everyone leave as he walked to the wagon to retrieve the stool that belonged to the piano. He quickly ran inside and placed it front of the piano.

Abigail still stood with her eyes covered; she never said a word as she continued to wait.

Jacob came back outside and walked up behind Abigail. "Can I look yet?" She didn't seem as happy as she had been when Jacob came home.

"Alright, my Girlie." Jacob put his hands over hers gently, taking them away from her eyes. "Keep them closed until I say." He walked behind her, guiding her into the house, being careful with each step. Jacob stood her in front of the beautiful piano, his arms around her.

"Before you open your eyes," Jacob quietly spoke in Abigail's ear, "I wanted to tell you how much I love you."

"I love you too, Jacob." Abigail smiled. "Can I look now," she added quickly.

"I know it's early, but I wanted to give you something extra special for your birthday," Jacob explained, knowing Abigail's birthday wasn't until the next month. "Are you ready now?" He grinned from ear to ear, knowing how crazy Abigail was feeling with waiting so long to see his secret present.

"Are you being funny? Of course I'm ready." Abigail started jumping up and down in one spot squealing under her breath.

"Alright, you can look," Jacob said all in one breath.

Abigail opened her eyes, taking a few seconds to adjust to the light while focusing on her surprise gift. "WOW!" She jumped up and down even more. She turned around while jumping, three times stopping in front of Jacob putting her arms around his neck. "How can we afford this? After the house? Buying new stock for the store-"

"Shhh." Jacob shook his head. "Don't … please enjoy your piano, you deserve it."

"You're too good to me." Abigail kissed her husband. She turned around and admired the beautiful piece of furniture. The upright piano was much fancier than the first one Jacob had bought for her. It was made of dark mahogany with carved scrolls on the front and sides as well as down the legs. There were candle holders protruding from the upper front at each side.

Jacob pulled out the piano stool for Abigail to sit down. It was a unique one, with a back on it, two twisted spindles supporting the backrest, with silver clawed feet that held a glass ball on the bottom of each leg. Abigail bent slightly as she tucked her dress under her legs and sat down. She lifted the lid and spread her slim fingers slightly apart, lightly placing them on the ivory keys. She closed her eyes, pausing for a minute, then began to play Joplin's "Bethena."

Jacob stood in amazement, listening to the beautiful music his talented wife was playing. For years, Jacob had admired Joplin's compositions, and now they both could enjoy the sweet sound from Abigail's fingertips. He couldn't have found a better gift for his Girlie.

"Just a minute." Jacob left the room, returning with the mantel clock he had given her as a wedding gift. He gently placed it on top of the piano, centring it carefully. He stood behind Abigail, putting his hands on her shoulders to admire it.

"There." Jacob smiled. "Now it's perfect." Abigail pulled her arm across her chest and reached for Jacob's hand, giving it a squeeze. They both knew what that clock meant to them, and in silence, they both counted their blessings.

Abigail continued playing, one song after another, for more than an hour. Jacob went outside, putting the wagon and horses away for the night, feeding them and bringing in an armful of wood. Abigail was still playing when he came back in the house. Jacob stoked the stove, adding wood, then he put the kettle on for a pot of tea, all while enjoying the music, the beautiful night, and feeling blessed beyond words.

The next day was Easter Sunday. Abigail was thrilled to be hosting the big meal of the day. It was a gorgeous day, with a slight breeze and a few clouds. Jacob got up extra early to make sure the stove was piping hot for Abigail to put the turkey in the oven. She wanted to be all prepared and ready before her guests arrived, which would be after church.

Abigail stuffed the twenty-pound bird with her mama's special recipe. She then placed it in a big rectangular roaster. She opened the oven door, placing the roaster on the rack, then she closed the door and dusted her hands off by wiping them together.

While Jacob was outside hitching up the horses to the wagon, Abigail peeled the potatoes, cutting them up and filling the pot; she covered the potatoes with water, placing the lid on top. Then she did the same with the carrots.

Abigail was pinning her hair up when Jacob came through the door with another armful of wood.

"We're going to be late," Abigail hollered to Jacob from their bedroom.

Jacob filled the stove again. He came into the bedroom to change into his Sunday clothes. Abigail was wearing her light pink lacy dress with a solid pink ribbon tied at the back. The sleeves were long with small buttons along the outer seam close to the cuff. The dress touched the top of her boots.

"You look beautiful," Jacob said to Abigail. "As always."

"Thank you." Abigail blushed at Jacob's reflection in the mirror.

Jacob and Abigail arrived at the All Saints Anglican Church in time to get seated in their usual pew. Jacob saw Bert, Alice, Gracie, and Ernest sitting on the other side; Jacob nodded as Bert smiled in acknowledgement.

Mr. and Mrs. Rodgers and Aunt Gladys were sitting in the pew in front of them. Peter, Missy, Sarah, Dennis, and the children came in after Jacob and Abigail and were sitting in the last pew at the back.

The church filled with people and Reverend Young stood, began to pray, and started his sermon. Once the service was over, the Reverend stood at the back, greeting everyone as they left the building.

"We'll see you in a little bit for dinner?" Jacob shook Reverend Young's hand.

"Yes, the wife and I are looking forward to it." Reverend Young said.

"Bring your appetite." Jacob grinned. "Abigail has been preparing for this for a long time." Reverend Young smiled.

Jacob and Abigail chatted with their neighbours and friends for a few minutes before heading home to greet their guests.

"See you at Jacabig," Jacob told his siblings as each climbed into their own wagons and carriages.

Jacob started the caravan towards Jacabig Place. Abigail's ma and pa first, then Peter and Missy along with Sarah and Dennis. Bert, Alice, Ernest, and Grace followed suit.

Jacob and Abigail reached the round house first. Jacob pulled up to the front door. He hopped off the wagon, walked around behind the wagon, and reached his hand up to Abigail. She placed her hand on his and stepped off the wagon carefully, holding her dress up with her other hand.

Jacob and Abigail reached the door and Jacob could smell something burning. He raced to open the door.

"What's that smell?" Abigail looked at Jacob.

"Smells like something's burning," Jacob answered as he unlatched the door, quickly opening it. Smoke seeped out of the oven door.

"Oh no!" Abigail yelled, running towards the stove. "The turkey!" Abigail grabbed the pot holders as Jacob quickly opened the oven door. Smoke gushed out the door as Abigail closed her eyes, avoiding the stinging while reaching for the roaster. She set it down on the table behind them.

Jacob waved his arms in the air to move the smoke around. He ran to open the door, but it swung open as he was reaching for the latch. He looked up to see his family standing in the doorway.

"Hello there." Jacob smiled with embarrassment, swinging the door wide open to let the smoke out.

Abigail was still in the kitchen mumbling. "How much water did I put in the roaster?" She was coughing, waving a tea towel in the air.

"I think I put too much wood in the fire." Jacob smiled weakly, hoping he could take the blame from Abigail. "Come on in," he said politely.

"Oh, my." Abigail came running over to the door as their company came through the door. "This is so embarrassing. I wanted everything to be perfect." Abigail felt like she had disappointed everyone and wanted to crawl under the bed and hide. The meal was supposed to be perfect, to show everyone what a wonderful cook and homemaker she was. But that was all ruined.

"I'm sure it's not as bad as it seems." Mrs. Rodgers said as she took off her coat. Mr. Rodgers stood beside her, holding his white hanky over his mouth and nose. Both his wife and Aunt Gladys gave him a disapproving look.

"We can help you," Alice tried to console her as she set down the basket she was carrying. Bert was standing beside her holding Grace.

"We brought buns." Ernest held them up with a shy smile, trying to say something to make Abigail feel better.

"There, you see. All is not lost." Jacob joked with Abigail. Everyone laughed. Abigail scowled at Jacob for teasing her.

"I'm sorry, Girlie," Jacob sympathized with her. "It's all my fault, love. I shouldn't have added those last two logs to the fire."

"No, it's entirely my fault," Abigail admitted quietly to him. "I think I forgot to add the water," she whispered, not wanting everyone to hear. Jacob felt sorry for her; he put his arm around her giving her a quick hug. His facial expression gave Abigail a bit of a lift. She decided to make the best of it, and finish making dinner.

"It'll be alright," Jacob said before he turned to see who was at the door.

"Is Jacob cooking dinner?" Peter teased when he appeared in the doorway. Missy gave him a smack on the arm and scowled.

"What? I'm only fooling," he told Missy.

"Just get in here." Jacob shook his head. He figured that Abigail had heard enough jokes for one day.

Peter, Missy, Sarah, Dennis, and the children took their coats and boots off, as well as their hats. Jacob placed all the coats on their bed.

"Smells good! What's for dinner?" Charles' smart remark floated into the room. He couldn't stop from giggling at the sight of the haze floating in the air and the smell of burnt turkey. By then, no one was laughing at the situation. It seemed that Abigail, her mama, Aunt Gladys and Alice had it under control. They were able to salvage the turkey and began cooking the vegetables on the stove.

"Don't worry, love," Jacob encouraged Abigail. "It'll be delicious, no matter what." He gave her a peck on the cheek and went into the living room to chat with the men. They had begun a competitive game of cribbage.

The children were running around the house, laughing and playing hide and go seek. The house was filled with love and laughter; it made Jacob happy and sad at the same time. He and Abigail would never see the smiling face of a baby who resemble her mother, or hear the giggle of a little boy who had his father's dimples. There would be no one to teach the family traditions to or to teach to pray. No little one to call him Daddy or let him kiss his finger better when he got it caught in the door.

Jacob's heart sank a little at that realization. He didn't begrudge Abigail for it, that was for certain. He'd known when he married her she didn't want to have children. But he'd never thought it would bother him until he saw Bert's little girl play with Missy's daughter. He watched as they chatted like miniature grown-ups.

"Your turn." Bert nudged Jacob. "Hello? Is anyone in there?" Bert laughed.

"Uh oh." Jacob returned from his thoughts. "My turn already," He played his hand, and the game continued.

There was a knock at the door. In came Reverend Young and his wife, along with Doc and Mrs. Johnson. Not far behind them were Jane and Claude.

"Come on in," Jacob greeted his guests. "Give me your coats." He took their coats to the bedroom, returning quickly.

"Here, have a chair." Jacob pointed to the dining room chairs. The house was getting fuller, and almost out of places to sit, but Jacob and Abigail wouldn't have it any other way. Family was the most important thing to them.

Jane and Claude were still standing by the doorway. Jane had a particular look on her face, but she looked rather well. In fact, she looked different than she ever had. Her hair was in a looser bun and she was wearing a bit of lipstick. Both of those things were unlike her. The mousy young woman, whom both Peter and Jacob said would never find a man, looked admirable. Jacob didn't think he was the only one who noticed either. Everyone in the kitchen seemed to be mesmerized by her appearance.

"Jacob," Claude looked at him, then everyone else in the room. "Everyone, we have something to tell you," Claude continued as he looked at Jane nervously. She stood beside him, holding his hand slightly awkwardly. Then Claude smiled at her, and her face glowed with happiness. Everyone stopped what they were doing. The whole house was hushed.

"Jane and I are getting married," Claude said in one quick breath as Jane squealed with delight.

Abigail was the first to dash over to her, congratulating them, hugging them both.

Jacob felt joy for his sister and even a sense of relief. That worrisome feeling left him, knowing his sister wouldn't be alone for the rest of her life.

"Congratulations, brother." Jacob walked up to Claude and shook his hand. "I am so happy for you both."

"Merci, Jacob." Claude smiled. "I owe it all to you, and that means a lot to me."

Jacob smiled. He stepped over to Jane, giving her a big hug. "Congratulations, dear sister." Jacob grinned from ear to ear. "May you two be so happy together."

"Thank you, Jacob," Jane gushed. "We're so happy." Her eyes spoke volumes.

The rest of the day was perfect. The turkey turned out better than Abigail anticipated; only the bottom and the outside were over cooked. Once she added the water and tried a little secret her mama showed her, the turkey finished beautifully. The company was as delightful, as Abigail and Jacob had hoped. They couldn't have asked for a better way to celebrate Easter, with their family and good friends. God was truly good.

chapter twenty-one

AFTER EASTER, IT wasn't long before plowing began. Jacob helped his father-in-law with planting. In fact, Claude came and helped as well, which made the work go by quickly. Jacob then, in turn, went to Crocus Flats and helped Claude and Peter with their seeding.

Abigail was working full-time at the general store because Jacob was working long hours. It worked out well as she loved the job and felt she'd found her niche. She enjoyed visiting with the ladies who came for their groceries, and she served tea daily to anyone who wanted to stay to chat. She dusted and cleaned once a week, restocked shelves when orders came in from the city, and re-ordered every two weeks. Jacob did most of the deliveries, but when he couldn't, he asked Charles to help out. Charles was more than willing to give a hand; between helping his father, the general store, and the Empire Hotel, it kept him quite busy.

Jane and Claude were married that July, between planting and harvest. It was a beautiful wedding at All Saints Anglican Church in Abbington Pickets, followed by an outdoor luncheon.

Jacob was Claude's best man, and Abigail was Jane's matron of honour. Jacob was proud to stand beside the new brother he would gain. He'd seen Claude go through so much, but he'd overcome even more. Claude reminded him of himself. God had seen him through his worst and given him his best. They were now truly family.

The summer had been hot and dry with little rain. Hay wasn't as plentiful as usual, but with the previous year's hay and what they could scavenge, there would likely be enough feed for the winter.

With the extra time before harvest coming on, Jacob took a day at the beginning of August and organized a rope-making bee. They hadn't done one in quite a few years. He was in need of more rope, for the horses' halters, strapping crates on the wagon for deliveries, and towing the stone-boat.

Anyone who needed rope made came to participate. It took at least three men to make each rope.

West of Jacob's carpentry shop, he pounded a post into the ground. He then mounted the four-strand rope maker on it.

About twenty men came that day. Abigail made iced tea, lemonade, sandwiches, and thimble cookies to serve to them while they were there. Each bought their own twine from Abigail at the general store. It was a great sales pitch and a necessary item to have.

Jacob started early that day, right after breakfast; first come, first served. They started with Mr. MacDonald's rope. Jacob set the rope up. He used a handmade wooden tension paddle, which separated the twine and kept the strands from tangling. Whoever's rope was being made turned the handle. The third man was the next one in line for his rope to be made and he was the swivel hook holder. This man would stand back as many feet as he wanted the rope to be.

Jacob tied the end of the twine to the swivel hook; Charles' dad held it and counted to twenty steps away from the rope maker. Jacob looped the twine on the left hook of the rope maker, then walked down to the swivel hook, looping the twine onto the large hook. He then took the twine back to the rope maker, this time on the upper right hook then back to the swivel hook. He then went back to the rope maker on the lower right hook then back to the swivel hook and then back to the last hook on the lower left side of the rope maker. Jacob repeated this pattern until there were four strands on each hook. Good thing Jacob's legs were long and his steps were big.

Jacob asked Mr. MacDonald to start turning the handle on the back side of the rope maker clockwise, turning slowly with a good rhythm. Jacob held the tension paddle between the twine sections and walked back and forth while Mr. Mac Donald turned the handle to keep the twine from tangling up. Charles' dad was still holding the swivel handle snug, trying not to let it go. The swivel began to turn.

"Alright, that's good," Jacob hollered as he began to walk towards the rope maker. The twine automatically started twisting together behind the tension paddle to form a nice thick one-inch rope. Jacob continued to walk until he reached Mr. MacDonald. He then pulled the paddle out from the twine that was still attached to the hooks. Jacob carefully removed the loops from all four hooks, placing them on the middle hook. He nodded at Mr. Mac Donald to turn the handle, which he turned in the opposite way to tighten the rope and keep it from unwinding. Jacob then took a piece of twine and wrapped the end of the rope about ten times, tying a knot at the end.

"You can bring it down here!" He yelled down to Charles' dad, who walked towards him. Once he reached Jacob and Mr. MacDonald, he took the loops off the hook and tied the end in the same manner as Jacob had the other.

"There you are sir." Jacob wrapped the rope around and around his elbow and hand to form a coil then handed it to Mr. Mac Donald.

It was a long day for Jacob with all the walking he did. By sundown, he was ready to hit the hay. One good thing he had learned from his pa was how to make rope.

Harvest came and went, as did winter. They spent Christmas with Jane and Claude at Crocus Flats. It was the first year since Jacob had left home that he had Christmas in that house. It was bittersweet for both he and his siblings. It was also the first Christmas they were all together without Andrew.

Alice had her second baby at the end of December. They named her Annie Julia, after Alice's mother. She was sweet as a button, but not near as small as little Grace had been. Bert was a proud pa again. Although Bert had told Jacob he was hoping their next baby would be a boy, he sure did love his little girls.

Jacob's father-in-law was doing well and seemed to be back to the way he had been before his stroke. His mobility was next to being perfect, and he no longer required a cane. His legs were strong, and he was able to do the things he used to. He thought the next year he would possibly buy some cattle and begin to ranch. It was what he'd wanted to do when he came to Canada, but for health reasons, he hadn't gotten that far.

Another spring went by. The heavy winter had brought extreme moisture, which made up for the previous dry year.

Jacob finished another order of tea tables to send to David Adair. Winter was the time that Jacob could work on his tables the most. He would construct more of them, then stockpile them for when he received orders from David.

It was a rainy day at the beginning of July. Jacob was working at the general store while Abigail stayed at home to do some baking for the church on Sunday.

"Good morning, Jacob." A gentleman came in the door, carrying the crate that held *The Leader* from Regina.

"Good morning, Stan." Jacob nodded his head as he was putting groceries in a box for Mrs. Smyth. She always left an order to be filled, then she picked it up after she had been to the flour mill and the post office.

"Better check out the headlines today," Stan told Jacob as he pointed to the newspapers.

"It's exciting, is it?" Jacob grinned, anxious to see what he was talking about. He was thinking that possibly it wasn't much, but he had to look. He reached in the crate for the paper and opened it up.

"Archduke Franz Ferdinand assassinated!" the headline read. "There's going to be a war for sure," Stan commented. "At least in Europe, that is."

Jacob thought about how it would affect Abigail's relatives in England if Europe went to war. He wondered how they would be feeling right then.

"Well, hopefully it won't resort to that," Jacob commented.

It sure got him thinking about how blessed he was to live in Canada.

After church the following Sunday, everyone got together outside for their picnic. News spread fast about the talk of war abroad. It was definitely a possibility. Of course, everyone had their own opinion and idea of what could happen if it came to that, or perhaps there wouldn't be a war at all. Maybe nobody cared that the Archduke was murdered in the first place.

The next time the paper from Regina came out, the headlines contained even more terrifying news.

"Britain Declares War!" Jacob read before he packed the wagon for another delivery.

"Good day." Jacob tipped his hat to Mrs. Smyth as she strolled past the general store.

"Good day, Jacob," she answered. "How's Abigail?"

"Great, thanks for asking," Jacob answered.

"Hello, Jacob." Reverend Young walked up behind his wagon as Jacob loaded crates.

"Hello, Reverend." Jacob nodded. "How are you today?"

"Very well, thank you," the reverend answered. "Where's the Missus today?"

"She's at her ma and pa's," Jacob informed him. "They're spending the day gardening apparently." He smiled as the reverend kept on going.

"Well, if it isn't my best friend in the world." Jacob looked up to see a smiling freckled face.

"Charles." Jacob smiled. "Aren't you supposed to be working?"

"I just got done." Charles grinned mischievously.

"It's only ten in the morning," Jacob pointed out. "A little early to be done work, don't think?"

"Doesn't take me all day, you know." Charles laughed as he took a puff of his cigarette, tipping his head back and blowing the smoke up in the air.

"You know that smoking isn't good for you," Jacob teased.

"You have no proof." Charles played along. "Besides, how do you know?"

"Because I do." Jacob grinned.

"How?"

"Because."

"You don't know what you're talking about," Charles confronted Jacob, keeping the joke going.

"Well, Charles," Jacob said nonchalantly, "I may not know everything, but I'm always right."

Charles burst out laughing, bending over and slapping his leg in entertainment.

"I thought I was the card." Charles continued to laugh. "But you, my boy, you have me beat."

"I am glad you think it's funny," Jacob said, pretending all seriousness. "But it's the truth." It was hard for Jacob to keep a straight face as he strung his buddy along.

"Well, I'm glad we got that all straightened out." Charles tried to put on his earnest face. "Now what's all this talk about war I keep hearing?"

"Doesn't sound good." Jacob grabbed the paper he had been reading and handed it to Charles.

"Oh, wow." Charles looked at Jacob. "Does that mean?"

"That Canada will go to war?" Jacob knew exactly what Charles was asking.

"Yes. Do you think we will?" Charles wasn't joking any more. In fact, he'd never been more serious.

"It's our duty as Canadians," Jacob stated. "After all, we do belong to the British Commonwealth. It would only be right that we follow suit."

"You're right again." Charles half-heartily smiled. "As always."

"Besides, Prime Minister Borden encourages it," Jacob added from reading the Prime Minister's letter that was published in the paper.

Jacob went home that afternoon with a heavy heart. His small world at Abbington Pickets was almost perfect. God had provided him with everything he needed and then some. He had a strong marriage with a beautiful, hard-working wife. He had two thriving businesses. His family was closer than ever. Abigail's father was healed and better than he was before. Jane had found happiness, and Claude had found the Lord. God had blessed him graciously.

But across the world, there was much more happening. The world was not happy or at peace. A war was breaking out, and there was nothing anyone could do to stop it. In fact, Jacob suspected it was only going to grow larger. How could he tell the love of his life what he was thinking? How could he not? Jacob was betwixt and between.

chapter twenty-two

"HAPPY ANNIVERSARY, GIRLIE." Jacob kissed Abigail's forehead. Abigail smiled as she stretched her arms up in the air. Holding her hands together. She rubbed her sleepy eyes as her head lay on her pillow. It was past dawn, the sun peeking through the clouds in the east.

"Happy anniversary to you too, Mr. Hudson." Abigail reached up to Jacob, where he sat on the edge of the bed, and kissed his lips.

"I love you so much," Jacob whispered as he held Abigail's face in his hands.

"I love you too," Abigail spoke softly.

"I made you breakfast." Jacob proudly showed Abigail the silver tray sitting at the end of the bed. Jacob stood up, picked up the tray, and placed it on Abigail's lap as she sat up in bed with pillows propped up behind her. Eggs, bacon, toasted buttered bread, and a cup of coffee were nicely placed on the tray.

"You're so sweet," Abigail gushed. "Pray before it gets cold," she suggested. She loved it when Jacob said grace. He did it with such tenderness and honesty. He was committed to the Lord; the more she witnessed it, the more she respected him for it. If it hadn't been for Jacob, she would have never learned to trust in Jesus as she did then. It melted her heart to be married to this wonderful, God-fearing man.

When Jacob finished the blessing, Abigail took a sip of coffee. "Mmm, that's good." She smiled as she dipped her toast into the egg yolk, taking a bite. "Aren't you having any breakfast?"

"I had a bite while I was cooking." He laughed as he watched Abigail eat her eggs, noticing how delicately she chewed.

"Well, you're a great cook." Abigail continued to eat. "Why am I doing all the cooking?" she teased.

"I know since we've had the store," Jacob started to explain. "Well, I mean, had the store full-time," he corrected himself. "We don't have the opportunity to go many places together."

"I love working at the store," Abigail insisted. "I get to visit with people every day."

"Oh, I know you do, Girlie," Jacob agreed. "I mean that because this is a special … *our* special day, I wanted to do something special." He grinned.

"Thank you." Abigail reached up and touched Jacob's cheek.

"Abigail," Jacob said as he put his hand over hers. "We need to talk about something."

"Alright," Abigail agreed. "Are you alright?"

"There's really is no way to say it," Jacob said quickly.

"Now you're scaring me." Abigail lowered her eyes, feeling the seriousness of Jacob's words.

"I am not trying to scare you, love." Jacob held onto Abigail's hand. He stared into her big brown eyes. "I'll just come out and say it, and forgive me for it," he pleaded.

"Jacob?"

"I'm going to war," Jacob point blankly said, and held his breath, waiting for Abigail's reaction.

Abigail's eyes widened and her mouth fell open, but nothing came out.

Jacob knew it was going to break her heart, but he felt he had no choice. He had an obligation to his country, to his family, and to himself. He felt helpless, but he needed to fight for the flag that flew close to their home, in the middle of their village, in the centre of their country. The Commonwealth needed his country's help to defeat the enemy. Jacob's heart ached at the thought of leaving his family, his home, and his dedicated wife, but he had a duty to uphold. He had to fight for freedom.

"Please don't go." Abigail grabbed Jacob's arms with her hands, holding tight. "You can't."

"Don't you see?" Jacob held her arms as well. "I need to do this for you and me, and for our family."

"No, I don't see." A tear rolled down her left cheek. "You don't just up and leave me, and our family."

"*Our* country needs me. *Your* country needs me."

"*I* need you, Jacob," Abigail argued. "We need you," she whispered.

"Men are already dying every day," Jacob told her. "They need men."

Abigail sobbed softly, not wanting to talk about it any longer. Their special day was no longer special. It was a day that they both would remember; the day Jacob broke Abigail's heart.

Jacob felt adamant about serving his country. Staying home wasn't even an option, in his mind. He would do what it took, at any cost, to fight for King and country.

"Our country needs me. Your country needs me." - Jacob.

The rest of the week wasn't pleasant. Abigail didn't understand Jacob's desire to go fight in another country and leave his family behind. Jacob could tell she tried hard to hide her disappointment in him and fear of losing her husband. He wanted to be able to take her fear and pain away, but there was no other solution.

Jacob didn't want to leave Abigail unprepared for the winter that was about to come. He already had enough wood cut and stacked for a year's worth of burning. He hauled hay from Goldenrod for Abigail, so it would be easier to feed the horses.

He finished and packed every tea table he had in the shop, sending them to Kingston. Of course, Mr. Rodgers reassured him that they would take care of Abigail. After everything Jacob had done for them, it was the least they could do to keep him from worrying about what was happening at home. Jacob did in a week what would have normally taken him a month to do.

Jacob, Charles, Claude, Bert, and Ernest all travelled to the nearest recruiting office, which was in Abbington Pickets, to enlist. Jacob, Charles, and Ernest were the only ones who passed the physical. Bert had a heart murmur; Claude had flat feet.

Apparently, that was considered a physical defect. As disappointed as the two men were, Jacob was slightly relieved. He knew Jane and the farm would be taken care of, and Bert could help Mr. Rodgers when need be.

Jacob, Charles, and Ernest would be taking the train from Abbington Pickets the following Friday, it would take them to Quebec to begin military training at CFB Valcartier.

The church held a farewell lunch that Sunday, after church, for all the men from the village and community that were headed to fight the war. The church was the fullest it had ever been. The young men who enlisted had all their family there to say goodbye. All of Jacob's family were there, including Sarah; she had travelled from Kingston with her husband Dennis, but left their children with his ma and pa, to make the trip less hassle.

It was a sad day, to say the least, especially for every mother; they took it the hardest. Reverend Young prayed over each young man and their families for strength, wisdom, and peace.

Jacob and Abigail drove home from the church in silence. When they drove up to Jacabig Place, he hopped off the wagon, making his way to Abigail's side of the wagon. He held his hand out to her as she stepped off the wagon. How many more times would he be able to do that before he left, and when would be the next time? He would never know.

"I'll make us some tea," Abigail said quietly as she walked towards Jacabig. Jacob sensed her sadness. They both felt it.

Jacob took the horses to the stable, where he unhitched them. He fed them hay and filled their water trough to let them drink. He tried not to take too much time, so he had the rest of the day to spend with his wife.

Jacob unlatched the door, took his coat off and hung it on the hook by the door. He grabbed his hat off his head and placed it on the second hook. He sat down on the bench beside the washstand. He pulled his leg up and unlaced his boots, pulling each one off, setting them on the floor, neatly, one beside the other.

"Tea's ready." Abigail stood at the table with the teapot in her hand, ready to pour.

"Thank you, love." Jacob half-heartedly smiled. He walked into the dining room, then into their bedroom. He opened the top drawer of his chest of drawers, pulling out an envelope. He walked back into the kitchen. Abigail was sitting at the table, stirring honey into her tea.

Jacob walked up behind her, bent down, and kissed the top of her head. Her soft hair felt like silk on his lips. He closed his eyes, breathing in deeply; the familiar fragrance reminded Jacob of the first time he'd held Abigail. She and her father had been in need of help the day Jacob and his family were out cutting wood. For their sake, Jacob was at the right place at the right time. He never wanted to forget that smell; he wanted to hold on to it forever.

Jacob held the envelope in front of her; she looked up at him with surprise as she took it from him.

"What's this?" She asked.

"Open it." Jacob smiled as he watched her intently.

Abigail delicately opened the white envelope, tearing the flap. She took out the piece of folded paper and proceeded to unfold it. The words on the paper danced in her mind as she read the letters Jacob so carefully had written.

Girlie,

I will always love you,
In the warm autumn breeze.
I will always love you,
In the moments stopped in time.
I will always love you,
When the flowers bloom in spring.
I will always love you,
When your breath reaches my face.
I will always love you,
When I leave your side,
And let go of your hand,
I will still... always love you.

Keep this close to your heart until I return to you, my love. You are the first thing I think of when I awake and the last when I close my eyes. I love you with all the love I have in me.

Pray for me, Girlie, as I will be praying for you and please, forgive me.

I will always love you, Jacob.

A single tear fell from Abigail's cheek onto the words Jacob had penned. The ink pooled in a transparent shade of black and ran down the rest of the paper. Abigail turned around in her chair as she wrapped her arms around Jacob's waist.

"Thank you," was all she said.

Jacob crouched down on his knees to her sitting level. He kissed her face where the tears had run from her eyes as if he could kiss it all better. Abigail's eyes begged him not to leave. Jacob's heart broke into pieces and it felt as though those pieces fell to the floor to shatter at her feet.

chapter twenty-three

IT WAS A sober day for everyone. Despite the sunshine and the cloudless sky, the day felt as gloomy as any rain-filled twenty-four hours. Jacob slipped the handle of his duffle bag over his right shoulder, carrying it to the wagon. Lifting it up, he placed it in the back of the wagon with the others.

Mr. Rodgers drove Jacob, Abigail, Charles, and Ernest to Abbington Pickets. Mrs. Rodgers had said her goodbye earlier and couldn't bear to do it again. It broke her heart to see Jacob leave, but it was also sad to watch her only child feel such heartache. She and Aunt Gladys stayed at home.

Charles had said his farewell to his ma and pa that morning in Abbington Pickets.

Alice didn't want to watch her only brother leave on the train and was distraught knowing he was headed to war. Bert brought him as far as Abbington Pickets to catch a ride with Jacob to the train. Ernest sat up front with Mr. Rodgers, and Charles sat right behind them in the wagon.

Jacob wanted to spend as much time as he could with Abigail.

They sat in the back of the wagon, close to the end. Abigail leaned her head against Jacob's shoulder as they rode. Jacob placed his arm around her, holding her tight against him. He lifted his chin over Abigail's head, breathing in the sweet smell of her brown locks. Oh how long before he would smell that familiar fragrance? How long would it be before he would touch her face again, feel her warmth, wrap his arms around her? When would be the next time Jacob would hear Abigail's British accent convey beautiful words as her face lit up while her big brown eyes smiled at him.

The rough ride to Abbington Pickets was usually long but felt much shorter on this day. The horses briskly pulled the wagon. The big wheels rolled over holes and rocks, producing a rocking motion. Everyone kept silent, each in their own thoughts about what they were leaving behind, about where they were headed. Jacob wanted to hold his Girlie one more time.

Abigail remained strong; Jacob knew it was for his sake. His heart was breaking as much as hers. Jacob also knew what he was doing to his wife. The huge responsibility he was leaving her with. The work that it entailed and the loneliness it would bestow upon her. He felt shame for leaving her and his family, but he had a duty to their country and their mother country, where Abigail was born.

Jacob could see Abbington Pickets in the distance, and he wished that time would stand still for a moment. He reached over and touched Abigail's cheek, gently pulling her face to look at him. He wanted to look into her eyes, touch her face, feel her hair before they stopped. They continued to embrace until the wagon came to a complete stop.

The CPR Station in Pickets was humming with people ready to board the awaited train. Their families were standing with them, saying goodbye as well. Charles and Ernest took their luggage from the back of the wagon. They both walked to the ticket booth to get their ticket. Mr. Rodgers went with them to give Abigail and Jacob privacy.

Jacob hopped off the back of the wagon. He reached his hands up to Abigail; she put her hands out and held onto Jacob's arms as he helped her down. The two of them stood there for a minute. A tear rolled down her cheek as she looked up at Jacob with sadness in her eyes.

"Write me every chance you get," Abigail told Jacob. "I need to hear from you often." Another tear fell.

"I will, Girlie," Jacob promised.

"Don't forget," Abigail persisted. "I couldn't stand if I don't hear from you."

"I promise." Jacob was a man of his word and always did what he said. He put his hands on either side of her face wiping her tears with his thumbs. "Don't cry. I'll be home before you know it," he consoled her.

Abigail closed her eyes, swallowed hard as she nodded.

That was the hardest thing Jacob had ever done in his life. He didn't expect it to be quite that tough. The pain pierced through him as though his heart was being ripped from his chest.

Jacob pulled Abigail to his chest, wrapping both arms around her, holding on tightly. Tears welled up in his own eyes, but he blinked them away.

"I love you, Jacob Hudson." Abigail backed away from him, still holding his hands. She looked up into his eyes. "You come back in one piece, do you hear me?" she scolded him like a child.

"I will, love," Jacob reassured her, not knowing what the future held. But he did know that God would protect him, and He would protect Abigail at home. That was his only comfort in leaving her behind. He had faith.

The loud whistle blew from a distance as the
train came roaring down the tracks.

The loud whistle blew from a distance as the train came roaring down the tracks. Puffs of steam bellowed out the top of the chimney. The screeching was deafening as the train slowed down to come to a complete stop in front of the station house.

Jacob knew that was it. The time was there to say goodbye.

He had dreaded the moment since he'd decided to enlist. Doing something right and good was sometimes the most painful thing a person could endure.

Jacob reached into the back of the wagon for his bag. He lifted it out, slinging it over his left shoulder. Abigail walked beside him, holding his other hand.

"I got the ticket for you, son." Mr. Rodgers walked towards them.

"Thank you, sir." Jacob half smiled and set his bag on the ground. "You take care of my girl, here." Jacob put his hand out to Mr. Rodgers to give him a handshake, but when Mr. Rodgers reached out, he grabbed Jacob's hand, then pulled him and gave him a hug instead.

"We'll miss you, Jacob," Mr. Rodgers' voice sounded sad. "Don't forget to come back to us." He tried to make light of the situation.

"Oh, I intend to," Jacob assured him. "I can't stay away from this little beauty." He winked at Abigail.

"Well, boys." Mr. Rodgers shook both Charles and Ernest's hands. "You boys take care out there."

"Thank you, sir. We will," they said simultaneously. Charles and Ernest picked up their bags and stepped on the train. They knew Jacob would be behind them in a few minutes and they wanted to give him the time.

"I'll be in the wagon," Abigail's father told her gently. "Take your time."

"Thanks, Pa." Abigail gave him a slight grin in appreciation.

"You take care of yourself and come back to us," he reminded Jacob again as he shook his hand once more.

"I will, Pa." Jacob watched him as he walked away from them. "I love you, Girlie," Jacob told her as he put his arms around her back, holding her close, "and don't you forget it." He smiled, clenching his jaw, as he tried to keep hold of his emotions. He flicked the end of her nose, and she gasped a half-cry half-laugh in his last attempt to tease her.

There were people rushing past them, noisy chatter, the train engine, horses trotting by, but Jacob could only hear one thing.

Abigail's voice. It was like they were the only ones standing in all the hustle.

"I love you too," Abigail said, looking up at Jacob. He bent his head down, kissing her one last time. "I'm not saying goodbye," Abigail informed him. "I'll see you soon." Tears rolled down both her cheeks. She couldn't help it any longer. The train's whistle blew, which made everyone rush even more. Their time was running out.

"I will see you soon," Jacob repeated, not wanting to say goodbye either and he quickly let go of Abigail. Instantly he picked up his bag, throwing it over his shoulder and turning towards the train. As he started to walk away, he felt a hand grab his arm. He turned around swiftly and looked at his brown-eyed Girlie. She leaned into his chest, hugging him tightly. He held her with his free arm, closing his eyes with the realization that leaving her was the worst feeling in the world. Again, the train's whistle blew, and the train master called out, "All aboard!"

Jacob let go of Abigail as she released him. He walked towards the train car door, reached for the support handle, and stepped up without looking back. He walked down the aisle until he reached the seat where Ernest and Charles were sitting. He put his bag in the overhead compartment and sat in the empty seat across from them. Looking out the window, he could see Abigail on the other side. She was slowly waving, her face tear-stained. Jacob touched his lips with his fingers, then placed them on the window as if to send her a kiss. He remained frozen in that position as the train began to move forward and the whistle blew. All he could see was a fog of steam surrounding Abigail as she waved in the distance.

"It'll be alright." Charles smiled. "We'll be back before they even have time to miss us."

"I hope you're right, lad." Jacob looked at his friend.

Ernest sat beside Charles without a word. The three of them were scared to death, but none of them would dare admit it.

Jacob stared out the window as the scenery raced by. He thought long and hard about his life, about his future, and about how God had never given him more than he could handle. He knew God would see him through, just as He had before.

The train would take about three days to reach the military training camp in Quebec. Night was falling, and Jacob started to doze off. He got up and reached for his bag above him so he had something to use for a pillow. He sat back down, placing his bag on his lap. He unzipped it to move some things around to make it more comfortable for his head. As he was shifting his clothes around, he felt something inside. He pulled it out. It was an envelope that read "Jacob" on the front of it.

He tore open the back of the envelope. Jacob pulled out the white folded paper, unfolded it, and started reading the penned words.

September 25, 1914

Dear Jacob,

By the time you read this, you will be miles away from me. I know I will have already missed you a hundred times over by now. I want you to go to war without worrying about what's happening here at home. We will be fine; I will keep the home fires burning. Make no mistake, I will miss you dearly and yearn for your touch, but I want to be strong for you and for this family. Keep yourself alive and well so you can come

*home to this patient wife of yours. When that
long- awaited time arrives, there will be someone
here who will be anxious to meet you. You see, I
am having a baby. The baby you longed for. The
baby you never thought we'd have. So when you're
fighting for your King and country, remember
your family. Your wife and child need you.*

*I love you with all my heart and
soul. I will see you soon.*

All my love, Your Girlie, Abigail xxxooo

Jacob held the letter in his hand, staring at the ink for several minutes in disbelief. His heart was pounding eagerly as he looked up and glanced at Charles and Ernest, sitting across from him. His sober lips turned into a slight grin.

"I'm going to be a father," Jacob said out loud.

The End

CPSIA information can be obtained
at www.ICGtesting.com
Printed in the USA
LVHW02s2009190318
570374LV00001B/2/P